I stepped over to the window to study the lamplit street below, but I could sense Christian moving up behind me. As he bent to kiss the nape of my neck, I gasped.

"Hilary, you are a lovely young woman," he whispered.

He raised his fingers to my cheeks. For a moment I simply stood there, my eyes closed; then I felt his lips brush my eyelids. I opened my eyes just as his lips claimed mine in a sudden fiery kiss.

"You'd better leave now," I said, moving to the window to look down at the street again. I did not even hear him open the door and leave the room.

It was not until later, after I had struggled out of my gown and was brushing out my hair, that I saw the folded note on the sofa. I laid the brush down and unfolded the paper that had been camouflaged by the floral print of the upholstery. I stared at the words printed in crude block letters:

HE DIES WHO GOES TO WIDOW'S MOUNTAIN

PATRICIA WERNER

HIDDEN GOLD OF WIDOW'S MOUNTAIN

ZEBRA BOOKS
KENSINGTON PUBLISHING CORP.

ZEBRA BOOKS

are published by

Kensington Publishing Corp.
475 Park Avenue South
New York, NY 10016

First Printing: April, 1993

Printed in the United States of America

Chapter 1

Brooklyn, September, 1855

I pushed the heavy oak door shut and slid the bolt into place. Clutching the eviction notice to my breast, I turned and ascended the narrow staircase. As I turned again on the second floor landing, my faded gingham skirts brushed the faded wallpaper in the narrow hallway. At the end of the hall, I couldn't help but glance through the double doorway to the master bedroom.

How many times in the last week had I paused on that slightly worn carpet and gazed sorrowfully into the room? Sarah Stafford, our landlady and lifetime friend, had inhabited this room until last month when she had followed her husband, Gunther, to the grave.

Now, mourning the woman who had raised my sister and me from childhood was colored with a new emotion. I grimaced at the legal document I held in my hand and then glanced up the stairs to the third floor. The most difficult part would be telling Fanny.

A hundred thoughts flew through my mind as I

ascended the final flight of stairs to the floor where we both had our bedrooms. I passed the door to my own room at the back of the house and went along the hall to the front room, where I knew I would find my younger sister, most likely still in her peignoir, even though it was past noon.

I myself had been up since before eight, busy with the responsibilities of the household. After Gunther passed away last fall, his wife seemed to fade, as if life without her longtime companion and faithful husband wasn't worth living. Since before Sarah Stafford died, I had taken on more and more tasks, getting the meals when Sarah could no longer work in the kitchen.

The door to Fanny's room was ajar, and I pulled it open. Lying atop rumpled bedclothes, her slippers tossed to the floor, my eighteen-year-old sister leaned on the pillows, her emerald eyes devouring the printed pages of a chapbook. Long tangled strands of blond hair, many shades lighter than my own curly brown hair, straggled over the pillows that were bunched up under her, the rose-colored peignoir hiked up over one knee.

The entire room reflected the same carelessness with which Fanny ignored the rest of life's necessities. Petticoats tumbled from the chaise in one corner of the room, and a trail of clothes led to the marble-topped dressing table, which was piled with combs, jars, and a bonnet whose ribbons trailed to the floral carpet square that stopped just short of the furniture lining the room.

Fanny hardly blinked when I entered. "It's past noon, Fanny. Aren't you going to dress?"

She let the book fall on the bed and rolled on her back, raising her eyes to the ceiling.

"Oh, Hilary. Don't tell me we're going out. And if

6

it's more help you want downstairs, my muscles are still sore from all that scrubbing you made me do in the kitchen yesterday."

"As a matter of fact, we've already had a caller," I said. "Were you so wrapped up in your story that you didn't even hear the door slam just now?"

Fanny turned her green eyes on me, undoubtedly criticizing my serviceable dress of brown plaid gingham and the neat bun and drooping ringlets I was able to manage in a quarter of the time it took Fanny to groom herself. I tried not to show how cross I felt.

But my words registered on her, and she half roused herself onto one elbow. "What visitor?" she asked.

I picked up a pair of stockings and took a seat on a faded upholstered chair. I did not look forward to the ill-tempered reaction I knew must come from Fanny at the news I had to break, but I couldn't put it off. So I simply said, "We have to leave the house. We have to move."

Fanny fell back against the pillows and drew her gently arched brows down into a frown. "What do you mean, move?"

"I'm afraid this house is no longer our home. Sarah and Gunther had a number of debts. The house must be sold to satisfy the creditors."

I had not been unaware that the Staffords were reaching the end of the money they had saved for their latter years, but even I had not been able to prevent the sinking feeling when Mr. Jeffries, the Staffords' lawyer, had handed me the eviction notice a little while ago. I had hoped it wouldn't come to this, but it had.

Fanny tilted her head as if not quite understanding, and I had to fight my rising impatience. My sister could be lame when it suited her. I was four years older than Fanny and had spent almost all of my life helping Sarah raise her since our own mother had died.

I held the document out. "We must be out in a month."

"A month!" Fanny kicked aside the covers entangling her feet and sat up. "It's not fair."

"Few things in life are fair," I said. "That's not the point." Then in a kinder tone, "I'm afraid we have no choice."

Fanny rose and took a few steps in her bare feet across the carpet. I followed her gaze around the room, staring at the worn damask drapes, the Oriental design of the old wallpaper that led the eye straight up to the crack in the ceiling plaster above the molding.

Our life in the Brooklyn row house had not been luxurious, and we hadn't had a real family, but it had been secure. I felt as bad as Fanny must at the sweeping away of all that was familiar. But I had an idea that might stem my sister's threatening temper tantrum.

I straightened and said, "How would you like to make a journey? Since we have to vacate the house in any case . . ."

Fanny remained petulant. "Couldn't we just stay a little longer—until suitable arrangements could be made? You know Hil, we could go out more, meet some people, well *you* know. We can't just leave now that we're *marriageable*. If one of us gets married, that would solve it."

I rolled my eyes. "Oh, Fanny, not Fifth Avenue again."

That was all Fanny seemed to want to talk about since one Sunday last year when Gunther had rented a rig to drive us up Fifth Avenue as far as Sixteenth Street. Fanny had immediately envisioned herself in one of the mansions built by New York's wealthy along the famed avenue above Washington Square, and from that time on she began to take on airs that I found ridiculous.

Not that I lacked the desire for better things in life, it was just that I was more practical. At least I always thought so. But what I was about to suggest would hardly seem very practical in Fanny's eyes.

I lifted my chin. "I think we should find Father."

"What!" Fanny whirled to look at me as if I were mad. "But we don't even know where he is."

I rose and went to the window. "Don't you remember the letter he sent two years ago from California saying he was going to the Sierra Nevadas to look for that valley he'd heard about?"

Fanny frowned and began tossing the clothing off of her vanity stool. She flounced onto the seat and glared at me in the mirror.

"How could we ever find him, even if we knew where he was? And what good would it do? The last time he made any money, he lost it all again in the blink of an eye. For once, my dear Hilary, I think you've lost your usual good sense."

I allowed myself a half smile. Our father had gone west to seek his fortune in 1837. In '49 he'd drifted to California with all the other seekers of fortune when the gold fever struck. There had been some money, and he'd sent home as much as he could, instructing Mr. Jeffries to set some of it aside as a savings for our future.

"It might seem that I've lost my senses, but we can't stay here," I said.

Fanny jerked her hairbrush through the tangles of her mussed tresses. "But if he's not where he said he was going two years ago, and we don't find him, then we're no better off than we are now. And besides, who can meet a suitable husband in some wilderness no one's ever heard of at the ends of the earth?"

Pushing aside the curtains, I glanced out the windowpane down at the horse-drawn delivery carts and buggies passing on the brick street below. The morning had been heavy with dark clouds promising rain, and now drops spattered against the pane.

"It's not the ends of the earth," I argued, watching the workmen and neighbors quickening their pace along the street to get out of the rain. "According to Father's letter, Yosemite Valley is on the western slope of the Sierra Nevada. It's a long way to be sure. We'll have to either sail around the Horn, and that could take half a year, or go by train and steamboat to St. Joseph, Missouri and take the stagecoach from there."

Fanny had paused in her violent hair brushing long enough to listen, but at the word *stagecoach,* she made a face and grunted.

I grew tired of my sister's protestations and turned, hands on hips. "I know it's taking a chance, Fanny, but it seems to me we can afford this one gamble. We've enough money in the bank for the journey, and if Father's done well enough, it would be our chance for a real home. Then you could meet your gentleman, maybe even in San Francisco. It's supposed to be a lovely city."

Fanny caught my eyes in the mirror. "Like New York?"

I shrugged one shoulder. "Nothing's like New York, but there are people in San Francisco, opportunities surely. We're strong able-bodied women. We can make our way somehow."

I turned back toward the window, glancing at my sister out of the corner of my eye.

10

"The only alternative would be to seek employment here. We'd have to rent rooms of course, but we could pay for them out of our wages."

I fingered the lace under the curtains, careful not to look at Fanny, who slowly placed the brush on the cluttered dressing table. The silence lasted a full minute, and I waited patiently while examining the sienna-colored brick of the houses across the street and the rain spattering the sidewalk.

I knew good and well that seeking employment was the last thing Fanny would want to do, though I also knew that a good day's work was probably exactly what she needed. I went on when I was sure my words would sink into her mind.

Dropping the curtain, I said, "Surely it's worth a try to find him."

Fanny swiveled in her seat and contemplated me. "We have the money Father sent us. Surely . . ." But the fight had gone out of her.

"It's not enough to set up housekeeping," I said more gently. "Not enough to last more than a few months. After that, we'll be as poor as church mice."

As Fanny stared at a spot in the air two feet from her nose, I could see that she was slowly coming round to my way of thinking. At least the first obstacle had been hurdled.

With more self-doubt than I cared to admit, the following Wednesday I stepped off the horse-drawn omnibus on Fulton Street and passed through the revolving doors of the New York Bank and Trust Company. I had already called on Lawyer Jeffries, and now I stood at the high wooden counter and asked to see the officer who always handled my father's

11

account. After a short wait, I was ushered through the half door and into a back office, where I was offered a seat.

I should not have felt so intimidated while explaining my situation to the balding man behind the cluttered desk, but I had never done this sort of thing before. Women didn't ask for money from a bank; it was paid out to us in small amounts.

Clearing my throat and stiffening my spine, I explained that my sister and I were going to join our father in California. Then I asked to withdraw our money.

The officer contemplated me for a moment over the rims of his spectacles, then excused himself to look up the account. He offered to give me some of the funds now and send the rest later, but I insisted that I needed it all now. After signing some documents, I succeeded in withdrawing the money.

Hoping that I was indeed doing the right thing, I stuffed the bills into my crocheted bead bag and marched back to the street. Outside, I took another deep breath as I plunged into the flow of pedestrians hurrying along the sidewalk. I clutched the handbag closer and caught the omnibus again, which let me off a few blocks from home. Turning my corner, I passed the modest brick row houses with their small yards until I approached our familiar stoop.

I sensed that there was something wrong before my foot even touched the bottom step. Glancing up swiftly, I saw that the front door was ajar. Perhaps someone had been to call and Fanny had left the door open? But as I hastened up the steps and pushed the door inward, I doubted that simple explanation.

"Fanny," I called from the entrance hall.

Then as I glanced through the double doors leading

to the front parlor, I gasped, my pulse trebling its beat. The shrouds that had covered the furniture were scattered on the floor. Cushions were tossed everywhere, stuffing spilled from huge tears in the upholstery, chairs were overturned.

For a moment I froze, staring at the disorder. I tried to call out again, but my lips were numb. I stepped into the parlor and over the braid rug, which was rolled back on itself, and went through the door that led to the combination study and occasional room beyond. Unconsciously, I dropped the bead bag at my feet as I surveyed the room, which was even more torn apart than the parlor.

Every drawer in the writing desk had been turned upside down on the floor, the contents rifled. The rug was turned back here as well, shrouds tossed in a corner. Finally the scream that had been building escaped my throat.

"Faaaannnny!" I cried as I ran through the hallway and flew up the stairs. I didn't stop until I reached the top floor, my feet flying over the runner, pausing at the door to my sister's room long enough to catch a single breath, the blood pounding at my temples.

In the center of the room, Fanny sat gagged and tied to a ladder-back chair, her eyes wide with terror, her cheeks nearly as white as the rag that cut through her mouth and tied at the back of her head.

"Good heavens, Fanny, are you all right?"

I threw myself to my knees beside the chair, my fingers straining at the knot in the white cloth.

"Hold still," I said.

I was afraid the cloth was too knotted to budge under my shaking fingers, but it came at last.

"T . . . two . . . m . . . men," stammered Fanny through bruised lips when I had released her mouth.

13

"They g . . . got in somehow and c . . . came . . . mum, up here."

"Did they hurt you?"

Fanny shook her head.

"Thank God. Now, I'll have to get the scissors to cut these ropes, they're too stiff." I squeezed Fanny's shoulder. "Everything will be all right."

Fanny gulped and watched with huge eyes as I flew out the door and into my room where I kept a pair of pinking shears that would be strong enough to cut the rope.

When I returned, Fanny was babbling, but I concentrated on the thick cords that had already chafed her wrists. Then I unwound the rope that snaked across her shoulders, breasts, and stomach and bound her legs to the seat of the chair. Finally freed, Fanny rose, rubbed her wrists, tears forming. I led her to the bed. I was shaking myself, but I knew I had to remain in control.

"You have to tell me exactly what happened," I said as we sat on the edge of the bed, and I handed Fanny a handkerchief with which to blow her nose. "What they looked like," I continued, "everything they did. We'll have to get the police."

Fanny struggled with the narrative of how she'd heard nothing until the two men threw back her door, startling her, rushing across the room, and overpowering her.

"I was ff . . . frightened," she said, shivering.

"I know, dear," I said, "but it's all over now."

I hugged her again and stood up. "I've got to inform the authorities. Will you be all right while I get one of the policemen downstairs? I'll be right back."

Fanny nodded, dabbing her eyes with her handkerchief. As I crossed the room, she spoke again.

14

"I heard them g . . . going through your room, then I heard the doors slam downstairs. Wh . . . What did they want, Hil?"

My heart turned over at her pinched voice. "I don't know," I said.

I suddenly remembered the bead bag I must have left downstairs, and hurried out of the room. Panic filled me as the thought suddenly occurred to me that the intruders might still be in the house. In my fright, I had left the bag with all our money in it on the floor downstairs. Suppose I had come back to the house before the thieves had found what they wanted, and they had hidden somewhere, seeing me drop the bag? Oh how could I have been so foolish!

My heart hammered violently, and with little thought for my own safety, I ran back to the study and shook with relief when I saw the little bag still on the floor. I sagged against the door frame, still too shaken to try to understand what had happened. I picked up the bag, checking inside to see that the money was still there. Then I went back up to my room, panting from the exertion. I picked up one of the dresser drawers that had been emptied on the floor, replaced it in the dresser, and stuffed the bag inside. Then I went back downstairs to find a policeman.

By the time the police had finished looking through the house and questioning Fanny, I had given the house a cursory search myself, and could not find anything missing.

"Not that we, that is our late landlords, had anything of value to steal," I said to the middle-aged, red-faced officer who was writing up his report on a pad balanced on his knee where he sat on the demolished sofa in the parlor. His nightstick and his high helmet lay beside him.

"The silver plate had been sold. There wasn't any money. I don't understand it," I said.

The very fact that nothing was missing left me with an uneasy feeling. A nagging thought was beginning to form in the back of my mind, but I was too frightened to voice it.

"You two girls living alone in this house?" asked the policeman, glancing again at the furniture, which he and his sergeant had put back in a semblance of order, all except the étagère, which was broken and still lay on its side on the floor.

I nodded, but hastened to add, "We're leaving a week from Saturday. The house is being sold." I explained about the Staffords.

"I see." He scratched his ear. "Well, for now we'll keep a man on the block, in case there's any more trouble."

"Thank you."

He folded his notebook shut, picked up his high helmet, placed it on his head, and strapped it under his chin. Then he pushed himself to his feet, retrieving the nightstick.

I felt a moment of doubt. He looked more like a kind, well-meaning fatherly type than an officer effective against thieves. Before he left, he gave me a whistle, which I was to wear around my neck. If I encountered any more trouble, I was to blow it, and the police force within hearing distance would come to my rescue.

I saw him out, then crossed the little entry hall to the stairs, leaning for a moment on the newel post for support.

The incident strengthened my resolve to leave as soon as possible. For if the intruders, whoever they were, had not found what they were after, mightn't they be back?

Chapter 2

Fanny moved herself to help prepare for our imminent departure. I calculated and recalculated the costs of the journey we were preparing to undertake. First there would be the railroad journey to St. Louis, then a steamboat up the Missouri River to St. Joseph, Missouri, and a night's lodging there to wait for the next day's stage.

The central-overland stagecoach route from St. Joseph to Sacramento, California was twenty-four days straight through and cost one hundred and fifty dollars apiece plus the night's lodging, if we chose to get off the stage and sleep at any of the way stations along the route. That would add time to our journey, but would probably be necessary, for sleeping night after night on the hard seat of a crowded coach rumbling over bumpy roads could hardly be considered restful.

What we would find in Sacramento posed more difficult questions. I sought advice from the ticket agent, who told me that the California Stage Line could take us as far as Mariposa, some fifty miles southwest of Yosemite Valley.

During the next week and a half, friends of Sarah

came and took away articles that I was sure she would have wanted them to have. By the middle of the day the following Friday, two leather-bound trunks, two smaller chests, and several carpetbags were nearly packed.

I was in my room trying to decide how best to carry the money when the doorbell sounded. I smoothed back my hair, which I had hastily stuffed in a snood at the nape of my neck, and ran downstairs to answer the door.

"Coming, coming," I muttered to myself as I reached the landing, and the bell sounded again.

I pulled the door open and stared at a tall dark-haired gentleman dressed in a black broadcloth frock coat, his black neck cloth tied around a turnover collar. He removed his high-crowned silk hat, holding it in front of him, revealing thick, dark hair parted on the side and brushed over the tips of his ears. He had a well-trimmed dark moustache and burnsides and eyes the color of murky skies after a storm.

"Miss Fenton?"

"Yes," I answered.

He smiled, gazing at my face with a look of curiosity.

"Forgive me for staring. May I introduce myself? Thomas Neville at your service," he said, sweeping the silk hat under him and bowing.

"Should I know you?" I asked.

There had been so many callers since Sarah's funeral that I had difficulty keeping some of them straight.

"May I come in? I will explain," he countered.

Already his eyes had flickered past me and were glancing around the entry hall. I stepped back, glancing around myself, as if there were anything but the hall stand with its mirror, empty pegs, and umbrella rails to look at. I removed the large checked apron in which I had been working and led the way into the parlor, which had been put somewhat to rights.

From his manner, Thomas Neville did not appear to be any friend of Sarah's. His frock coat was impeccably cut, his elastic-sided street boots polished to a shine. He was a good six inches taller than I was, his face was tanned, and he appeared to be in his midthirties.

I gestured to the covered sofa. "Please sit down, Mr. Neville. I apologize for the appearance of the house. My sister and I are leaving tomorrow."

His eyes, which had taken in the ghostly shrouds that covered the remaining furniture, came back to settle on me.

"So I understand."

He sat gingerly on the sofa and nodded almost as if to himself. Then he said, "Please allow me to explain and to apologize if I have come at an awkward time. I learned from Mr. Jeffries of your circumstances."

"Mr. Jeffries? But how—" I sat on an ottoman beside the sofa.

He held up a hand. "This may come as a surprise to you, but I am a friend, actually a former colleague of your father's."

"My father's?" My hand flew to my breast in surprise.

"Did he never write to you of Thomas Neville?"

"Thomas Neville," I said, trying to remember. Then the pieces began to fall into place, and I recalled where I had come across the name. I rose. "Excuse me a moment."

I went into the adjoining study, located a scrapbook

19

I had laid aside to put into my trunk upstairs, and returned with it to the parlor.

"Yes," I said, sitting down again and flipping open the pages. "Father did mention you. Here, I knew I had kept it."

I moved beside Neville and pointed to a newspaper clipping with a daguerreotype of three men. "Father sent this to us two years ago."

In the picture, three men stood in front of a wooden store front. The names were printed below. Thomas Neville, Gaspar Fenton, and a third man dressed in a fringed leather jacket, leather breeches, and high-laced boots.

"Yes, that's myself, Gaspar, and the other man is Christian Reyeult," Neville said. "Your father must have told you that the three of us worked a claim together in California for a time. Made a modest profit, too."

"Yes. That was when Father sent half his share to the lawyers for our support and invested the other half in the general store to supply the miners. That was the store that burned, isn't it?"

"That it is. I decided we'd make more money supplying the miners than trying to be miners ourselves. Gaspar and Reyeult agreed, so when we had made a little money, we sold our claim and opened up the store for business."

He shook his head. "The fire took everything though, and we ended up as poor as when we started."

I continued from there. "Then Father went to explore the Yosemite Valley. He sent a letter telling us."

Neville seemed to look inward, smiling at the memory. "Old Gaspar was always the explorer."

Then he cleared his throat. "I myself returned East.

My father had passed away and I was needed to run the family grocery business."

"I see."

I glanced idly at the picture. "What happened to your other partner, Mr. Reyeult?"

"Last I heard Reyeult went to trap beaver in the Oregon Territory."

I shut the album and set it on a shrouded side table.

"Since you saw Mr. Jeffries, you must know that we are going to California in the hope of finding Father. Do you wish me to deliver a message to him?"

"No, not at all."

Neville rose and walked slowly to the mantel, resting an arm on it. The mirror above the mantel needed resilvering, and I felt slightly embarrassed by it, though I knew I should not have.

"Quite the contrary," he continued. "I have business in California myself, and coincidentally I plan to leave immediately. When I learned from Mr. Jeffries that you were planning the trip, I hastened here to offer you escort. It would be the least I could do for my old friend and former partner."

"Escort?"

I unconsciously fingered my skirt. What was it about this man that I didn't like? Was it the way he looked at me, as if he were looking for the similarities between myself and my parent? I glanced away from him. We had only just met, but already I wished he would leave.

"I assure you it would be an enjoyable task for me," he said. "And two young women traveling alone would surely not be safe from petty thieves and highway brigands. Strangers would be less likely to trifle, on the other hand, if said young ladies were with an escort."

He cleared his throat and straightened his neck cloth, leveling his dark eyes at my hazel ones. "I would be a most reliable escort."

I studied the tall, dark man in front of me again, noticing now the tiny creases around his eyes and at the edges of his mouth. I was unprepared to accept his proposal, and yet I could find no logical reason not to do so. Perhaps pride made me want to undertake this journey on our own, and yet that was silly. As travelers we would necessarily rely on the help of others along the way. Why not accept the offer of assistance from the start?

Just then Fanny came into the room. I made the introductions. Fanny sat down docilely on the sofa Neville had just vacated and smoothed her blue striped grosgrain skirt. She had taken care with her appearance and looked quite fetching with a ribbon around her yellow curls and a bow at the back of her head.

As I considered Neville's proposal, he strolled about the room, glancing at a crate of knickknacks I had packed in straw stuffing. His gaze fell on the broken étagère lying on the floor, and he paused, looking at it curiously.

"That happened last week," I said. "The house was broken into."

I told him briefly what had happened. When I came to the part about Fanny being tied up, I saw a muscle in his jaw flinch.

"You were not otherwise harmed?" he asked, his brows knitting in concern.

Fanny blushed and shook her head.

"Was anything taken?" he asked.

"There was nothing of value really," I said. "But whoever it was did a thorough job of searching through everything. We had an awful time getting it all cleaned up."

"I'm sorry to hear it. Nothing of value, you say?"

"No. There was only some silver plate, and that had been sold recently."

He cast his eyes in the direction of the door to the study.

"You're sure there's no hiding place you might have overlooked? Possibly your, er, landlady hid something that you didn't know about, perhaps under a loose floorboard?"

I shrugged. "I can't imagine. The Staffords lived so modestly. When they fell ill, they ran up debts. That's why the house is being sold."

"Oh, yes."

His glance came to rest on me once again. "Did they search the entire house? The attic as well?"

The question surprised me. "Why no, that door was locked."

"I see. Well, you can understand even better my concern for two young ladies such as yourselves. After such an incident, I feel sure your father would not want you to travel alone."

A feeling of irritation flashed through me. "I don't see that the break-in had anything to do with us. Common thieves most likely, just out to see if there was any money lying about."

His gaze rested on Fanny, who blushed a deep shade of crimson.

"You were fortunate that no harm came to Miss Fanny," he said. "If I were you I wouldn't take any chances."

"We are grateful for that," I said, further annoyed at Neville thrusting himself into our affairs. I rose.

"Thank you for your concern. Since, as you say,

23

you are planning your own journey to California, I cannot help it if our plans coincide. But please do not consider yourself responsible for us."

Seeing that he was being ushered out, Neville picked up his hat and brushed a piece of lint from it.

"Good day then. I look forward to the possibility of our being traveling companions. At least I hope you will allow me to send a cab for you on Saturday. That is tomorrow, isn't it?"

"I don't think—"

But Fanny cut me off. "Why, how kind of Mr. Neville. I'm sure Father would appreciate it."

Fanny's comment caught me off guard, and while my expression continued to protest, I could think of nothing more to say. We would have to take a cab in any case. We might as well let this high-handed Mr. Neville pay for it, but that didn't mean that we owed him the favor of our company for the rest of the journey.

As promised, the black horse-drawn cab pulled up in front of our house early Saturday morning. At least Neville wasn't in it. A note explained that he had some last-minute business to attend to. The cabby loaded our trunks onto the roof and our baggage into the boot. Giving one final glance around the downstairs, I pulled the door shut and turned the key in the lock. Then I placed the key under the doormat, where Mr. Jeffries would pick it up later this morning.

Several of the neighbors stood in their small yards or watched from the stoop, as they all knew we were leaving. A few came to press our hands and offer last-minute advice.

"Remember," said our next-door neighbor, Mrs.

Childers. "If things don't work out, you come right back here. There's always room at our table."

I hardly thought so, for her husband just eked out a living for their five children as it was, but I thanked her.

The butcher's wife presented us with long, smoke-cured sausages to take on the train with us.

After many goodbyes, I followed Fanny into the cab and sat back, fanning myself against the heaviness of the air. I was dressed in a green percale traveling costume with a peplum overskirt that had been remade for me from Sarah Stafford's wardrobe years ago. Fanny looked fetching in a tiered dimity skirt and round-necked bodice, trimmed with blue satin ribbon we had bought when we were more flush.

The cab swayed as the driver strapped the trunks to the luggage rail and then climbed into the seat with a "Giddap" for the horses.

I watched the row of houses and the waving neighbor women with their small children clinging to their skirts as the cab rolled away, but my mind was so occupied with last-minute details, that I spared little thought for nostalgia. A phase of life was over, but perhaps it was just as well.

As we drove along the crowded brick streets and made our way to the ferry that would take us across to New Jersey, I tried to still my nervousness, hoping we were doing the right thing. Beside me, Fanny sat with mouth downturned, but when I shot her a look, she shifted in her seat and attempted to transform the pout into a more congenial expression.

The cab deposited us at the ferry terminal, where we took the steam ferry across to New Jersey and the train station there. Perspiration was dripping from our brows by the time we located our compartment and watched our trunks and baggage being loaded into the luggage car. I held out hopes that the interfering Mr. Neville would fail to join us, but just as we got seated and the steam began to billow from under the wheels, his black-clad figure in stovepipe hat appeared at the door to our compartment.

"Ladies," he greeted us with a bow.

Fanny threw him a closed-lipped smile and fluttered her eyelids. I frowned and angled my knees so that he could sit down on the leather seat opposite.

"My compartment is next to this one," he said. "But I wanted to make sure you were settled."

Neville threw his glance around the entire compartment as if making sure every corner was secure, his eyes traveling over the smaller luggage stowed above us, and then finally looking over us, as if assessing our appearance.

Fanny looked straight ahead, fanning herself with her leghorn straw bonnet, the feathers and cloth flowers brushing her chin as she cast Neville an occasional glance. I arranged my skirts and leaned into the corner of the compartment, a hatbox on the seat beside me.

The train jerked forward, and I knew our journey had begun. As we rumbled away from the station, Neville commented, "Truly a marvel, these iron horses, aren't they? Why we'll be in St. Louis in a matter of days."

"None too soon," I commented.

"Ah, then begins the hard part. Steamboat up the Missouri to St. Joseph, then the stage along the central-overland route."

I sighed, looking out at the white clapboard houses that began to pass quickly.

"Twenty-four days." I looked at Neville. "Do you intend to make the journey straight through?"

Neville took a moment before answering, and when he did, it was with a question of his own.

"Surely ladies like yourselves will wish to refresh yourselves at the way stations. Bouncing on hard leather seats from St. Joseph to Sacramento can do nothing to enhance your lovely appearances and health."

I dropped the subject. The conductor took the tickets, and finally Neville slid back the door to the aisle to go to his own compartment. But he insisted on escorting us to the dining car for dinner.

I spent the first few hours of the journey reading, while Fanny worked on some embroidery, wincing once when she pricked a finger. Seeing that Neville refused to leave us alone, we followed him to the dining car later.

Over coffee, he began to talk about Father. Of all Neville's conversation, I was at least interested in hearing about my own father and found myself curious about the business relationship shared by Neville, my father, and that other man, Christian Reyeult.

"How did you come to work the claim together?" I asked him. "Father really told us very little."

"Ah, I am pleased that there is at least one topic I have to offer that interests you." His curved lips and dark eyes challenged me.

I suppressed my immediate reaction and forced a smile instead. "You were going to tell us how you started."

He described how the three of them arrived at their claim at the same time and how rather than fighting it out, Gaspar suggested they do business together.

"I liked old Gaspar immediately," Neville chuckled. "He seemed a shrewd man, one I could do business with. I didn't trust the French Canadian, Reyeult, but your father pointed out that with three of us, we could keep each other honest, so I agreed."

I couldn't resist querying. "And did you?"

"What?"

"Keep each other honest?"

Instead of the quick repartee I had expected from such a remark, Neville's eyes darkened slightly. But in a moment the sober look was gone, and he flashed his white teeth in a beguiling smile.

"Honest as this world goes," he said.

For a long moment, Neville and I stared into each other's eyes as if assessing the quality of the person that lay behind the social trappings. At first Thomas Neville had struck me as a man I did not want to know. Now I was beginning to think there might be things about him I needed to know, if only to learn more about my father's life.

Back in our compartment after dinner, I stared out at the gathering darkness, my thoughts turning to the picture of the three men who had worked the claim together, made a profit, started a general store to supply the miners, and then lost it all.

"I admit," said Neville later that evening, "that I found it hard to work for anyone but myself. I was not sorry to leave California and return to take over my family's business. But I never forgot Gaspar, no ma'am. In fact, I am more than curious to see how far his adventurous spirit has led him. I admit I have become tempted to join you in your journey all the way to Yosemite Valley."

I dropped my crocheting. "Whatever for?"

Neville crossed his ankles lazily. "It would be a shame to cross the continent and not see this Yosemite Gaspar was always yammering about."

He lifted an eyebrow, fastening his gaze on me.

"Besides, that part of the country can be dangerous this time of year. By the time you get there it will be October, and snow can set in as early as November."

"It won't be necessary to accompany us any further than Sacramento," I said with emphasis. "We plan to hire a guide for the trip into the mountains, for of course we would not attempt the trail by ourselves."

He touched his hat brim in a salute, then folded his arms across his chest and stared out the window. I returned my eyes to my crocheting, the rhythm of the wheels on the rails below hammering in my ears.

From St. Louis, we took a steamboat up the Missouri River to St. Joseph, where we checked into a modest hotel. I was appreciative of the night's sleep in a soft bed and a chance to bathe and eat a meal in a room that wasn't moving. But early the next day we left for the stage that would carry us on the overland trek across the continent to California.

I surveyed the heavy wooden coach suspended from its straps of tough steer hide, curved at the bottom like a hammock against which the coach body rested. The advertisement promised "comfortable travel in luxurious Concord coaches," but I was no fool. Twenty-four days and nights in the thing, sleeping on the seats, walking when hills were too steep for the team, or through sand or mud, would prove anything but luxurious.

A portly gentleman of about age fifty had made our acquaintance. "Consider yourself lucky, my dear," he said to me. "At least you have to go only one way. Had you the return to contemplate you would most likely be coming back by sailing ship."

Finally we boarded, and once in the coach, which

seated nine, private conversation all but ceased, for which I was thankful. But I noticed how Neville, seated by my sister this time, took every opportunity to catch her arm or support her with his leg when the coach took a sharp turn and she was thrown against him.

Fanny always laughed shyly when Neville gave her a little pat or squeeze. Such gestures made my stomach turn, and more than once I met Neville's gaze with a threatening one of my own. I hoped he was not seeking encouragement from that quarter. Fanny was too young and inexperienced to realize what her coy looks could do to a man like Thomas Neville.

The days and nights seemed endless, the dust seeping into the coach so that it burned our eyes and lungs. When the trip proved too strenuous, we recuperated with a night's rest at a way station, failing to shake Thomas Neville even then.

Several times we had to alight and walk up a rough rocky trail while the horses and coach went ahead, and Fanny and I appreciated the opportunity to stretch our legs. On one morning's walk, Neville was talking to a gentlemen who had recently boarded, so I took the opportunity to speak to my sister.

"I do hope you're not encouraging Mr. Neville, Fanny."

"Why, Hilary, just because you insist on being rude to him doesn't mean I can't talk to him. He's only trying to be entertaining and help us pass the time on this horrible trip."

I yanked my skirt free from a bush that seemed to reach out over the side of the road. "Don't forget when we reach Sacramento he'll be occupied with business and will have little time for entertaining us."

"Why, I believe you're jealous," she said slyly.

"Oh!" I frowned and pressed my lips into a stern line.

My little lecture was having no effect, and I despaired of trying to warn my little sister to stay out of Neville's way, for I still did not trust the man.

On the tenth day out, at a small, rickety way station situated on a prairie that swept eternally to the horizon in every direction, we dined on bread, tea, and fried steaks of antelope, the thin walls at least protecting us from a threatening dust storm.

Talk had again turned to the mining days. As evening drew on, Neville was recounting the night of the awful fire that had burned up all their profits.

I commented, "There was nothing left to do, I suppose."

I had meant it as an idle contribution to the conversation, but Neville's gaze sobered, and I could see him contemplating his next words. For some reason, I felt more compelled than usual to pay attention.

Finally, he turned sideways, stretching his feet to the rough-hewn rude bench opposite, and crossed one boot over the other as he stared at the fire the host had built in the rude stone fireplace.

Gone was the devil-may-care attitude or the almost overbearing way he usually directed our conversation. Instead, he spoke as if he were carefully weighing his words before he uttered them.

"When we were partners," he began, not looking at anyone. "Gaspar and Christian and I often played cards together to while away the long evenings. On the night before the fire, the stakes ran high. Gaspar won."

He glanced at me, as if to make sure I was paying attention. I nodded, wanting to hear the rest of the story.

31

"Reyeult accused Gaspar of cheating, paid half of what he owed, swearing it hadn't been won honestly. I didn't have cash on me and had to give Gaspar my IOU. I'll tell you now that is the real reason I want to go to California, for I wish to find your father and discharge my debt."

I creased my brow. I wondered if it would seem petty of me if I pointed out that since Gaspar's daughters were seeking him, Neville could simply give us the money and we would deliver it to our father when we found him. But for some reason, I said nothing.

Neville returned his gaze to the fire. "Now that I have the money to pay him, I want to see it through."

I thought that was the end of it, but Fanny asked, "What about the other man? He accused Father of cheating."

Her comment roused Neville from his reverie. "Oh yes. The two of them would have fought it out, but I forced Reyeult to apologize, and for Gaspar to accept Reyeult's IOU for the other half of his debt as well."

"And so that is how you left it?" I said.

"Yes. Your father and the Canadian finally shook hands, but you could see by the look in their eyes, it was the end of the partnership. The next night, there was the fire."

"Well, did Father really cheat?" Fanny asked.

Neville smiled benevolently. "I saw him do nothing dishonest, but then I wasn't watching for it. A dishonest man is often more suspicious than others," he said, implying doubts about Reyeult's integrity. "And if Reyeult thought your father pulled a card from his sleeve, I never saw it."

Neville lifted his coffee cup and studied the bottom of it. "But then I never believed your father was a cheating man."

Chapter 3

The stagecoach rumbled for days over the road to the gold town of Mariposa. There Fanny and I settled into a bedroom with sitting room in a two-story hotel with a balcony along the front.

In the morning, I approached the desk. The manager, a small, clerkish-looking man, looked up and gave me a thin smile. "Good morning, miss. What can I do for you?"

"I need to hire a guide. My sister and I need someone who can take us to Yosemite Valley."

He took off his spectacles and polished them, not meeting my gaze. "Good guides cost money," he said.

"We can pay. I am looking for someone who was last known to be there—my father."

"Who might your father be?"

"Gaspar Fenton. Do you know of him?"

He frowned in concentration, replaced his spectacles and scratched his bald head.

"Fenton, yes the name sounds familiar, but . . ."

"And a guide for the trail?" I reminded him of my other question.

He considered me. "If you're determined to penetrate Yosemite Valley this late in the year, the only man for the job is Christian Reyeult, if you can get him."

I blinked. *Reyeult here?*

My father had written me that his erstwhile partner had gone to the Oregon Territory, and Neville had made no mention of the possibility that Reyeult might be here. But if he was perhaps he might know where Father was. My pulse quickened at the possibility.

"Where can I find Mr. Reyeult?"

"You can leave a message for Reyeult at Bertha Johns's boarding house where he stays when he's in town, but that's not very often. Keeps to himself mostly. Doesn't seem to like people much."

I stared at the prim little manager a moment, still assimilating the news. "Thank you."

He gave me directions on how to reach the boarding house, and I crossed the lobby, coming out to stand on the boardwalk in front. Bearded miners and tradesmen crossed the wide dirt street or lounged in the shade of the wooden awnings in front of the few falsefronted buildings. Several men lounging against the rails stared boldly at me, and I pulled my paisley shawl tighter around my shoulders.

Christian Reyeult was actually in this area. And now Neville was on his way here, too. Neville's business had kept him in Sacramento, but he promised he would follow on the next day's stage. I felt a tingling in my spine and could not help but wonder if there was any connection. Why would the two expartners converge on the same area at the same time after not seeing each other for over two years? Though Neville had not said anything about it, was it possible they had planned it?

The boardinghouse was a two-story clapboard affair at the end of the street. A tilted sign had the word *Rooms* painted on it and hung from the porch roof by one nail.

Following a wooden walk up to the porch, I knocked on the rickety screen door. It was answered by a matronly woman with gray hair pulled back in a bun and small black eyes that examined me from behind spectacles balancing on the end of her nose. She wiped her hands on her white apron. The screen door screeched as she opened it.

"Come in, miss. I'm Bertha Johns. What can I do for you?"

I followed her inside. "I'm looking for some information."

"Come in here, then," she said, directing me to a tiny parlor with a window that looked out to the street. "The place isn't much, but I can give you a cup of tea."

"Thank you."

"You wait here. The water's already boiled, so all I've got to do is let her steep."

She rustled out and I took a seat in a faded upholstered chair and gazed at the homely parlor with its assortment of mismatched furniture, potbellied stove in the corner, and a pair of yellow shaded lamps with beaded fringe. Mrs. Johns was back in a minute with crockery rattling on a tray which she set on a scratched coffee table, and soon I was sipping tea from a white china cup as I sat stiffly on the edge of the chair.

She poured her own tea and gave me an appraising look as she sat back in her creaky rocking chair.

"Now, what kind of information is it you'd be looking for?"

"I'm looking for my father. Have you ever heard of Gaspar Fenton?"

"So Gaspar Fenton's your father."

35

She rocked and squinted. "I guess I coulda told you that by lookin', but my eyes aren't what they used to be. Well you've come to the right place. Haven't seen him in a long time though. He was here in July, I think it was, stocking up on supplies. What's your name, child?"

Relief swept through me. I had not imagined that it would be quite so easy to track my father. So many people must come through this part of the country, it was a miracle that the first two people I'd talked to actually knew who my father was.

A confusion of emotions suddenly spilled over as I realized how near I was to actually seeing him, and I unexpectedly choked on my words.

"I'm so glad," I said. "How is he?"

"Last time I saw him he was ornery as a fly in currant pie. How long since you've seen him?"

I blinked. "Well I was four years old when my mother died. He left shortly after that. He came back to visit us one Christmas when I was ten, I think."

I shrugged, suddenly embarrassed to be confiding these personal facts to a complete stranger. But Bertha Johns peered at me, her interest obvious.

"You must be about twenty, I'd judge."

"Twenty-two."

"Then your father's not seen you in over a decade." Her leathery face finally split into a smile, and I noticed that she had a tooth missing. "I reckon he'll find you changed."

"He might not even recognize me," I admitted. "But I have to find him first."

Bertha scratched the bridge of her nose with a finger, setting her teacup down.

"If I remember correctly, he planned to build himself a cabin and stay on Widow's Mountain all winter.

36

Folks told him he's crazy. He'll be stuck there from the time the snows come till spring thaw in the passes, though there's sun in that there valley in winter, he swears."

A sly grin passed over Bertha's face. "That Gaspar, he used to pass his evenings with me when he was here. He could tell a tale."

I hid my look of curiosity by lowering my eyes to my teacup. Apparently my father had an admirer in Bertha Johns. When I had sobered my expression, I said, "With a competent guide, do you think I'll be able to find him?"

"It's late in the year for traveling in the mountains. You should've come in the early part of the summer."

"Yes, I know."

I told Mrs. Johns about our circumstances in Brooklyn and why we had come. She rocked back and forth, watching me as I spoke.

"Yes, I suppose Gaspar Fenton might like a home with his grown-up daughters," she said. "But you couldn't get him to stay under your roof all the year round. There's too much of the adventurer in him. He does have to do his exploring. Didn't I hear all about it? He even showed me his map, the one he shows no one."

I looked at Bertha curiously. "What map?"

"The one he got from the Indians, the Ahwahneeches. It was the reason he went into Yosemite Valley in the first place."

"Father said nothing to me about a map or any Indians," I told Bertha. Of course Father had always been looking for gold. Maybe the Indians knew about some gold and had drawn a map for him.

Outside, the sun was setting, and the room darkened as Bertha began to tell me the legend left behind by the

37

Ahwahneeches who had been driven from the valley three years ago by a battalion that went in to bring them down to a reservation on the plains. They had not wanted to go.

"They knew where there was gold in the mountains," she said. "So much gold it blinded the eye to look at it. Many a white man looked for the Ahwahneeches' gold, but no one who ever went into Yosemite Valley to look for it ever returned alive. Or if they did, they were half crazy. No white man can confront the ghost horse the Indians left to guard the gold. Has hooves of silver. Once you're struck, there's no recovering. I warned Gaspar not to go after that gold, but he wouldn't listen."

She shook her head. "I don't mean to worry you, my dear, but I fear for him. It's the Indian curse. If Gaspar isn't careful, he'll be its next victim. I wouldn't go into that valley, not I," she said. "Haunted by the Ahwahneeches, it is."

I set my cup and saucer on the coffee table, no longer feeling jubilant. The story she told me was unsettling.

"I'm also looking for Mr. Christian Reyeult," I said. "The hotel manager said I might be able to leave word for him here."

"Ah now there's a fine specimen of a man. Arms and legs that could wrestle a bear, and have. Strange one though, keeps to the hills a lot. Can't say when he'll be here, but I'll give him the message if he does come."

I went on. "I had wanted to hire him as a guide, to try and locate my father."

"Well he's a good one at that. Knows his way around those mountains. Always make a room up special for him, I do. I tell the man a few nights in a bed instead of sleeping on the ground won't hurt him. Course he frequents the Bull Whacker's Rest sometimes when he's here. He's no less susceptible to whiskey and cards than any other man."

I thought of the daguerrotype I had seen of the man, unconsciously smoothing my skirt.

"I'm rather anxious to try to reach my father, since it is so late in the year," I said.

"If I hear from either of those rascals, I'll be sure and let you know. You just count on old Bertha."

She grinned her odd grin, the gap in her teeth giving her a wild look. "These parts can be rough on womenfolk, and if you need a place to hole up for a while, why you just bring yourselves along to me."

I thanked her, but there was something about the dim boardinghouse that made me feel I wouldn't be comfortable staying here. I scribbled a message on a piece of paper for Christian Reyeult and left it with Bertha.

"Tell me," I said as I was leaving. "Did Mr. Reyeult ever mention my father? They used to be partners, but I don't believe they came here together."

She folded the note, tucking it into her apron. "He may have mentioned your father's name, but if he did, he didn't say anything about 'em bein' partners."

"Well thank you, Mrs. Johns—"

She held up a hand. "Now, now. I'm Bertha to those that know me."

I smiled. "All right, Bertha, and I will call on you if I need anything."

Bertha patted my hands and then watched me as I went down the wooden steps to the boardwalk that led back to the hotel. The sign hanging on its nail squeaked in the breeze behind me.

New fears assailed me, and I thought perhaps we'd

come too late. In the sunlight, I tried to tell myself not to believe the legend, that my father would not be harmed by an Indian curse, but I couldn't rid myself of the nagging concern.

Bertha had said that Christian frequented the Bull Whacker's Rest, so I decided to try my luck there.

The Bull Whacker's Rest appeared to be the noisiest saloon on the street. Even in the middle of the day, the tinny sound of a piano issued forth from its open, arched doorway. I stepped to the door to look in.

As my eyes adjusted to the dim light, the piano music stopped, and there was only the clink of gold pieces and the rattle of glasses at the bar.

"Well, well, well," I heard a man's voice say. "What have we here? Come on in, miss. What can we do for you?"

I made out the figures of several groups of men hovered over smoky round tables cluttered with bottles of whiskey and cards. I wanted to turn around and leave, but I forced myself to project my words firmly, so that I would not seem timid.

"I'm looking for a Mr. Christian Reyeult. I've been told he often comes here."

Loud guffaws came from the men, and the one who had first addressed me walked toward the door and slouched against the door frame.

"We try to separate him from his money in here from time to time. Sometimes we're successful. You a friend of his?"

Again, the laughter. But at least I had found out Christian Reyeult was known here.

"No," I said rather snappishly. "I've never met him. I've been told he's a good guide, that's all."

"Well now, if it's a guide you want, we got plenty of those."

The man, who was none too clean and had several teeth missing, motioned to some of his friends, and I heard their chairs scrape against the wooden floor.

"No thank you," I said as I began to back out of the door. "I believe I'll wait for Mr. Reyeult. I've left messages for him elsewhere."

And I turned and hurried down the street, I would have to be more careful. Such dens of iniquity were dangerous to young women like myself. For a moment my imagination ran away with me, and I imagined Fanny and myself being sold into white slavery.

Then I stopped on the street corner and took a deep breath. If I was careful, I would be all right here. Some of the people in this town seemed decent enough, and I would just watch the company I kept.

I spent the rest of the day making inquiries about my father and about Christian Reyeult. Most of the shopkeepers I spoke to said they'd heard of both men but didn't remember when they'd been in town last, and no one had ever seen them together.

There was no word the next day from Bertha, so I decided to look at pack animals myself. Finding my way to the livery stable, I introduced myself to the large, muscular black-haired stableman named Smitty and told him my plight. He scratched his head, looking me over, but I stopped him when he started to try to discourage me.

"Please, Mr. Smith, I've already been told my enterprise is foolish, and I'll spare you the reasons I feel it necessary to make this trip at this time of year. Please just show me the animals that might be useful on such a trip. At least I can get an idea of the cost."

"Well, miss, and if you're that insistent . . ."

He took me to the corral where a number of long-eared, sleepy-looking mules were tethered to the fence. He pointed out their attributes.

"Sure footed they are, even if they look dumb and lazy. But they'll carry your packs over trails a mountain goat would sneer at."

He waxed eloquent over the value of mules. "Their facility to acclimate, their sedate temper and resistance to fatigue make them the most valuable creatures man has ever used to serve his needs." He stopped to pick something from his teeth with a piece of straw.

"I see."

"You'll need a mount yourself, of course," he said.

He led me back to the stable and along a row of stalls where horses hung their heads over the ends of the stalls, waiting for a possible treat. He stopped halfway down the row. The Indian-red mare in one stall eyed Smitty and reached out to nuzzle his pocket.

"Delilah's a fine mare," he said to me. "Sturdy and gentle for a lady."

Delilah swung her head in my direction, and I reached up to touch the velvety nose, trying to picture myself on the mare's back ascending the steep trails into Yosemite.

The scrape of boot heels announced another visitor and a musical baritone voice touched with a French Canadian accent said, "Ah, I disagree, Smitty. Delilah's a fine mare, but shouldn't you show the young lady the best you've got?"

I turned toward sunlight streaming in the stable door, and the tall silhouette stepped forward and became a blond man wearing a buckskin hunting shirt which hung below the waist and long leather leggings with fringe and scarlet cloth along the seams, the leggings stuffed into high-laced leather boots. His stiff wool hat was wide-brimmed and high-crowned with a scarlet band around it that held a tuft of wild bird feathers.

He reached into the furthest stall. Running his long fingers along a mouse-colored mare, he said, "Now this old girl is what you are looking for."

The man I recognized as Christian Reyeult went on. "Gabrielle might not look very pretty, but she's sure-footed. I've been with her on the trail many times and she's never led me wrong, have you my girl?"

"That is true, Christian," said Smitty, leaning against a post and crossing his arms. "But I did not know how much Miss Fenton wanted to spend."

Christian Reyeult paused in his ministrations to the mare and looked at me. The amused smile under his blond moustache and his blue eyes held a look of interest, and after a moment surveying me, he said, "But allow me to introduce myself. I am Christian Reyeult, and you are . . . ?"

"Hilary Fenton."

I straightened and extended my hand nervously. At last I had found the man I had been looking for. I regarded the blond hair that came to his shoulders and framed the rugged face, the blue eyes with silver flecks, lit with *joie de vivre,* and the drooping moustache that partially hid what promised to be a well-shaped mouth.

"As I said, Miss Fenton," he continued in his rolling accent, "Gabrielle knows the trails, and she is worth the money. But perhaps we should talk privately, eh?"

"Then you received my message?"

"I did."

His easy gaze raked over me, and he jutted his chin toward the door. We left the stable and walked out to

43

stand in the sunlight. Christian stopped and faced me again, making no attempt to hide his curiousity.

"I am intrigued by meeting Gaspar Fenton's daughter, but alas, I must disappoint you."

"Have you seen my father?" I took a step closer in anticipation. "He didn't say anything in his letters about your being here."

He shook his head. Hands on hips, he rested his weight on one leg.

"No. I haven't seen him. I have no idea where your father is, so you see, I can hardly accept your money to lead you to him."

My heart sank, and my voice rose in a sudden feeling of desperation. "I must find him. My sister and I have nowhere else to go."

He studied me as if my face reminded him much of old Gaspar, his expression turning to amusement.

"It is too late in the year to begin such a journey for those unfamiliar with the trail."

Sick to death of the same advice over and over again after we had come all this way, I shook my head and turned away from him. I gazed down the dusty street behind the stable and out to the hills where miners' cabins dotted the banks of the streams.

"I really am determined to find my father. And I can pay you well."

He cleared his throat, moving a step nearer.

"The trip into the valley takes several days," he said. "It's far too dangerous for a woman, even one as determined as you, my lovely."

I refrained from mentioning Fanny, who was much less determined and certainly more timid of such a venture than I.

"Does no one winter in the valley?" I asked. "I

understand my father is building a cabin for the winter."

"Hmm. That may be. But the accommodations in Yosemite are not what you are accustomed to. Even old wall-eyed Drusilla Earley and her husband, Franz, close up their ramshackle hotel and come down when the last of the visitors leave."

I opened my mouth to continue with my queries, but Christian stopped me. "No more, eh? I came to town for one reason, mademoiselle. I have a great desire for a good meal. I cannot listen to the badgerings of a female, even such an attractive one as yourself, on an empty stomach."

His eyes teased me as he continued. "Since you are so interested in hearing about your father, if you will dine with me this evening I will tell you all I know of him and of the beautiful Yosemite Valley where he has probably disappeared until spring."

Impatience coursed through me. Christian Reyeult was just as bad as Thomas Neville. He had the same hungry look in his eye, and I wasn't fooled by his pseudo gallantry. At the moment I did not know which of them was the less honest. For standing in front of me was the man who had once accused my father of being a cheat.

I wanted with all my heart to refuse to dine with him, and it thoroughly annoyed me that because I was a woman, I was forced to rely on these arrogant men to take me where I wanted to go.

"All right," I said, feeling I had little choice if I wanted information about my father from this French Canadian.

He stepped closer to me, bent his head, and said in a voice meant only for my ears, "Do not be so annoyed with me, my lovely. I have been on the trail for many weeks. An evening's relaxation and conversation with a woman of beauty like yourself will surely put me in a more congenial mood."

His eyes roamed over my curls. His glance took in my face and figure. His meaning was all too obvious.

"I will tell you of the valley you wish to see," he said, his voice coaxing. "Of walking through rainbows over waterfalls, such as you've never seen. Of sleeping in groves of tapering pines. That is what you wish to know?"

For moment I stood transfixed, his words soothing my temper. Then I swallowed and gave him the name of our hotel.

I examined myself in the mirror while Fanny sat on the bed giving me advice about my hair. I wished I hadn't put on my good off-the-shoulder indigo evening dress, but Fanny had persuaded me to wear it. The thought of Christian Reyeult looking at my bare shoulders made my face warm. I turned from the mirror and started toward the trunk that was open at the foot of the bed where Fanny and I had rooted through the clothing earlier. I would have to change.

"I hope," Fanny said to me, stopping me from reaching for the pile of more sturdy, modest clothing that spilled out of the trunk, "that you're not going to treat Christian Reyeult the way you treated Thomas Neville. If you continue with your high-handed manners, we'll never get to Yosemite."

I paused, and Fanny led me back to the vanity bench, fussing over my hair. "A winning smile will go farther to persuade this Frenchman than all the stubbornness in the world," she said. "He will never take us to the mountains if he dislikes us."

46

I considered my little sister in some amusement. I should have realized that hearing her offer advice on how to get what I wanted from a man was typical of her growing coquettishness.

"He isn't French," I said, allowing Fanny to arrange curls on either side of my face. "He's French Canadian. There's a difference."

At seven, I descended to the hotel lobby, tightly clutching a cream-colored cotton lace fichu, which I had draped over my shoulders at the last minute, claiming I would be too cool without it. Across the room, Christian Reyeult rocked on the heels of polished black boots as he waited next to a square supporting pillar. In frock coat and starched collar he looked very much the gentleman. The leonine hair curling over his ears and the moustache, swept upward, did not seem out of place in these surroundings where mountain men, businessmen, and miners lounged in leather chairs and smoked cigars.

I crossed to him and his gaze slashed from my carefully arranged coils to the satin slippers peeking out from under my generous skirts. He bowed before me, then offered me his arm.

We took seats at a corner table in the small hotel dining room and ordered venison, potatoes with gravy, greens, and thick slices of bread. When the food arrived, I was forced to loosen the knot in the fichu and drape it across the back of my chair so that it wouldn't fall into my plate.

Christian kept his lips compressed, but his eyes betrayed something of his thoughts.

The food seemed to satisfy him, and he commented that the the wine warmed him. When he sipped it, his eyes never left my face. I listened with interest as he described the giant sequoia trees in the Mariposa grove, my blood quickening that we might soon be there. He said these unusual trees were thought to be thirteen hundred years old, and he made me want to see such a wonder.

"You are still determined to find your father, in spite of the danger?" he finally asked.

"Of course."

"Then I will consider it," he said.

"You will?"

He grinned. "It is very hard to say no to the beautiful daughter of my old friend and colleague."

I felt relieved. "I am glad you will take us."

"You cannot blame me, my lovely. You did not have to dress in such a way as to fetch my attention."

In spite of myself, I could not deny his charisma. I had meant to persuade him to take us into the mountains, but I had not meant for it to lead in the direction he seemed to construe. I decided his French Canadian blood had endowed him with a natural prowess and charm—a charm I should beware of.

He gave a guttural laugh. "How dare old Gaspar sire such a tempting morsel of a daughter and for fate to place her within my grasp?"

When we had finished, he rose and held my chair, his fingers brushing the smooth skin of my back. I stiffened, fighting the pleasant sensation of his touch, which was unsettling after the mellowness the wine had caused me.

He led me out of the dining room, across the lobby, and up the red carpeted staircase. At the landing he turned to me.

"Which room?"

I gave the number, and he followed me along the

carpeted hallway, waiting while I put the key in the keyhole.

I pushed the door open, and before I could stop him, he had followed me into the sitting room. Fanny was nowhere to be seen. She must have gone to bed. He took my hand in his and held it for a moment, looking into my eyes.

I reclaimed my hand and turned away from him. I stepped over to the window and was studying the lamplit street below, but I sensed Christian moving up behind me. As he bent to kiss the nape of my neck and ear, I gasped. I turned in a reflex motion, even though his lips on my skin sent a tingling sensation rushing through me.

He held my shoulders with his hands, preventing me from moving, forcing me to look into his silvery blue eyes.

"Hilary, you are a lovely young woman," he whispered.

He raised his fingers to my cheeks. I drew my breath inward at the contact, my body suddenly shaking. For a moment, I simply stood there, my eyes closed, and Christian, emitting a sound of pleasure, bent and kissed my eyelids.

"You'd better leave now," I said shakily, moving to the window to look at the street again.

He stepped backward two steps then turned. His tread was soft as he walked to the door. I was staring out the window again and did not even hear him open the door to pass through.

It was not until later, after I had struggled out of my gown and was brushing out my hair in the sitting room so as not to wake Fanny, that I saw the folded note on the sofa. I laid the brush down and unfolded the piece of paper that had been camouflaged by the floral print of the upholstery. I stared at the words printed in crude block letters.

HE DIES WHO GOES TO WIDOW'S MOUNTAIN.

Chapter 4

I stared at the note for a long time, trying to understand where it might have come from and who might
have written it. Someone was trying to warn us or was
trying to dissuade us from our trip. Any number of
people were trying the latter, and if the note was meant
merely as a deterrent, I did not appreciate the melo-
dramatic approach of the author.

I slept uneasily that night. I hid the note among my
things and did not mention it to Fanny. The notion
even crossed my mind that she had written it as a sort
of prank, for I knew that she did not look forward to
going any further into the wilderness. And if she
hadn't written the warning, it might only serve to un-
nerve her, and the last thing I needed was more of her
hysterics.

Naturally the next morning she plied me with questions about my dinner with Christian Reyeult, and I
told her little, except that he had agreed to take us. She
was miffed that I remained so reticent.

Later in the day, I set out to make a few purchases
at the general store and at the pharmacy. Dark clouds
had gathered, and it started to sprinkle while I was

doing my errands, but I thought I would be able to get back to the hotel before the storm broke.

Thunder rumbled in the sky, and as I was dodging wagons and riders in the middle of the street, the rain began to come down in earnest. I clutched my parcels to me, and finally made it to the other side, but not before I had gotten a good soaking.

The wet gown doing nothing to improve my mood, I went up to change. Fanny was out, so I patiently undid all the hooks and eyes myself and got the wet garment over my head. I had spread it over the back of a chair in the bedroom and walked to the open trunk to get another, when I heard a footstep in the sitting room. Thinking Fanny had come back, I went to the bedroom door. Then I gasped. Thomas Neville stood in the center of the sitting room.

"Oh," I said, holding the dry gown, which I had fortunately in my grasp, in front of me.

His eyes took in the sight of the naked arms holding the half-folded garment covering my camisole and cor-set-clad form. Amusement filled his eyes, and he removed his wide-brimmed hat.

"Pardon me," he said, though he didn't move.

Caught off guard, I stammered, "I thought you were Fanny."

Then I spied the dressing screen to my left and made a dive to it, gritting my teeth behind the screen at Neville's behavior. Why didn't he leave?

"I see I've caught you at an inopportune time," he called from the other room. "I'll wait here while you change."

Seeing that I could do nothing to make him leave, I struggled into my dress, my fingers clumsy with the fastenings. I had suspected that Thomas Neville was no gentleman, and I could tell by the sound of his voice that he enjoyed the idea of the state of my undress.

I pulled on muslin petticoats, furious with resentment that I had to dress so quickly. When he was gone I would simply have to change again, for my camisole and corset were damp and I could not change them without Fanny to help me lace up.

When I was ready, I reappeared, and he gazed at me from his seat on the sofa. He had removed his hat, and from his slightly rumpled frock coat I judged that he had come directly from the stagecoach here. I stammered out an inquiry about his journey.

"Satisfactory, though every mile I looked forward to again being in your lovely presence and that of your sister."

A slight lift of the chin was all the acknowledgment he got from me.

"I have come to invite both of you to dine with me this evening." His tone was smooth and solicitous as usual.

I was about to decline when the door opened again, and Fanny came in. Her eyes shot to Neville, who rose and bowed over her hand. She blushed and lowered her gaze.

"I was just telling your sister," he said, "that I am in hopes both of you will dine with me this evening."

"I'm afraid—" I began.

"How nice," said Fanny, raising wide eyes to his and giving him a smile that would move a statue.

"Very well then. I'll call for you at seven. We shall catch up on news, shall we not?"

He reached for his hat and was at the door before I could make a move. Drat. The last thing I wanted was dinner with the man. But I couldn't leave Fanny alone with him either.

"I wish you weren't so enthralled with that man," I snapped.

"Oh, Hil, he's only taking us to dinner. It will be nice."

She flounced into the bedroom, over to the dressing table, and sat, spreading her wide flounces around the vanity bench.

Biting my lips to keep from making any more bitter remarks, I opened my parcels and put away the toiletries I had purchased. I supposed I ought to feel satisfied that soon we would be on our way to Yosemite, and I tried to spend the day reorganizing the belongings we would take and packing them in the saddlebags Christian sent over.

He had also sent a note naming his price. If I had no objections he would spend the next two days obtaining supplies and looking for a cook to take with us.

I sent a note to the boardinghouse in reply, agreeing to the price and the arrangements. I should have been happy. Instead, I found myself irritable and sulking. Luckily, Fanny seemed to sense it and kept out of my way.

That evening I suffered through dinner in the hotel dining room with Fanny and Neville, contributing little to the conversation, and shooting warning expressions to my sister when I felt she was making a fool of herself. I finally dragged her away, and perhaps Neville was relieved to see us go, for as he tipped his hat to us when we began to ascend the stairs, he turned and headed for the saloon on the other side of the lobby.

The next morning, Fanny and I put on outdoor dresses and our braided Zouave jackets and proceeded downstairs for our breakfast. Today we would have to see about split skirts for riding astride on the trail. I had already noticed that the mercantile had enough ready-made bloomer style skirts that we ought to be able to find some that fit.

The friendly host took our order of catfish, ham, eggs, and milk, and then I looked up in surprise to see Christian Reyeult come through the door that opened onto the street. Seeing us, he came directly to our table, and without being invited, pulled out a chair.

"Bonjour, ladies," he said. He smiled cheerfully at me and then cast his gaze at Fanny, waiting to be introduced.

"May I present my sister, Fanny Fenton," I said. "Fanny, this is our guide and Father's former partner, Christian Reyeult. He will be taking us to Yosemite."

She batted her eyelashes prettily and nodded her head. Then the host came to pour our coffee.

"Ah," said Christian. "I'm just in time. A hearty breakfast is just what a man needs before setting out on a day of business. I have good news to report. I have found our cook, a Chinaman I know well and who is trustworthy on the trail."

I hardly listened to Christian's report of what he had accomplished in the way of preparing for our trip, so stunned was I that he was accepting coffee and a plate from the host. No doubt I was treating him to breakfast. He must have assumed it was just another one of his expenses.

I tried to stifle my irritation with his behavior and bring my attention back to what he was saying. After all, it was our money he was spending on the supplies and this cook he was talking about. He was talking about the pack animals he had purchased for us and the loads they would be carrying.

"We will go by way of the Mariposa grove," said Christian. "It is on the way, and you will not want to miss seeing the giant trees."

It crossed my mind that the self-confident French Canadian was making this a sight-seeing tour, costing us extra money, when our real objective was to find our father, and I said as much.

"Mr. Reyeult," I said in my most businesslike manner. "Please remember that we are not here for pleasure. We want to find our father as quickly as possible. I must insist that you keep that objective in mind."

He smiled at me in amusement, sending my heart lurching to my stomach and upsetting my stiff resolve. The man's dreamy glances were irritating beyond belief. No wonder he was a mountain man. I could see that his easygoing, relaxed manner would be good for nothing in the world of hustle-bustle I was used to.

I had grown up around people who worked from dawn to dusk for a living, and this man seemed to float through life needing nothing more than a campfire over which to cook meat and the ground to sleep on. At the time I did not see how he could call what he did work.

Just because he had spent his life in the mountains and therefore could guide people through them did not seem a very good excuse to call what he did earning a living. I had more than one opportunity later to see just how wrong I was. I believe on that morning Christian was having a good laugh on my account as he sized up my grim manner.

We were all distracted by the sight of Thomas Neville entering the dining room. When would we be rid of the man, I wondered.

Then I glanced at Christian, remembering that the two men were former partners. To my surprise, the

56

joie de vivre fled from Christian's face. He scowled as he watched Neville approach our table.

Neville was dressed immaculately as usual and carried his hat in his hand. The fixed smile also slipped from his face when he got near enough to recognize Christian. Then Christian's chair scraped back and he rose to confront the other man.

Neville's eyes narrowed slightly, and I saw the muscles in his neck stiffen. I was surprised. Neither man seemed glad to see his erstwhile partner, and their reactions further confused me. Fanny and I simply sat there with our mouths opened slightly, watching the two men close in on each other. I heard Christian audibly exhale a breath between parted lips.

Neville was the first to speak. "Well, this is a surprise. But then I should have known you might be in the area. It's been a long time, Reyeult."

"So it has," said Christian. Neither made a move to shake hands.

I was stunned. They might not ever have been close friends. Even I found their characters to be too different to expect them to share much camaraderie. And they may have parted with some animosity, but even I, who did not entirely understand their situation, was surprised at the depth of unpleasant feeling that seemed to pass between them. My mind whirled with questions. Both men had known and worked closely with my father. How did he fit into their small circle?

But there was not time to speculate. Neville went on. "I see you have met the Misses Hilary and Fanny Fenton."

He gave a smirk that he must have supposed passed for a smile. "Was it their own unmistakable beauty that lured you to their presence or knowledge that Gaspar Fenton's daughters were in the area?"

"It was I who sought out Mr. Reyeult," I said rather snappishly and then blinked at my own defense. But I could not stop there, for now everyone stared at me. "I have hired Mr. Reyeult to guide us to Yosemite to find our father."

Neville's eyes narrowed again. "So you still persist on this foolish venture. If you're not killed by a grizzly bear, you will be buried in an avalanche."

"We will leave before the snows," I said, having just discussed the matter with Christian.

Christian's blond brows raised slightly and his blue eyes betrayed a look of ironic amusement as I swung to the defense of his plan. But there was no time to consider my actions. Neville lost even his ironic swagger as a cloud of undisguised disapproval descended over his face.

"It will be dangerous even so," he insisted. "The trail is steep and difficult, even for the experienced, so I have heard."

Christian was eyeing him speculatively. "It seems you have looked into the matter quite thoroughly yourself."

"One cannot be very long in Mariposa without hearing a great deal about the Yosemite Valley. The name of the place is on everyone's lips, whether or not many plan to visit it themselves. It seems to be the latest wonder of the world."

With his last sentence his covert mockery seemed to return. I was uncomfortable sitting in the middle of the ill feelings that emanated from both men and was relieved when Neville took his leave. He gave a small bow of the head.

"I plan to be in Mariposa another day or two. I will call on you two ladies at a more convenient time."

I breathed a little easier when he left our table, but

I was still full of questions for Christian. Then I remembered what Bertha Johns had told me. As soon as Christian resumed his seat, I turned to him.

"Have you ever heard of the curse of the Ahwahneeches?" I asked.

His look darkened as he glanced sharply at me. "I have heard of it. What do you know of this matter?"

I repeated what Bertha Johns had told me. Christian sighed and drummed the checkered tablecloth with his long fingers.

"What has happened to the Ahwahneeches is most unfortunate. They have considered the Yosemite Valley their home for many generations. Indeed their home is rich with legends. They never expected to be forced to leave such a place. They thought their trails in and out of the valley were unknown to men outside the valley. Indeed it was many years after the valley was first sighted by a starving party of fur trappers that a way in was found.

"The Indians would have been safe had it not been for the determination of one Major James D. Savage. He was the man whose job it was to persuade the Ahwahneeches to make treaties. But when his messengers attempted to enter the valley, the Indians would roll down great rocks on any white man who ventured near. The soldiers would not enter because they believed there were many witches there."

My heart missed a beat when he said it and I imagined that the sun went behind the clouds. I glanced at Fanny, whose face was drawn tight with apprehension.

Christian saw her face pale and sat back. "It is true that the Indians have powers that most of our kind don't understand. But it is also true that legends are born of nothing more than one man's desire to keep

59

another from finding something. I would not worry about curses, if I were you. I would be more concerned about the difficulty of the trip. Have you purchased suitable traveling clothes?"

"We plan to do that today," I said. I told him of our plans to visit the mercantile after breakfast.

"Good. Then everything will be ready by tomorrow morning. We will leave at seven o'clock. I trust you can be ready by then?"

"Of course," I said.

I mentally counted backward, thinking how early I would have to drag Fanny out of bed.

Christian gave me an itemized bill for the purchases he had made so far and we settled up. He also estimated what he would need for the rest of the outfit and I advanced him a portion of it. I was rather proud of my abilities to negotiate. I refused to give him all the money he thought he would need. How did I know he would not simply leave town with it? I did agree that all the purchases would be paid for before we began the trip.

When we had settled our business and eaten our breakfasts I settled that bill, too. I felt an uncomfortable worry at seeing our money being spent at so rapid a rate. Fear asserted itself that we might never find Father and would end up in Mariposa penniless. Then what would we do?

However, I did not let my anxiety show and hustled Fanny off to the mercantile where we were waited on by a tough-looking middle-aged woman of generous proportions who told us her husband ran the saloon next to the hotel. Her name was Dora Mertz and she assisted us with trying on clothing, boots, hats, and warm wraps for the cool highlands.

There were so few women in Mariposa I felt inclined

to visit with her. She seemed to have no regrets about settling here and was proud of her store, which she felt sure would serve many customers as more and more travelers heard of the wonders of Yosemite.

"Have you seen it then?" I asked as she was wrapping our purchases in brown paper and tying them with string for us to carry back to the hotel.

"No, never seen it. The trails are steep, and there ain't many mules want to carry this body over them. But my husband predicts the day good roads'll be built there and stages'll get through. If I'm still alive maybe I'll be able to take a coach there and back."

"Well then," I said, "if the place draws that many travelers I'm sure your business will thrive."

"We're countin' on it," she said. "Like I said, if I live that long."

We bid her goodbye and I left her store with mixed feelings. Looking at the rough little town it was hard to imagine it as a thriving metropolis. Some of the residents seemed to feel that Yosemite Valley was an undiscovered wonder. Would it really draw travelers here someday in such great numbers as to boost the businesses of the town? It seemed as unlikely as my father's dreams of gold. And would travelers venture there if the place was cursed?

We took our packages back to our hotel room and busied ourselves arranging them and laying out what we would wear tomorrow morning. Fanny went through the motions, but there was no spirit in her. I began to feel guilty about bringing her here. But what choice did I have? There had been no one I could have left her with. Our neighbors in Brooklyn had always been kind, but I couldn't have afforded to board her anywhere, and I knew she was not anxious to work for a living.

61

After we had our things arranged, Fanny walked to the window and looked dejectedly out. Then uttering a great sigh, she turned.

"I think I'll take a walk," she said. "Perhaps I can call on that boardinghouse woman you spoke of, the one who knows Father."

I pressed my lips together. Of course Fanny was bored, and this would be the last day she could walk out in one of her day dresses and petticoats. I also realized that we ought to thank Bertha Johns for helping us find Christian Reyeult and let her know that we were leaving tomorrow. It was only courteous.

"Very well," I agreed. "Please thank Mrs. Johns for her interest in our affairs and tell her of our plans. But don't be gone too long. And stay to the main street. This is a mining town, Fanny. Some of the men here are very rough in nature. You must be careful."

She sniffed. "I can take care of myself."

After she left I continued to fold and refold clothing. A knock on the door startled me and I went to answer it. Thomas Neville stood there. I simply stared at him, surprised at seeing him so soon after this morning. He glanced past me into the room.

"May I come in?" he said.

I stepped back so he could do so. The minor irritation I felt whenever I saw him crawled up my spine, but I decided to be civil. After all, our plans were set, we would soon be on our way to finding Father.

Neville circled the sitting room, and I picked up a few things and took them to the bedroom to stuff into our baggage. I would have to arrange to leave our trunks here, with the clothing that would be impractical in Yosemite. Neville cleared his throat and I turned around.

He wasted no time with foolish frippery and came to

62

the point. "I have come to try to persuade you one last time to reconsider what you're doing," he said.

"I have reconsidered it," I said, stuffing a petticoat into the trunk.

"I want to warn you about your guide."

The ominous tone of his voice made me stop and glance up at him. "Why?"

"I have already told you of the argument between Mr. Reyeult and your father. He carries ill feelings. I fear what might happen should the two men find each other." He raised a dark brow. "There are many natural dangers in Yosemite Valley, to say nothing of the unnatural ones. Supposing Christian Reyeult means harm to your father. You would be leading Reyeult right to him."

I met Neville's gaze with a steady one of my own. I knew what I was about to say was based on nothing but my own instincts, but I felt obliged to defend my position.

"Suppose, instead, Mr. Reyeult seeks my father for the same reason you do. Suppose he wishes to pay him the money he owes him."

The idea had not occurred to me before I said it, but it was a possibility. I did not know either of my father's former partners well and could hardly have expected to understand their motives. I only posed my premise for the reason of argument. But perhaps that was the moment when I first realized that my mission consisted of more than finding Father. There was a mystery here, and I was about to be drawn deeper into it.

Neville lifted his chin a fraction. "I doubt it. I suggest you find another guide. You would be better off."

I straightened. "That is impossible. There are no

other guides available, and I have already advanced Mr. Reyeult half of his fee. We leave tomorrow."

He stared at me in exasperation for a moment and then lifted his shoulders in a slight shrug.

"Very well. I have done what I could to warn you. If you are fortunate and succeed in your mission, I will benefit as well. As I informed you, I also have a debt to pay Gaspar, and I would like to see him after all these years. It is my sincere hope that you bring him down from the valley. The hotel will always know my whereabouts."

"When we return, I will make sure he knows how to reach you," I said, leaning on the word *when*.

Neville bowed and strode to the door. His gestures were those of important business having been concluded. How ironic, I thought as I closed the door behind him. We hadn't concluded anything. In fact, we had only just begun.

Chapter 5

Christian stopped by later to pick up the saddlebags we had packed so that all would be ready when we met him the next day. He did not dally for conversation, but took the bulging bags with him.

The next morning Fanny and I rose just as the sky was beginning to turn a dull steel color. Fanny moaned and groaned as she sat at the dressing table brushing out her hair and then sat there stupidly until I pointed to the clothing she had laid out the night before.

"Hurry up, Fanny. We must be ready by seven o'-clock. I am not in the mood to withstand any smirks from Christian Reyeult if we are late. We can get breakfast in the dining room at six-thirty."

We dressed, laced up our boots, and groggily made our way downstairs. After placing our breakfast order, I found the manager and finalized our departure plans. He would look after our trunks while we were gone.

When we were ready, we went out to stand on the porch in the sun that had now penetrated the flinty sky and turned it a clear blue.

As expected, we found Christian moving about a train of pack mules tied to each other with rope halters. Cording and strapping bound a load to each beast of burden in one awkward mass, and he examined the knots that held the precarious supplies bundled onto the mules' backs. Then he went to our riding mounts, tightening girths. The mare Gabrielle was waiting for me, at least so it seemed, for she turned her head to look at me when I stepped down from the porch.

Now I noticed a strange bent figure hovering about the train of animals and at first thought he might be a beggar. But then I saw that when Christian gave him orders, he followed our guide's direction. It wasn't until he turned from one task and faced me that I saw the Oriental features of a rather flat face and realized this must be the Chinaman who would cook for us.

Then Christian directed the Chinaman to get on the other side of the lead pack mule. Each man took hold of the ends of the ropes that passed around and around the poor animal. Christian put a foot against the side of the mule's load, and with a shout, both guide and cook strained against the ropes as if trying to choke the mule between them.

I wondered how the poor beast could breathe. A faint grunt came from the solid animal, and I heard something within one of the parcels crunch, but Christian seemed not to think it mattered. He secured the knot and then grasped the top of the load and shook it hard. Not only did the load of pots, pans, and boxes vibrate, the mule did too.

Christian gave a satisfied chortle and stood back, his hands on his hips.

"He'll have to lose his skin before he can lose that,"

he announced and then turned to acknowledge our presence.

I stepped up to him, looking at the line of horses and mules, nodding in satisfaction. I was trying to remember that I was the employer, but of course if there had been anything to find fault with in Christian's preparations I would not have known it.

Fanny followed me into the sunlight, her eyes wide and tentative, and when she looked at the Chinaman, she jerked back.

Christian followed her gaze and waved a hand.

"Allow me to present our most estimable cook, Duignan," he said.

The Chinaman bowed.

"Duignan has been with me in many a camp and knows these mountains better than his own homelands," Christian said. "Should anything happen to me, you would be in safe hands, for Duignan's unerring sense of direction would lead you out."

He wore a traditional Chinese blouse over plain trousers, and his black hair was pulled into a long braid that hung down his back. But his felt hat was wide-brimmed and floppy, and it tied under his chin like a Mexican sombrero.

I nodded to the Chinaman, who bobbed again, but I hoped we would not have occasion to test Christian's theory about the cook's sense of direction.

Fanny looked doubtful about the whole proceeding, but Christian gestured to the train of animals as if pleased with himself at the beasts he had assembled. He then led us to our horses. I was to ride Gabrielle and remembered Christian's reassuring words about her at the stable the day we had met. He handed me some sugar to give her, and knowing that horses are

aware of a human's feelings toward them, I determined to make friends with her.

I had been around many horses, but most were the
work horses that pulled their loads through the streets
of Brooklyn. Once Gunther had sat me on the back of
a policeman's horse when I was small, but I had no
experience riding one, and the thought of guiding this
mount through the mountains sent a wave of apprehension up my spine.

Christian must have sensed my fear and quickly put
me at ease.

"You and Gabrielle will get along fine, eh? She is as
experienced in these mountains as old Duignan. Climb
onto the saddle and I will show you the touch of the
reins she likes."

He brought the mare out of line and led her to a
mount block. I stepped up on it so that I could more
easily put my booted foot in the stirrup.

"Take the reins in your left hand," Christian instructed smoothly, "and place the hand on the horse's
withers, just so."

He took my hand in his and laid it on the horse.
"Keep the reins light as you mount. Don't pull the
reins though or she'll back as you swing into the saddle. Understand?"

I nodded, holding the reins as he showed me.

"Take hold of the cantle with your right hand. As
you lift up, swing your right leg over, but don't bump
her with your toe. It is more courteous."

I did not know if he was joking, but he used his
hands to help hoist me into the saddle, and had I not
been so nervous about the horse, I might have objected to the way his hand slid down my hip and thigh
as I got settled. But he did not betray that it had been
anything more than an accident.

He adjusted the stirrups to my height so that my knees were slightly bent, my heels lower than my toes. I patted the mare's neck, and she snorted in what I took for pleasure. I began to relax as something of the old mare's dependability communicated itself to me.

Christian showed me how to hold the split reins.

"Ah, very good," he said, examining my seat. "You sit straight, but relaxed. The shoulders are square, you don't slouch."

He cocked his head first one way and then the other, much like someone examining a painting in a museum.

"Your weight should not be too far back on the cantle as you will then be out of balance with the horse. You see, sitting this way you will guide Gabrielle not only with the reins but with your legs and weight as well. And do not be tense."

It was a challenge to remain relaxed and I did not know how I could possibly retain the perfect seat through all the miles we must travel to get to Yosemite. I felt that Christian might be having some fun instructing someone as green as I was, but I tried not to be intimidated.

Fanny had watched me, and now Christian led an Appaloosa out of the line toward her. I saw her frown at the odd-looking horse, gray in front with spotted hindquarters. I curved my lips in irony but said nothing to Fanny's obvious displeasure at being asked to ride such an unattractive horse.

"Monty is a good stock horse and surefooted," Christian said to Fanny.

He led the gelding to the mounting block and helped Fanny into the saddle as he had done with me. She frowned and stiffened, and Christian spent some time speaking to her in his soothing, melodious voice until she surrendered her petulant look. I knew it was not so much for Fanny's pleasure that he did so, but for the horse. It was important to match horse and rider on this journey, I knew. We needed every advantage if we were to succeed.

When he had finished Fanny's riding lesson and watched her walk the horse once around in a circle, Christian took hold of my bridle and led me back into line. Duignan had mounted a long-eared mule that had fewer parcels tied to him, and after Christian gave one last critical look at the pack train, he gracefully swung himself onto a chunky palomino, the color of a newly minted gold coin.

Without even looking back, Christian led off. The other animals followed, with Duignan bringing up the rear. I should have felt elated that at last we were on our way to look for Father in the valley of Yosemite and that we were lucky to be with one of his former partners. But as we left the dusty town behind, it was with more a sense of foreboding that I gazed at the hills around us that hid the High Sierra from view.

I glanced at Fanny, who sat stiffly on her Appaloosa. Her eyes were wide as she stared straight ahead, and her face was white. My heart missed a beat. We were walking placidly on flat ground and she looked as if the jaws of hell had opened up to swallow her. What would she be like when we were on the high-winding trails that would take us to Yosemite?

I turned back in my saddle, feeling more desolate and lonely than I had since we had left the comfortable Brooklyn house. I stared at Christian's swaying back. I had entrusted our lives to a man I did not know. Neville's warnings came to mind, and I shivered.

What had really happened on the night of that card game? And did the fire have anything to do with it? It would be hard to imagine that one of the three partners had deliberately set the fire that had cost them everything, but stranger things had happened.

We followed a road that led us toward the mountains, past miners' cabins in clusters or singley, situated by every gulch and ravine we passed. I spent the time musing on the relationship among the three former partners, now that I had met them. My memories of my father were sketchy and subjective, but I had seen enough of their personalities to try to draw a picture in my mind. And I had to say, the whole arrangement struck me as odd.

Oaks and evergreens began to cluster in denser growth. We stopped for a cold lunch at an elevation of about three thousand feet where the timber was magnificent. Compared to eastern woods I had seen, there was little undergrowth here. The forest had an open feeling, which made me feel that we humans were very much the intruders. Many of the sugar and pitch pine grew two hundred feet high and seven to ten feet in diameter. When we gathered in a small area where Duignan circled the mules, he solemnly handed round dried beef, bread, and fruit.

"We'll have a fire tonight," Christian said, stretching his legs out in front of him as he leaned against a generous tree trunk. "We will camp in the Mariposa grove. You will be glad that we did not waste time here and that we'll spend our evening among the giants. You will not be disappointed."

I nodded in agreement and wondered silently to myself at Christian's air of being a tour guide. But I bit off the jerky and chewed on it. I did not want to constantly nag him with the reminder that we were on a very serious mission. I had the feeling that he was aware of my desperation, but that he lived his life on a different plane.

He was part of the mountains and when he spoke of them it was not only his wish to point out natural beauty, but I had an intuition that he was revealing himself and the things he cared about.

It did not take us long to finish our lunch. Fanny and I stretched our legs for a few steps and then Christian gave the order to remount.

This time I got on the horse by myself, using a stump for a mounting block. Christian assisted Fanny, and soon we were on our way again. Growing tired of speculations about my father and the men who knew him, I began to enjoy the autumn scenery around me. By the end of the afternoon, I learned that Christian had not in the least exaggerated the wonders of the Mariposa sequoias.

We came into the sylvan grove as the sun slanted near the horizon of the hills around us. These were not giant trees, they seemed more like the feet of giants themselves. I stared in astonishment at the base of one sequoia that I swore was as wide as our row house had been. I nearly lost my balance as I strained my neck back to look upward, but the height of the trees was lost in the circle of leafy tops that stretched as tall as the Trinity Church spire in New York.

The trees rose from their broad bases, slowly tapering. A breeze sighing through the trees' high tops seemed like the echo of storms that must have done battle with them for hundreds of years. We all gazed upward in silence, and then I heard the creak of the saddle as Christian got down.

"Thirteen hundred years old," he said as he came to stand between Fanny and me. He gazed upward as we did.

Such great age made me think of legend and antiquity. These trees breathed the history of our world.

Barbarians were overrunning Europe when these trees were young. King Arthur and his knights were meting out justice when they were in the vigor of early maturity, and the world had seen the last of the Dark Ages before these trees creaked with old age. What they could whisper about lost races made my imagination take flight.

Finally I brought my head down again, dizzy from looking at the heights. The big trees stood widely apart with many pines and firs in between them, and the sunlight streamed in golden slanted highways. The air was gloriously pure, and I knew that we were at an even higher elevation now.

At that moment I caught a glimpse of Christian's palomino, shaking his cream-colored mane. The way the sun caught the golden horse I was reminded of the ghost horse with its hooves of silver Bertha Johns had told me about. In this light I could almost believe that the ghost horse was among us.

But my mood of contemplation was broken as Duignan and Christian circled the animals in a shady spot they had selected for our camp. I got down and stood, holding Gabrielle's reins. I wondered if I was to receive a lesson about unsaddling my horse, but Christian came to take the reins from me. He gestured with his head toward the nearest big tree.

"We will set up camp and Duignan will prepare the meal. You are free to enjoy yourself. Examine the trees close up, eh? Over there you will find a stream. You'd better take the opportunity to refresh yourselves."

Fanny joined me and we took soap and towels from our saddlebags and strolled off together. We found the stream, and I bent to dip my hands in the ice-cold water. I splashed some on my face, for I had perspired and collected grime. Then we took off hats, boots, and stockings and splashed around.

After seeing to our needs as best we could in the private spot, we dried ourselves with the towels and returned to a campfire that Duignan was coaxing along in a shallow recess of red dirt within a circle of stones. Fanny, who usually had no trouble voicing her complaints, had retreated into a sullen silence. Yet I felt worried. Her usual petulance, even when giving me her silent treatment, was tinged with fear. But I could hardly blame her. She had never been out of the crowded metropolis of Brooklyn where the dangers were of a different kind.

Yet in spite of feeling uneasy at our strange surroundings, I was not unmoved by the beauty. While Duignan poured cooking oil into a large iron skillet and deftly mixed ingredients from small packages, Christian came to talk to us.

"It will be a while before dinner. Would you like to see some of the grove?"

I thought we were already seeing it, but I agreed. I started to follow him, but Fanny remained rooted to the spot.

"I believe I'll sit by the fire," she said stiffly.

"All right," I said. "We won't be far. Call us if you need anything."

I'm not sure what made me wander off with Christian. Perhaps it was my innate curiosity. I felt that Fanny would be safe with the taciturn Chinaman, and I wanted a chance to get to know Christian better. I had plunged my sister and myself into an unusual situation. Only my stubborn fortitude allowed me to do so. But since then I had felt obligated to find out as much as I could about the man who led us.

I had half formed questions about Christian's relationships with my father and with Thomas Neville, but after we had walked a little ways, he distracted me.

We were in a small clearing surrounded by a ring of the sequoia trees, not quite as large as the giant by which we camped. A sprinkling of pine needles made a soft carpet underfoot. Christian surprised me by sitting down on them.

"Join me," he said, gesturing to the expanse of pine needles on the ground.

I frowned. I was comfortable standing.

He gave a chuckle. "I want to show you something, but you will be more comfortable viewing it from here."

I still felt perplexed, but I sat down. He smiled at me, his blue eyes holding a secret. Then he slowly lay on his back, sprawled on the ground.

I was about to make an interjection, when he interrupted me.

"Look above you," he said.

I leaned on one hand and did as he said. Then I saw why he had taken the position he had. The perfect circle of trees around us tapered upward, their leafy tops seeming to lean in and touch. He was right, the illusion was unusual and beautiful.

Feeling uncomfortable with my neck strained, I slowly lowered myself to the ground beside him. Then I could more easily view the dizzying trees and the evening sky. I allowed myself to relax enough to get the full effects of the peaceful forest and smell the woody scents. After a few moments of soaking in the natural beauty I spoke.

"I've never been in such a quiet place," I said, almost in a whisper, not wanting to break the spell.

"Few people have seen it," he said. Then he raised

himself onto one elbow, still gazing at the forest I realized he loved so well. "But that will change."

I could not tell from his tone if he thought that was good or bad. "You think more people will come here eventually."

He jerked his head, his blond hair falling over his shoulder. "It is the way of things. The Indians would not have been asked to leave if the white man did not want this place for something."

He spoke as if he were neither white man nor Indian, but considered himself set apart from both. Thinking about the Indians I felt my senses sharpen.

"Do they really haunt this place?" I asked, listening keenly for I don't know what.

He moved his head imperceptibly. "Not here, perhaps, but the valley?" He paused. "Yes . . . I think they have left their spirits behind. And some of them have vowed to return themselves."

The thought troubled me. "Do you think we might see Indians then?"

He leaned toward me and grinned. "I do not know. What happens in Yosemite is, well . . ." He gestured with his free hand. "Out of time. You will see. Once in the place, all becomes different. You cannot say what will happen."

My pulse quickened, though I did not quite understand what he meant.

"Is there some sort of magic there?" I asked, feeling my eyes round in fearful wonder.

His eyes slid over my face and his lips curved in a pleased expression. "Magic," he said, softly, looking at me curiously. "Yes, there is magic there."

My heart pounded. With his face so close I could not be unaware of his sensual mouth, the inviting expression in his eyes. Perhaps I was already giving way to the wildness of the nature surrounding us. Or perhaps it was the thin air at the altitude to which I was unaccustomed, but as Christian moved his hand to touch my cheek, I did not move. I lay on the ground spellbound, trapped by feelings I had never experienced, drinking in the luxury of the evening. We were alone. I should have hastened to rise and return to the camp. But I did not.

But he did not move to kiss me. Rather he looked into my face as if the pleasure of gazing at me were enough.

"Your beauty is like this forest," he said, his accent making his words sound like music. "It is natural, untouched by artifice. Your heart beats to the same things that drew old Gaspar here."

"What . . . what do you think drew him here?" I asked, helpless, still resting on the ground as Christian's gaze pinned me there.

"New horizons, the search for gold, the wish to be where other men have not gone, the wish to expand his soul, the wish to experience a little bit of heaven on earth."

His words made little sense to me, but I did not argue. I thought he was going to kiss me, and as he bent his face closer to mine, I closed my eyes, unresisting. But all he did was brush his lips across my forehead. Then he sat up and took my hand.

"The meat will be roasting. It is time we returned."

He helped me sit up and brushed the pine needles off my jacket. We stood and I immediately remonstrated myself for not thinking of Fanny all this time.

"Of course."

He laughed, breaking the mood. "Are you hungry?"

At his mention of it, the hunger pangs in my stomach made me aware that it had been a long time since breakfast and the cold lunch we'd eaten had not been very satisfying.

I returned his smile, beginning to yield my strict attitude as levelheaded employer. "I'm very hungry indeed."

"Duignan will not disappoint you."

Christian was right. I do not know how he did it, but that evening we dined on roasted rabbit in thick gravy, fried potatoes and onions, and baked apples.

"It was very good, Duignan," I said as the silent cook gathered up our plates to take them to the stream to wash.

He split his mouth in a smile and spoke rapidly. "Good food is specialty." At least that's what I thought he said.

He boiled water for coffee, and Christian poured a drop of whiskey into our cups. "It will help you sleep," he said with a wink.

As we sat huddled up to the fire, sipping the hot, tasty black liquid, the forest around us receded in darkness. The flames danced in front of our faces, and I again felt the sense of being in a special, dreamlike place.

"Tell me, Christian," I said, relaxing into the use of his first name, "about the card game Neville spoke to us about. He said that the night before the fire, you three played a game of cards. He said my father won, but that you accused my father of cheating. Did he really cheat?"

I looked at Christian over the rim of my tin mug as I took another sip. His eyes glistened in the firelight and he raised his eyebrows, clasping his bent knees with his arms.

"Is that what he said?"

I heard the sarcasm in his voice.

"Yes, why?" I replied.

Christian grunted and changed position, stretching out on his side, leaning on his elbow. He still focused his gaze on the campfire, the way we all did. But I listened to the rise and fall of his musical voice as he told us quite a different tale.

"Yes, we played cards that night. The stakes went high. But no one wanted to quit playing."

Christian squinted his eyes as he recalled the memory, then went on.

"Gaspar finally ran out of money and pulled from his pouch a map he'd traded from some Indians that he said located a valley of gold somewhere in the western slopes of the Sierra Nevada. Neville and I took a look at it and accepted it as stakes.

"I won the hand and took the map, not knowing if it had any real value, or if it was merely an Indian myth. But I decided that it would pay me to explore the location and see if there was really a valley of gold."

He winked at me. "Gold or no gold, how could I refuse the chance to explore country I had not seen? Besides, I did not care who won the hand. Like other men, I play cards for the playing. It does not matter so much to me who wins."

I blinked at him in confusion. "You mean to say you won the hand?"

He nodded slowly, the firelight glinting off his gold hair.

"I did."

My mouth dropped open. "But Neville said . . ."

I repeated the story as we had heard it from Neville.

Christian raised a brow and shook his head. "Thomas Neville was never overly fond of the truth."

The implication made a shiver run up my spine, but

79

I was too fascinated by this conflicting tale to let him stop. Fanny, too, had lost some of the dazed look she had carried with her and was frowning in concentration at Christian. Both of us sought an explanation.

"Neville said you accused my father of cheating," I asked again. "Did he cheat?"

Christian glanced up, making sure of his audience. "He may have cheated during the evening. It is not so unusual, even among partners. But if he cheated it did not help him, for I won the hand. We ended the game amicably. Neville owed us both a little money. But," he shrugged, "no one was overly concerned about it. Another night, another game, and he might have reversed the debt.

"That night, while I slept, the map disappeared from my pack. I decided to take it out after breakfast the next day, but I could not find it. Neither of my partners had seen it, at least so they said."

I stared at Christian. "Someone stole the map?"

He nodded, then sent me a meaningful gaze. "Perhaps Gaspar could not bear to part with it after all, eh? Or perhaps Neville took it for himself. I always felt that man's greed would get the better of him one day. In any case, the map was no longer in my possession. I have not seen it since."

I swallowed and nodded. "What happened next?" I asked.

Christian dragged his gaze back to the fire. "There was the fire to deal with after that. And we dissolved the partnership. I thought little of the map for some years. Trapping and exploring brought me to these mountains, and I was reminded of Gaspar's Indian map. What had become of it? I wondered.

"I decided to look for old Gaspar when I found out he was in this part of the country as well."

Christian put a pine needle in his mouth to chew on thoughtfully. He glanced at Fanny and then at me. "It wouldn't be right to let another man steal what I'd rightfully won, would it now?"

I could not tell if his voice was teasing or serious. I shivered, nevertheless, wondering if I should have heeded Neville's warning. Christian Reyeult's words were honey-coated when he spoke poetically of the tall sequoias and misty mountains, but he admitted he was looking for my father. He might mean him harm.

I could not stop thinking of the strange events surrounding this Indian map, and when I rolled into my blanket on the hard ground next to the fire, I lay with my eyes open, the tops of the trees lost in the darkness above me as they stood like sentinels around us.

If Christian spoke the truth, then Neville had lied about my father winning the hand of cards. But why?

Chapter 6

I don't know how many hours of sleep I finally got, but I awoke to the tantalizing smell of coffee. After our morning ablutions at the creek, I gratefully accepted a cup as Duignan fried bacon and eggs. Food never smelled so good.

I banished thoughts of the strange story about my father and the map and concentrated on getting under way. Perhaps I could not confront the fact that I had led my sister and myself into danger and in the light of day tried to convince myself that I was still doing the right thing. That with Christian's experience as tracker and mountain man, he would find Father for us.

We ate a satisfying breakfast and got underway. In spite of my concerns, I could not help but notice the colors, light, and shade in constantly changing combinations that brought a thrilling sense of pleasure. I found myself smiling at the sense of freedom I felt in this venerable forest, comparing it to the routine of work from dawn to dusk in order to eke out a living in our crowded Brooklyn neighborhood.

But the moment I thought it, I chastised myself. We had had a decent, simple, hardworking life in Brooklyn, and our future at the moment was anything but certain. However, my eye continued to be drawn to the spots of autumn color set with intense power against the mass of evergreen. Deeper in the forest, the colors seemed even richer.

We spent the morning crossing streams and climbing hillsides, and sometimes we came out of the close-standing fir trees on a promontory to view long vistas. We began to pass broad outcroppings of granite, and as we attained the heights, we could see the High Sierra peaks beyond.

At noon we stopped in a meadow for lunch, but soon pressed on. I rode with expectation, though I could not explain why. Christian informed us that we were at an elevation of seven thousand feet, and perhaps I felt a little light-headed. Though I repeated to myself again and again I had not come here merely to see Yosemite Valley, I found myself looking forward to seeing the place that from all descriptions sounded otherworldly.

At last I glimpsed a wall of rock through the trees. I sat up straighter, ignoring my hard saddle and the plodding steps of my horse. A little way more and we rode into a clearing surrounded by tall pine trees. Christian dismounted and tied his reins around a secure branch.

"Wouldn't you like to stretch your legs and see the view?" he asked, turning toward us.

I nodded and clambered off my horse. My legs felt bowed, but I stumbled forward, turning to wait for Fanny. As she started to dismount, she pulled too hard on the reins, and her horse danced to the left. Duignan appeared by her side, grasped the bridle, and held the horse while she got down.

I brushed by some chaparral and then gasped as I came to stand next to Christian.

"The soldiers who first passed by here called it Inspiration Point," he said.

A long, narrow valley spread far below us, though from where we stood I could not see how we would get down to it. Far below, a nearly level floor was spread with broad meadows and deep grass. A sinuous river was lined with every manner of tree. Above that, ferns crawled across mossy ledges.

But most impressive of all were the walls of the valley, some smooth and sheer, some intricately carved, some rising to domes or spires, separated by wooded ravines and shadowy canyons. Snowy white waterfalls leaped down the granite walls like ribbons of gauze. It truly seemed like we had come to the valley of Shangri-La. No wonder the Indians had felt so possessive of it. Thinking of the Indians, something seemed to grasp my heart, and I almost imagined I could see them, running among the foliage far below, dipping in the wide, flowing river. And then in the next instant, the vision was gone.

"Look, Fanny," I finally said. "Isn't it breathtaking?"

Out of the corner of my eye I saw Christian smile at my reaction. I glanced at Fanny to see what she thought.

Her hardened expression had softened somewhat as she gazed over the precipice on which we stood.

"But how do we get down?"

Christian laughed. "A very good question and one often asked by the first explorers to these parts. Indeed the first men who saw it were starving. They knew that if they could reach the valley floor they would find sustenance aplenty. But alas, they were unable to get down."

Fanny turned to him sharply, a look of fear in her eyes. "Then how shall we? Have you brought us all this way for nothing?"

"Of course we will be able to get there, Fanny," I said. "Christian knows the trail." *Doesn't he?* I wanted to say, but I kept the question to myself.

A fleeting thought of my father's map entered my mind, though I did not know why. It was just possible, I thought, as I stared at the dizzying drop to the valley floor, that Christian had brought us this way for some ulterior reason of his own.

I stole a sideways glance at him. I dared not let myself think that he was anything other than what he presented himself to be, but nagging doubt seized me. Indeed, I had to make a great effort to control it lest it turn to outright panic. Christian may not be telling the truth about my father or the map, but now was no time to press him.

Let us get to the hotel he spoke of in the valley. Like the starving men who once gazed longingly at this spot, I believed that once we got into the valley we would have a firmer base from which to operate. I would have plenty of time to get better acquainted with our guide and find out what he might really want.

We remounted and began our descent. It was no wonder I had not seen the trail. It twisted and turned, and I found that I had to grip my saddle horn and give up guiding Gabrielle. The mare would know best where to set her feet, and it was all I could do to stay in the saddle.

Trees sheltered us most of the time, and still when I dared look up, the vista presented was breathtaking, the different shades of the granite walls majestic, serene, and silent. Now and then I heard the babble of a stream, trickling pleasantly along as if unaware of the giant leap it must eventually take to reach the mighty river below.

Our descent of three thousand feet took several hours, and I scarcely glanced at Fanny. As we neared the valley floor, the open meadows, groves of trees, and the winding river were more visible. I became aware of the parklike quality of the place with its high natural boundaries keeping the rest of the world out. I spared a thought for Christian's prediction that some day people would penetrate this valley in greater numbers. To seek the solace of its beauty? Or was there gold here? The reason my father had come.

Just as we got down, evening closed quickly. Christian picked a camping spot and we dismounted and made our camp where black oaks laced their branches overhead. In the distance a huge falls sprang over the wall in a breathtaking leap. The upper falls sparkled in the last rays of setting sun and then as if wrestling with spirits, it plunged into a wild spray that eddied down in formless mists and showers. Though we were some distance from the water, I imagined I could feel the spray in my face as I stood there in the eerie valley.

Far to the east, rising above all, two spires projected against the fading eastern sky.

"Cathedral Rocks," Christian said. "The Indians have a different name for them."

I had not heard him approach, but he must have been aware of my staring at the surroundings and my curious squint at the two rocky spires he had just named for me.

"Most unusual," I commented.

He nodded, looking at me speculatively as if we

both knew that words could not describe what I saw and what I was experiencing.

There was an eerie presence in the valley that I could not quite name. I attributed it to the altitude, for though we had come down from a great height, the valley itself lay at four thousand feet, a considerable distance for one used to sea level. But I did not think altitude alone could produce the feeling of isolated sanctuary, but a sanctuary whose spirits did not want to be disturbed.

I moved off toward the horses. Wanting to make myself useful I removed the saddlebags from Gabrielle and then returned to where she stood, thinking I might attempt to unsaddle her. I knew I was paying Christian to take care of all such details, but I was not by nature an idle person and thought that if I could do some of the necessary work while we were en route it would only speed our trip.

I lifted the left stirrup up over the saddle and reached for the cinch the way I had seen Christian do. He glanced at me from where he was unsaddling his horse, and I felt embarrassed. I should have simply asked for his help, but my pride did not let me do so. Instead, I fumbled with the cinch until Christian came to help me. He reached for my hands and though it appeared he was helping me finger the straps, his hands on mine felt like a caress, and I caught my breath.

"Like this," he said in a voice that seemed meant only for my ears. He showed me and I tried to nod as if he had done nothing unusual.

"I see," I said.

He was standing so close to me I could feel his breath tickle the back of my neck. He reached his arm around my shoulder and slid his hand down my right arm, lifting it and guiding my hand toward the cantle, where I took hold. I reached for the pommel with my own left hand before he could guide it in the same way.

"It is heavy," he said into my ear as if he were whispering words of love. "I am not sure you will be able to lift it down by yourself."

I tried to turn my head to the left to argue that I could lift it, for I was used to heavy housework, but when I turned, my forehead bumped his cheek and I thought he encouraged the pressure. However, I faced the saddle again.

"Let me try," I insisted. "I am stronger than you might think."

I believe my words contained a veiled threat, trying to impress upon him that should he have anything untoward in mind I would not be so easily overcome, that I was used to fending for myself.

He immediately released his hands and stepped back. "You are the boss, mademoiselle."

I ignored the teasing in his voice, grasped the saddle, and heaved. Gabrielle bobbed her head, but the saddle only slid to an awkward angle. I glared at the thing and tried again. This time it came off her back, but it was so heavy that I stumbled backward with it and did a sort of spin, letting it fall at my feet.

Christian had his hand to his mouth as if trying not to laugh.

"Well, it is heavy," I said.

When I bent to pick it up again, he strode over. "Allow me, mademoiselle. Perhaps you would bring the saddle blanket."

I glanced up at the saddle blanket which had been knocked askew but had not come completely off. Gabrielle stretched her head around toward me with an expression in her large eyes that told me I had better remove the annoying thing quickly. I grasped the blanket, pulled it off, and followed Christian.

Finding things I was more suited to do, I helped set up camp. Fanny sat and watched Duignan for a while, but growing bored with that, she got a chapbook out of her saddlebag and sat on her blanket to read it in the fading twilight next to the fire the silent cook had started.

I did not see how she could read when our lives right now were far more challenging than any novel could be, but I didn't nag at her. The trip was difficult enough without my telling Fanny how to behave. It was obvious that she was so miserable I halfway didn't blame her for her little escape. For myself, I could hardly slow down the thoughts that spun in my mind, thoughts of Father and Christian, and a growing desire to know more about Christian himself. I asked him to tell me of his background while he sat by the fire, whittling a stick.

He gave me one of his curious looks and said, "There isn't much to tell."

I sat very straight, much like a schoolmistress.

"Oh, but there must be. Your life sounds like it must have been so different from ours. I mean we've lived in Brooklyn all this time. This is our first trip West, you know."

Of course he knew, if he knew Father at all.

He shrugged and continued his carving. "I was born in St. Louis. My wife's father had a fur trading company, and for a while I worked in the company store."

"Oh." I stiffened further. "I didn't know you were married."

"Was," he said, not looking up. "She died trying to give birth to my son."

I swallowed. "I'm sorry. I didn't mean to pry."

89

"No matter."

We were both awkwardly silent. Finally I spoke.

"Did . . . your son live?" I felt nervous saying it, but for some reason I wanted to know.

"He did. He lives with his grandparents."

"How fortunate." I was honestly relieved. Though it must have been difficult for him to have a wife die, at least he had a son. "What is his name?"

I saw the pleased light that came into his eyes though he still did not look up. "Ceran."

"A French name. It's nice."

"Thank you. He is a good boy."

"Do you get to see him often?"

Christian shrugged and finally looked at me. "Not often. He is ten years old. Perhaps in a year or two he will come West."

"That . . . would be nice for you."

He gazed at me thoughtfully for some time and then Duignan's banging of utensils reminded us that dinner was being prepared. I moved to ask the reticent cook if I could help. He allowed me to boil water for coffee.

My second night on the ground was no more comfortable than the first. I awoke several times feeling the hackles on the back of my neck stand on end. I thought I heard distant singing of some kind, but I wasn't sure it was not part of my dreams. I felt the eyes that stared at us from the darkness and hoped that animals did indeed keep a safe distance from our fire. But I must have slept for Christian had to shake my shoulder vigorously to wake me in the morning.

After breakfast, we packed up and mounted. If I had anticipated a comfortable ride on the valley floor that day, I was wrong. We followed a long level of ground, passing groves of pine and cedar. Our mood was quiet, watchful, adding to the sanctuary feeling of the place. A thick carpeting of sienna-colored pine needles covering the ground hushed the animal's footfalls. Pillared trees formed vistas that stretched like a long aisle through the sylvan depths. The tall cathedral spires that Christian had pointed out yesterday gleamed in the sun.

The valley through which we passed appeared to be about a mile and a half wide and I asked how far it stretched.

"About six miles. But we will be going further. Drusilla's hotel is beyond Tenaya Canyon on Widow's Mountain. We'll be there tonight."

Widow's Mountain. I remembered the warning.

I looked at the acres of meadows and glades we passed and wondered why the hotelkeepers did not locate their inn here in this pleasant, fruitful location, but did not voice my question. Christian felt that my father would have gone that way, and so we would follow. But I asked myself again how he was so sure.

By midday we stopped near the Merced River, which we had more or less been following as it wound through the valley.

"This is the best place to ford," Christian said, riding back beside me. "We must cross the river in order to ascend Widow's Mountain."

Again I was startled. Cross the river? I had not anticipated such a challenge. I gazed doubtfully at the wide, swiftly flowing river. There was no raft.

Christian read my thoughts. "We must swim the animals across."

"Swim?" I was afraid it sounded fainthearted.

"The horses are used to it. You will be safe. Your legs will get wet, but that is all."

Fanny and I dismounted and watched while Christian and Duignan spent the next half hour securing everything to the mounts. Finally Christian decided everything was ready and told Fanny he would take her across first. She cast round eyes at me, but I tried to reassure her.

"Do as he says, Fanny. I'm sure it will be all right. An adventure, is it not?" I tried to make my tone sound lighthearted and hoped she did not see my quaking knees.

Fanny got on her horse, and Christian took her bridle. "Hold on to the pommel," he told her.

Then leading her horse, he pressed his heels into his own mount and urged the horse forward. The palomino snorted, but walked forward into the chilly water. Still Christian talked to the horse, urging him forward until water swept around his shoulders. Then I could see the horse's powerful shoulders change motions and the horse was swimming, head stretched forward.

I could not see Fanny's face as her Appaloosa plunged in, and I was glad I could not. My own heart constricted for I knew that the poor girl had never done such a thing in her whole life. But she held on gallantly. Then Christian's horse seemed to touch ground, for he lumbered out of the water and climbed ashore. I breathed a sigh of relief as the Appaloosa followed.

I noticed that the two horses came ashore some distance downstream from where they had left. Christian led Fanny's horse onto high ground then dismounted to help her down.

I saw from my side of the river that she was talking and gesturing, but I thought the expression on her face was more one of excitement than of fear. Perhaps she

92

felt proud that she had forded the river. When Christian led his horse to the water again, Fanny waved at me and I thought she smiled. Perhaps the excitement of the river crossing had awakened her from her dull somnambulant state after all.

Fanny sat on a log and took off her wet boots, and Christian mounted again and rode his horse back into the river.

"You see?" he said as he splashed ashore, grinning. "A little swim, that is all."

I surrendered my reins and he prepared to lead me into the water. I gritted my teeth and held on to the pommel, squeezing the horse with my knees and pulling my heels up as high as I could and still keep them in the stirrups.

Both horses plunged into the water, and the palomino lunged forward as he began to swim. Just then Gabrielle shied and twisted her head, jerking her head up. The reins flew out of Christian's hands. He looked back in surprise, and his eyes met mine in horror. I could not let go of the pommel to grasp for the flailing reins, but it would have done no good even if I had. My horse had panicked and was splashing around in the deep water now.

Christian turned his horse, but it was too late. A current seized Gabrielle and me and swept us downstream. The horse was swimming now, but we were parallel with the bank, and her strokes took us farther away from our goal.

Sheer terror filled me as the water whipped around us. The shores seemed to recede as the icy water swept us along. I tried to command my mind to think, but my wits were as frozen as my feet, and I was at the mercy of my frightened horse.

I saw something streak by on the shore to my right

and then saw that Christian and the palomino were on the opposite shore racing past us. I clutched my saddle and clung to my horse in numb fear.

In a daze I watched Christian spring from his horse and race to where a log had fallen in the water. He shoved it into the water and then leaped on it, letting it carry him to the middle of the river, and then he dove into the water. His strong strokes brought him to us, and I was sure we would all be swept to our deaths.

Instead, he captured the bridle and turned Gabrielle's head, so that she was swimming at an angle. The current was still very strong, but we headed in such a direction as to run into the log, which Christian used as a sort of raft to push against. Finally, he succeeded in turning Gabrielle toward shore, and once she could see it, she realized her goal.

"Fight the current, girl," I heard Christian call, and somehow he must have helped the horse to understand. For she was swimming as hard as she could. Christian kicked and held to the saddle with one hand, and then I felt the ground beneath us.

Christian stood up and Gabrielle carried me to shore. I must have been holding my breath, for I now expelled it and leaned over the saddle in complete exhaustion.

Gabrielle shook off her head and neck, and I felt Christian's hands on my waist to help me down. I kicked free of the right stirrup, pulled my leg over with an effort, and then literally fell into Christian's arms.

I hung onto his neck as he carried me a few feet upshore and set me on a dry rock.

"There, there, now. You're all right. Nothing to worry about. Gabrielle decided on a bit of an adventure, didn't she?"

The crooning words melted over me as I sat and

shivered. I heard my name being called and then saw Fanny running over the ground toward me.

"Hilary, Hilary, are you all right?"

She stumbled and threw herself on me, nearly toppling us both over the log. We hugged each other and then she held me away from her so that I could see her face was white.

"I'm all right, Fanny. There wasn't any danger really. Christian's fast thinking saved us."

"Oh, I'm so glad. I was so scared."

Indeed, she was shivering as hard as I was. Christian had shed his wet jacket and was gathering wood for a fire. In the distance I saw Duignan's head bob above the water where he was swimming across with one of the mules. Either the mule's stubbornness headed off the current or they knew where to swim to avoid being pulled very far downstream by it.

In a few moments Duignan had joined us together with the dripping mule. But the parcels of supplies that had been piled high on top of the mule had remained dry, and Duignan applied a match to Christian's kindling, and soon we had a fire. We all helped gather more wood, even Fanny, and soon the fire was blazing. We peeled off our outer clothing, and Duignan handed round dry blankets. I calmed down considerably, almost laughing now at my fright.

I did shiver though as I looked at the gushing waterfalls leaping down the granite walls rising above us. I breathed a prayer of thanks that our little mishap had taken place in the valley and not above on the ridges where the rivers dashed rapidly toward the falls.

We spread out our clothes to dry, and made camp. Christian had undoubtedly planned to go farther today, but seeing that we were in no condition to travel with so many wet things, we made camp early. I knew this would mean perhaps another night on the trail if it was too far to go to Drusilla Earley's hotel tomorrow. But then I had no knowledge of the trail ahead.

Chapter 7

The next day we followed the river back to where we had intended to ford it. From there we headed in a direction that I could have sworn would have taken us straight to the bottom of a sheer wall of rock. The scenery was still magnificent. At the far end of the valley a very strange formation rose in a hump. It looked as if a giant god had taken a knife and sliced off the front, so sheer was the face.

"That's Half Dome," Christian shouted when he saw me staring at it, my hand shading the sun in my eyes.

I'd never seen anything like it.

Just when I thought Christian had lost direction or else he was going to take us right through a solid wall, a cut in the rocks appeared before us. It was hidden until we were almost upon it, and then I could see that a small trail led up between the walls of rock. Christian rode back to speak to us.

"This is an old Indian trail," he said as Duignan got off his mule and walked up and down the pack train checking cinches and fastenings. "It takes us up Widow's Mountain. I don't think the soldiers who were here ever found this. When I first discovered it, there was no sign of anyone having passed by here but the Indians."

I squinted at the narrow passage we were about to squeeze through. "You can't mean that this leads to a hotel? What kind of place could be up there?"

I frowned at Christian. "I do not understand why hotelkeepers have not located in this peaceful valley. It is such an ideal location. How can they expect their guests to follow some old Indian trail?"

I sounded snappish. No doubt the rigors of the trail were getting to me. After being dunked in the river yesterday, now I was going to eat dust again as we climbed upward. But Christian only smiled mysteriously.

"The Earleys did not build their hotel for traveling guests from the valley floor. There are other routes from the east and the north. But let us waste no more time talking. We have a long way to go, eh?"

In other words we were taking the longest and hardest route! How exasperating. But then I knew of no other stage stop in the area. Whoever the Earleys served must travel on foot or on horseback. Well, there was nothing for it but to push on.

We followed Christian through the cut of rock and along a narrow passageway. I glanced back out of curiosity to see if the heavily laden mules would manage. Christian and his cook must have been this way before. I noticed that Duignan's loads had been shifted higher on the animals' backs since fording the stream.

In another turn, however, the trail widened and we came around a large boulder and onto a narrow ledge. The sudden view of the valley again was startling, and I would have feared the ledge would be too scary an ordeal except that bushes and trees clinging to the side of the hill masked the drop-off.

Then the trail turned once more and we went among rock outcroppings again, the valley hidden behind us. Truly, this seemed to be a hidden trail. But perhaps the Indians had made it so, needing to escape from enemies quickly while at the same time having the vantage points of the valley floor.

I was fascinated by the terrain as we quickly ascended. We came out on the side of the mountain again and were able to gaze back down the cut to the valley, framed now by the sides of the mountains that formed the little canyon up which we twisted and turned. The pack mules were strung out far below, but moved along slowly and surely.

The trail twisted and climbed so suddenly that my horse seemed to be walking along just above the heads of the animals coming behind.

A mist descended on us, and then I was amazed to see white misty clouds drifting around us. The sounds of the animals' hooves dislodging rocks were distorted, and sometimes the whiteness right in front of my face prevented me from seeing ahead at all.

I had given up steering my horse when we began the ascent, trusting the animal's surefootedness and the fact that she would follow the others. I simply clung to the saddle horn, trying to see through the mist when I could.

At every turn I peered behind to see Fanny, wavering in and out of the misty clouds like a wraith. She waved at me once, and even the movement of her hand seemed like slow motion. Her blond hair floated down her shoulders and I had the odd premonition that I was looking at an angel. At least she wasn't complaining, and I wondered again if my being plunged into the river had aroused her from her spoiled reverie.

Perhaps she had become aware enough of the present both to appreciate what she was seeing and to respect it. For it could hardly be emphasized enough that the trails we rode were challenging at best and dangerous at worst. And I had the feeling, sometimes, that we were being watched.

Perhaps it was just the tales of the Indians who had not wanted the white man to invade his beautiful valley. Did their spirits linger here? Or were some of them hiding behind bushes and rocks, watching our progress. I had enough to worry about without speculating as to our being watched, but several times I turned my head and fancied I saw movement, as if someone withdrew behind cover.

Our lives were in the hands of our guide. But after Christian's quick action in pulling me from the river, I felt more confident of his abilities. I should have known that even his fine-tuned abilities could not protect us from all threats, both natural and unnatural.

A breeze came up, and while the wind blew the clouds aside, I feared a storm, for now the sky overhead had taken on a leaden cast, and clouds began to roll toward us from the Sierra peaks. The going became slower as now the horses strained against the wind as well as the ascent.

Ahead, Christian dismounted. He trailed his reins and walked back to me.

"I know a cave not far from here," he said. "We'll have to take shelter there."

I nodded. As I had suspected, yesterday's delay was preventing us from making the hotel tonight. I did not look forward to another night on the ground, but already I felt drops of rain, and I was anxious to find shelter. I had been wet once today. Another cold soaking might bring us all down with pneumonia.

He checked the cinches on our horses before remounting again. Then we plodded onward. I leaned forward in my saddle, and ducked my head to avoid the large drops, so that I was not paying attention to the surroundings. But I heard Christian curse, and Gabrielle nearly bumped into his horse, he had stopped so shortly.

I followed Christian's gaze upward, then I gasped. Above us, standing on a high cliff, a white horse stood, pawing the ground. Eerie sunbeams encircled it as the sun's rays suddenly streaked from behind a dark cloud. The horse had a luminous quality. A chill ran down my spine. "The phantom horse," the words broke from my lips. Christian glanced at me, having heard.

"Could it be?" I asked him, lost in thought. "The one that carries the spirit invoked by the Ahwaneeches to help protect their valley?"

I expected Christian to deny it, but he said nothing. I remembered his reaction to the Indian legends. I looked up again, but the horse was gone.

Christian urged his horse onward, and I followed. Behind us came Fanny, Duignan, and the mules. I didn't know if they had seen the mysterious horse, but the impression of the sight would not leave my mind.

Christian turned aside from the trail. Again I thought he was headed for sheer rock, but when he pushed some brush aside, I saw the mouth of a cave. He got down and led his horse inside, then reemerged to guide us in.

The opening was narrow, but when I got off my horse and led her in, I saw that the room opened considerably. Christian showed me where to lead the horses, and then helped Fanny come in. My eyes got accustomed to the darkness as Christian unsaddled the horses. Fanny joined me, hugging herself.

"How far is it to the hotel?" she asked me as we stood close together in the chilly cave.

I shook my head. "I don't know, Fanny. But it's too far to go tonight. But we'll be safe and dry here."

She made a face. "Dry maybe. But I'm getting so tired. My muscles are sore from riding, aren't yours? I hope this is all going to be worth it."

"Of course it will. All we have to do is get to the hotel and then Christian will find Father and let him know we're here. You'll see. Things will settle down then."

I hoped my words sounded encouraging, for they did little to boost my own spirits.

Duignan tied the mules outside, and the two men brought in supplies that needed to keep dry. I wondered where we would get dry wood and was surprised when Christian walked to the back of the cave and picked up wood stacked there. Evidently he knew this trail well and had discovered the cave on an earlier trip. Again I thanked our luck that we had hired such a competent guide. At least he knew the territory over which he was leading us.

I helped carry wood, and then Fanny and I rolled out our bedrolls. In no time Duignan had a small fire going. But I jumped at the sudden flash of light followed by a loud crash of thunder. Fanny grabbed me, and we hugged each other.

"There, now," I said, after a moment. "Only thunder."

But she was shaking and I held my arm around her a moment longer.

"I've never heard it so loud," she said, her eyes wide.

Damp hair straggled around her face, and I realized I must look a sight as well. I pushed at my own damp locks self-consciously, at the same time criticizing myself for caring about my appearance. Naturally we looked a mess and would until we got to the hotel and were able to bathe and change into fresh clothing. I knew also *why* I cared, and chastised myself for it. Christian must think I looked a mess.

The storm got worse, and Fanny and I huddled near the fire. With every crack of thunder, we flinched, and I had difficulty eating the supper Duignan handed me.

We spoke little, but I do remember Christian commenting idly as he put his plate down and watched the torrential rain, "This is an unusual place. I know of no place else where so much of the terrible and the beautiful can be found together."

I felt damp and irritable and longed for decent shelter, and his words were anything but encouraging. We made our beds near the fire. All night long I listened to the rain pounding on the shelf of rock above us and wondered where the phantom horse had gone.

In the morning we got underway with few words. The trail leveled off and we rode along the back side of the mountain. Soon a dull roaring became louder, and when we came to a rocky ledge we paused and gazed at a huge waterfall that seemed to block our way.

Christian turned and gestured with his arm. "We will lead our mounts behind the falls," he said. "It is magnificent, you will see."

I was doubtful, but we dismounted and took hold of our horses' bridles. When we were ready, Christian started off, and we followed his lead. Sure enough, the trail came out on a flat ledge wide enough to accommodate us behind the falls. Spray covered us, but the unbroken curtain of torrential water plunged over our heads in a deafening noise to a drop of several hundred feet only a few steps to our right.

I was caught between awe and terror. The experience was so unique I held on to every second, trying to memorize the sound, the quality of unreality of walking behind a waterfall. The rock wall to my left rose like a wall of masonry. Gabrielle's eyes were wide open, her ears forward, and she snorted, flicking her tail at the mist, but otherwise, she did not seem to mind the experience.

The rock ledge curved and Christian came out into sunlight. I followed, and did not even look back. Surely Duignan would bring the mules safely. If a mishap occurred, I did not want to watch.

We walked away from the falls and out onto a rocky slope. The trail curved and twisted ahead, and I tried to follow it with my eyes. Live oak clung in crevices to small patches of soil, and the fragrance of bay and evergreen oak was pungent. Then my eyes moved upward and I pointed to smoke rising.

Christian smiled. "You have found it. That smoke comes from Drusilla's fireplace. It is not so far now."

I felt relief to see our goal at last. Yet when I thought of how far we had come and how difficult the ascent, I realized how far indeed we were from the rest of civilization.

The trail widened, but I could see where cliffs above us had fallen in, and avalanches of rock had wreaked destruction on their way down the slope. Large boulders had knocked down trees as if they were mere straws tossed on the wind.

Eventually we came out on a high, lush mountain meadow. The spiral of smoke seemed to lead upward from a grove of trees just a little above the grassy meadow.

We quickened our pace, and I felt my anticipation rise. This high valley seemed peaceful, and the slope with a view of the snow-capped Sierras off to our right boosted my spirits. The roar of the falls was present, but dim, reminding us of the powerful force we had just passed.

We straggled across the valley, and then the trail, well marked now with rocks lining the edge, took us back into the trees. The forest, except for the trail, was thick with pine, cedar, and oaks, the latter often laden with mistletoe. The sun was hidden as we rode through the dark, cool forest, and a breeze whispered in the branches.

Then suddenly we stopped in front of a ramshackle building that I at first took to be an abandoned outbuilding. But then I realized we must be looking at the hotel itself, for there was no other building visible, other than an outhouse some way up the hill and a barnlike structure some distance to our left.

The hotel sat on the incline so that the front of the first floor was built on stilts, but the back of the clapboard building was built into the hill. Four small windows faced out of the top floor, and several boards, with gaps between them, formed a porch on stilts. A steep stairway with splintery railing led to the porch from where we stood.

I must have been staring blankly for some minutes, for Christian led his horse into the barn and then tramped back to us. I could not hide my consternation, and fatigue and anxiety did not contribute to my good humor.

"This is the hotel?" I said in disbelief.

Christian simply bowed and swept his hat in front of him. "Mademoiselle. It may not look like much, but here you will rest comfortably, I assure you."

I could hardly bring myself to face Fanny, knowing what her reaction to the place would be, so I stiffened my neck and led Gabrielle into the barn.

"Allow me to take care of your horses, ladies," said Christian, following us into the small, damp structure. "You will be wanting to get settled."

I still thought it was mad to build a hotel in so isolated a spot, and I even wondered if Christian had spoken truth when he had said that gold-seekers came to the hotel from the opposite direction. He handed us our saddlebags and led the way back outside.

Christian grasped the railing and climbed the rickety steps, more like a ladder slanting upward to the porch with nothing behind it except the air beneath our feet. I eyed the steps suspiciously, but when Christian reached the top I could do nothing but follow.

Once on the porch, I did not see how this place could stand against the strong winds that surely must blow from the High Sierras. But we followed Christian across the porch, being careful not to get a heel caught in the openings between boards obviously handsawed.

Christian opened a creaky door and we crossed the threshold to find ourselves in a large entry hall. A door frame without a door led to a room on the right. To my amazement, a large cedar tree grew right through the floor and out the ceiling in what looked to be the parlor.

Odds and ends of furniture, rocking chairs, and footstools were scattered around the tree, and there was a rude stone fireplace on the southern wall. It appeared that the hotel had been built around the tree, but I refrained from comment.

I had not heard anyone else come into the entry hall, but a footfall beside me made me start. I heard Chris-

106

tian's words of introduction, but they did not penetrate my brain, for I had turned and was staring at our hotel proprietor.

Drusilla Earley, for I did hear Christian say her name, stood before me, her body bent slightly from some deformity of the spine. A yellow apron covered her drab, gray work dress, and sleeves hung loosely under a short cape around her crooked shoulders. Her head jutted forward under an octagonal button bonnet with a brim that seemed to reach out toward me. But it was her glass eye that startled me most.

Her good eye looked us up and down while the stationary eye seemed at the same time to hold me in place. Christian had finished the introductions and I knew I should say something to this strange-looking personage, who did not at all seem to have the warm and welcoming characteristics I expected of an innkeeper.

A bit of hysteria passed over me and I thought of the fairy tale, *Hansel and Gretel*. Fanny and I were the children lost in the woods and Christian had brought us to the witch.

I nodded my head stiffly. "We are glad to be here," I said. It sounded stilted and I knew it. "We've had a strenuous journey."

"You got yer choice of beds," she said in a nasal twang. "The rest left two weeks ago."

I understood her to mean the last of the guests left two weeks ago, not the beds. I glanced sideways at Fanny, whose eyebrows were raised and eyes were round as she stared at our hostess.

"Thank you," I said quickly. "If you will show us the way."

Drusilla turned and started toward a steep set of stairs and I was only distracted from her hobbling gait by a small, silent man dressed in dark trousers, red flannel shirt, and suspenders, who stood watching us from just inside a door that led to a room on the other side of the hall. No one introduced us, but I presumed that this must be Drusilla's husband, Franz.

We followed her up a narrow stairway that was not less steep than the entry ladder outside. We came out on the second floor that I saw at once was all one room. Muslin sheets hung from clotheslines stretched across the room, separating the space into sections. These, I took it, were the "rooms."

Drusilla held up the corner of one of the sheets. "I wouldn't sleep on the ends," she said. "Too much wind comin' through the cracks in the walls. If ye sleep here, ye'll get the mornin' sun."

I nodded, just as if she were showing me to an elegant hotel room, and stepped into the partitioned area. A small rope-sprung bed with a thin mattress stood against the neighboring sheet. The rest of the furniture consisted of a washstand with a porcelain bowl on it, a bench, and a hand-hewn chair.

"Thank you," I said. "Perhaps my sister can sleep in the next bed."

Drusilla bobbed the top part of her body up and down, which I took to be a nod and went back through the opening in the sheet. I caught Fanny's glare as she stood outside my room, but I had nothing to say. Drusilla scuffed along and showed Fanny similar accommodations. Then she came back to me.

She named the price, which included three meals a day, but before I agreed to it I had a few things to ask her.

"We don't know how long we'll be here. We've come here to locate my father, Gaspar Fenton."

She gave me an odd stare, which was not too difficult since her expression hadn't quite looked normal since I had met her. But I perceived a change of expression. Finally she spoke.

"I know him. He shows up here every now and then. Came here lookin' for gold, but I think now he's more interested in trappin' bear."

"Good," I replied. "Then perhaps Christian will not have trouble finding him."

"No tellin' where he's wandered off to this time of year."

"But you do think he's in the valley?"

Doubts that we had come all this way for nothing made me more apprehensive than I was already.

She shrugged her elevated shoulder. "Can't say." She waited another moment. "Beds all right?" she asked.

"I suppose they'll do if you have enough blankets to keep us warm."

"We got plenty of those and a nice warm fire downstairs."

"Very well." I could hardly argue. I didn't have a choice.

I paid her for three days in advance, then she left us to unpack our things. Of course there were no drawers to put them in, but I found some nails driven into the plank walls and supposed that this was where we must hang up our clothes.

After Drusilla left, Fanny flipped the sheet between us over the line and stood in front of me looking as displeased as she could, her green eyes snapping, her blond hair straggling down to her shoulders.

"This is horrible," she said, looking at the miserable accommodations. "We should have stayed in Brooklyn."

I felt myself stiffen. "Don't say that, Fanny. It won't

109

do us any good. We're here, we might as well make the best of it."

Her lips trembled, and I was afraid she was going to cry. Guilt for getting us into this circumstance warred with my impatience that Fanny must always be the victim.

"At least we have a roof over our heads," I reminded her. "Even if it's not a very attractive one. This is a temporary arrangement, Fanny. As soon as we find out what's happened to Father, we can make permanent arrangements."

My own forbearance was being strained, and the resentment sounded in my own voice as I spoke.

"We didn't choose our circumstances, they chose us. Now we must show some courage until things are sorted out."

I took a deep breath and surveyed the little room. "Someday we'll look back on this and laugh about our trials."

I risked a glance at Fanny. Her face was screwed up as if she were trying to keep from crying.

"I just don't understand it all," she said. "How did things turn out this way?"

"I'm trying to tell you, dear Sister, that they haven't turned out yet at all. This is a transition to a better life. I'm sure of that." I wasn't really sure at all, but I had to sound confident.

Fanny sank down on the rickety little bed and sighed, cupping her chin in her hands.

"Oh, dear me," she said. "I'm saddle sore, hungry, and filthy. I don't know which is worse."

"Well, we do look a sight," I agreed. "I think we should make getting cleaned up a priority. I'll see what we can do about a bath."

I left Fanny and went back downstairs in search of

Drusilla. Not seeing her in the front room, I proceeded in the direction of the room in which I had seen the silent little man. He was not there, and as I stepped into the room I saw now that it was the dining room. A long table stood in the center of the room, and two benches stretched down either of its sides.

The dim room had only two windows, as if the Earleys were afraid to let in too much sunlight. Drusilla wasn't here either, so I headed for the door opposite. A short corridor led me to another door which opened into a kitchen. Drusilla and Christian were bent in deep discussion over two glasses of whiskey at a work table in the center of the room. They both looked up when I entered.

"I'm sorry to interrupt," I said, "but Fanny and I would like baths. Can that be arranged?"

I thought I saw amusement in Christian's eyes before he knocked off the rest of his glass and got up.

"I'll be seeing to a few things," he said. He touched his hat brim and exited through a rear door that I saw led down another set of stairs on the side toward the barn.

Drusilla hobbled to a clothespress at the side of the room and took out two towels, which she handed me. Then she crossed the kitchen again and opened a free-standing cupboard next to the cookstove. She rummaged around and came up with a bar of soap, which she also handed me. Then she pointed to the door through which Christian had gone.

"Take those there stairs. Path takes you right to the stream. There's a hot springs a quarter mile yonder."

A stream. A hot springs! Surely she didn't expect us to bathe outdoors. I stretched to my full height.

"Mrs. Earley, we have been bathing and drinking out of rivers since we left Mariposa. Your bedrooms

111

don't even have walls. Surely your exorbitant fee covers the basic necessities."

I pointed to a large pot. "Now surely water can be boiled in that pot. Am I to believe that you have no tub?"

She glared, and her mouth made chewing motions. Her shoulder seemed to twitch, and I sensed her indecision.

"We got a tub if ye' insist," she finally conceded.

"Good. May I see it?" I wasn't trusting her to anything at this point.

She hobbled to a small pantry and pointed to a tub lying upside down on the floor.

"May I turn it over?" I said politely. After all, it didn't sound like it had had much use if the guests were used to trekking to the woods for their ablutions.

She shrugged one shoulder. I approached the round wooden tub and grasped its sides so as not to get too many splinters. I heaved it on its side and rolled it a little way out, then set it down on its bottom. It was a perfectly good tub.

"Satisfactory," I said as I stood up again, my hands on my hips. "Can your husband bring it upstairs? And the water, too?"

One corner of her mouth twisted up slightly, but she nodded. "I reckon so. But it'll take three trips to fill it."

"I understand," I said. "Have you any more pots to boil the water in?"

She didn't answer but trudged back to the kitchen and from another corner extracted another pot. I saw that she was fully capable of providing her guests with a bath if she wanted to, though she must only do it when pressed.

"I expect the water will be boiled within half an hour. Your husband can bring up the tub now."

And I turned on my heel and left. I was used to doing such chores and could have drawn the bath myself. But if I was going to pay this woman to stay at her hotel, then she had to earn my patronage.

On the way back to the stairs I ran into Drusilla's husband. I remembered Christian saying that his name was Franz. No longer willing to stand on ceremony, I looked him in the eye.

"I am Hilary Fenton," I said to him. "I presume you are Franz Earley?"

He looked out of his narrow eyes suspiciously, but nodded an inch.

"Your wife is drawing us a bath. Please bring the tub up to our floor now." I could not bring myself to say "room."

Without waiting for an answer, I swept past him and tromped up the stairs once more.

Chapter 8

Upstairs I found Fanny hanging her clothing on the nails meant for the purpose.

"The water is heating for our baths," I said, holding up the soap and towels.

She took them from me and looked about for a place to set them down. The bench being the most likely place, she moved to set them there, and the soap fell out of her hand. She wasn't quick enough, however, as it did not land on the floor. Rather it slipped between the edge of the split planks and the wall. We heard it bounce down to the lower floor.

I struggled to hold in my own exasperation, knowing that of the two of us, I was the one who must demonstrate control.

"I will fetch the soap and see how the water is coming," I said and left her.

On the stairs I ran into Christian coming up. I stopped to let him pass, but he paused a step below me.

"Have you found everything you need?" he inquired, gazing at me with that mixture of humor and challenge that I found characteristic of him.

"We are doing the best we can," I said, my chin hoisted an inch to show my determination not to betray weakness even in my displeasure.

He leaned against the opposite wall and let his eyes slide over my face.

"It is a rude place, but what can you expect? The trails are difficult and all the lumber must be hand-sawed. One day the trails will be wider and lumber will be brought up by mule train."

I did not care what the valley would be like in a few years. Our immediate physical needs were too pressing.

"We will manage."

I was beginning to feel uncomfortable being pressed into the narrow stairway so close to him. But he hadn't moved enough so that I could pass. I either had to stand and face him or retreat upstairs again.

"It will not seem so bad after a hot meal, perhaps a toddy to relax you, hmm?" he said.

He had not moved an inch toward me, but with looks and voice he could send my blood pulsing through my veins in a most disconcerting manner. He went on in his maddeningly tantalizing tone.

"A fire in the fireplace and a change of clothing can do wonders to refresh you. You will see, by this evening you will swear that you want for nothing."

I tried to clear my throat, but I am sure it sounded like I was strangling. "I hope so," I finally managed to get out.

I attempted to give him a pleasant look and move on, but he still did not move.

"I believe the high mountain air suits you," he said, his gaze drawn from my eyes to my lips.

"How . . . why do you say that?" I stammered.

115

He lifted his hand to my face and let his fingers drift over my cheek.

"There is a blush on your cheek," he said, shifting his weight back on both feet and looming closer to me. "It makes you more beautiful."

He braced his arm above my shoulder on the wall. I knew he was about to kiss me, but thankfully the dragging steps of Franz carrying the tub toward the stairs interrupted us. Christian glanced downward, and the spell was broken.

I slid past him and got to the bottom of the stairs just as Franz arrived with the tub.

"Thank you, Franz," I said. "My sister is upstairs. We are most anxious for a bath."

He gave me his narrow-eyed look and hoisted the tub on its side so he could carry it up the stairs. Christian came to stand at the foot of the stairs to let him pass.

"Well," I said to Christian, not quite sure how to end our conversation, for I did not feel like simply walking abruptly away. "The parlor is most unusual, is it not? Why did they build it around that cedar?"

He walked with me into the parlor. He gave his nonchalant shrug.

"The wood for the frame was maybe a little too long. The tree was there. Rather than tear down the frame again or try to saw through so big a tree, they built around it. A logical solution under the circumstances, don't you think?"

I could not tell if he was teasing me or not, but I didn't answer. Instead I changed the subject.

"When will you look for Father?"

"Ah, I have already inquired about him and have noticed signs he left when he was last here. You see? I do not shirk my duties. I will set out in the morning."

I nodded. At least there was something definite in his plans. "Good."

We didn't seem to have any more to say to each other, so he gave me a nod and picked up the rucksack he had dropped on the stairs when he had encountered me. I went on to the kitchen to check on our water and realized that if Christian was still upstairs when we were ready to bathe, we would have to ask him to leave. But surely he would see the proceedings and be gentleman enough to do so. But then Christian Reyeult could hardly be judged by any standards I could fathom.

I went to search for the soap in the dining room where I thought it had fallen and found it near the side of the room. Luckily these floorboards fit tightly to the wall, otherwise we might have lost our soap to the ground below.

In the kitchen, Drusilla ladled the boiled water into several buckets for ease of carrying, and when her husband returned, he took one up. I took one, and Drusilla brought the third. Like a little train we carried the water upstairs and poured it into the wooden tub that Franz had placed in Fanny's "room."

When Drusilla and her husband had left for more water, I dropped the flap that served as the door to Fanny's bedroom.

"Why don't you bathe first, Fanny," I said, being polite. "I packed a sponge in my pack somewhere."

I heard Christian rustling around in the space next to mine and knew he must be unpacking. I did not know how to ask him to leave the premises, I was far too embarrassed about the subject. So I stayed in the "room" with Fanny, making noises in preparation of the bath, hoping Christian would take the hint.

When I heard footsteps on the stairs, I opened the

flap so that Drusilla could pour in more water. Her husband waited at the entrance and traded buckets with her. At least some men were sensitive to the rights of ladies' privacy. But Christian still had not left.

When Fanny had undressed down to her camisole and drawers, I said, "Go ahead, Fanny. I will guard the door."

I was feeling more indignant by the minute. I believed that the muslin sheets between us and Christian would prevent him from seeing us in our state of undress, but it was the principle that he was so pointedly ignoring common decency that irritated me. I was torn between standing by Fanny while she bathed and marching down to Christian's quarters and confronting him.

I had worked myself up in preparation to do so, when I heard the *whoosh* of his door flap and his heavy boots cross the floor. Then he took the stairs. When I heard him reach the floor below, I expelled the air I had been holding in my chest.

"Well," I said, "left alone at last."

Fanny had discarded the rest of her clothing and stepped into the water, which was warm, but not too hot. I handed her the sponge and the soap, and she sank gratefully into the water, her legs folded so that her knees met her chin.

"Oh, Sis, this feels wonderful," she said. "I could stay here for hours, but I won't do that. You wouldn't get to bathe."

"Hmmph. If our hostess had had her way, we would be bathing at the stream."

"Ugh," Fanny said, wrinkling her nose. "We've done enough of that."

"My sentiments exactly."

I sighed and fetched a brush from Fanny's pack and

sitting on the bench, I brushed out her hair so she could wash it. Drusilla lumbered up the stairs bringing more water, which I instructed her to leave.

"We will need this water dumped in about half an hour," I said to her. "Then fresh water for my bath."

Her glass eye seemed to look at me accusingly, as if to ask why we could not share the bathwater, but I met her stare with a defiant one of my own that brooked no argument.

Fanny finished her bath and dried off with a towel. She had dressed in a fresh shirtwaist and gored skirt by the time I heard footsteps on the stairs again. Drusilla shuffled across the floor and then with an empty pail began the laborious process of emptying water from the tub into the pail and throwing it out the window at the back of the room facing the hill. While her good eye seemed to concentrate on the work, the glass eye seemed to stare at me each time she turned around until I could stand it no longer.

"I will undress in my quarters," I said.

It seemed like the baths would take up the entire day, but in a place without the slightest convenience I had to force myself to be patient.

I made several trips with water, undressed, returned to the tub, and stepped into the bath. The feel of the warm water and a good scrubbing with sponge and soap was worth the effort to obtain it. Fanny brushed out my hair as I had done hers, and I soaped it. Then she poured fresh water over it so I could rinse it. At long last we were both finished and dressed, and by that time it was nearly time for the evening meal.

When Christian joined us at the long dining table, it was evident that he too had bathed, but most likely in the hot springs. His hair was damp, as if from washing. And he wore a fresh yoked shirt that laced at the neck.

It hung loose over his leather pants. He had replaced his heavy boots with soft Indian moccasins.

As he sat down opposite us at the table and leaned forward in anticipation of the meal, I was uncomfortably aware of the way his sinuous movements affected me.

"Drusilla is an uncommonly good cook," he said, winking at us. "You'll see."

Though my stomach growled with hunger, I was prepared for a very plain meal. Everything else about this place was rude, so I could hardly expect the cooking to be exceptional. However, I was wrong.

Drusilla shuffled in with a platter of catfish that surprised me. We dished portions on our pewter plates when she returned with another platter of venison. Good food never seemed like such a luxury. The meats were complemented with rolls, baked apples, and some kind of cooked root.

We ate ravenously, all acknowledging the tastiness of the food. Christian grunted with pleasure as he stuffed venison and catfish into his mouth and more than once caught my gaze as pleasure filled his eyes.

We washed the food down with fresh coffee, and then after thanking Drusilla, we left her to clear away. I automatically headed for the parlor, where Franz was coaxing a fire. I could almost believe that we were in civilization, so much better did I feel after the bath and food.

I seated myself in a scoop-backed chair near the fireplace. Christian seated himself in another chair and propped his feet on a small stool. Fanny went upstairs to retrieve some knitting she had brought along for quiet evenings. Soon the fire was roaring, Fanny's needles were clicking, and the evening settled around us.

I heard the uneven shuffling steps of our hostess and was not surprised when she joined us, taking a seat in a rocking chair between Christian and Fanny. I was in a relaxed mood, ready to be entertained, and so when Drusilla and Christian began to speak of things related to the valley, I listened with interest.

Several times Drusilla turned her strange gaze to me, but I could never tell if her look was curiosity, accusation, or warning. I wondered if I would ever learn to look her straight in the face without feeling self-conscious.

When the conversation lagged, I asked her a question. "Do you get many guests in the summer then?"

She rocked back and forth. "A fair amount, you might say. Most folks can't put up with the steep trails. But more'll come. You can't keep 'em out once they know there's something worth comin' for."

"Do you mean the scenery or the gold?" I asked, remembering that other prospectors besides my father must have come this way.

She glanced at me and then at the fire. "Depends what they're after."

After a moment of silence, she continued. "The valley ain't kind to all of 'em what comes though. There's plenty who don't want people hereabouts."

A little tingle ran up my spine. "Do you mean the Indians? I've heard of the Indians' curse."

Her good eye passed over me as if she didn't really see me.

"Can't say if it's the curse or not. But many's the man who's lost his life tryin' to climb these here mountains."

Her words made my stomach feel uneasy, but I still tried to sound casual.

"Oh, really. How recently was that?"

121

She didn't pause in her rocking. "One prospector was found at the bottom of One Way Gulch. Never knew who he was or how he fell. He was spread-eagle at the bottom of a cliff."

My throat went dry and my eyes widened. "You say no one knew who he was?"

She took my meaning and said, "I saw him. They brought him here. It wasn't so long after that when Gaspar came by. I warned him not to go by way of Devil's Point."

"Devil's Point?" I asked.

"More'n one traveler lost his life there. Some er lucky and jes' lose their horse. Christian can tell ye that. It's above here, farther up on Widow's Mountain. A jutting ledge with nothing 'neath it but air. Steep wall of rock beside the trail. You know it when you see it."

Fanny and I exchanged glances then both turned to Christian for explanation. He had removed a small silver flask from his pocket and was drinking from it. He jerked his head to glance at Drusilla when she mentioned his name, then frowned and took another swig from the flask.

"You can get around these mountains if you know how," he said. "It's fools who lose their lives. You take risks, you do foolish things, then you're tempting fate, eh?"

His words sounded sensible, but I was not sure how reassured they made me feel. Outside, night covered the mountains and I shifted a little closer to the fire. Fanny scooted her chair up also.

"Bertha Johns said people lose their minds here," I said tentatively, not looking at anyone. "Is there any truth to that?"

If a person had lost his mind, he might very well do

foolish things and take risks that he would otherwise not normally take.

The pause before Christian answered was just too long for comfort. He must have had to think of an answer.

"Well, I've been here many a time," he finally said. "Perhaps the gods favor me, but I'm still in possession of my faculties. You cannot believe all these tales you hear."

I shivered slightly, even though the fire crackled a few feet from me.

"No, but people *have* lost their lives," I said.

"I told you they took unnecessary risks," replied Christian. He drank from the flask then held it on his stomach and stared at the fire.

For a long moment no one spoke. Drusilla's rocker creaked in a regular rhythm, punctuated by the wind that had risen outside.

"What about the man who lost his horse?" I finally asked.

Perhaps it was the atmosphere, or my insatiable curiosity that made me ask, but I would not leave the subject alone.

Christian bestirred himself and recrossed his ankles on the stool.

"Funny thing that. It was two winters ago. Snow was beginning to cover the trails, and I was leaving the valley by way of Tamarack Flat. I had made most of the descent when to my surprise I came upon a preacher, leading his horse along the trail. He was determined to winter among the Indians and convert them to Christianity.

"I told him to turn back. I pointed to the trail he must take, and gave him firsthand information as to what it was like, having just come that way. But he wouldn't listen. I warned him not to go. I was low on supplies myself and warned him that if he ran into trouble he would be on his own. He thanked me for the warnings, but he was stubborn, and he went on his way.

"Every once in a while, as I went on down the trail, I would turn back and see him, a small speck, climbing the steep trail. I watched as he made his way along the stony defile, high above me and around shelving rock where one false step would send him and his horse to certain death two thousand feet below.

"But I dared not delay. I went on. Just before I made my last turn, I heard an echoing cry and turned. The man stood on the side of the rocky, snow-covered precipice. But his horse twisted and turned as it plunged to the rocks below."

"And the man?" I asked.

Christian shrugged. "I had warned him."

I shifted nervously in my chair, my hands clutching the arms until splinters dug into my palms.

"You didn't try to help him?"

Christian moved his head from side to side. "The snow was heavier by then. It would have been certain suicide."

Then he looked at me as if wanting to say something to soften the blow. "He was near the top of the pass. He had already climbed the most difficult part. Who knows? Perhaps he made it on foot and lived among the Indians as he wished."

I met his gaze with difficulty, trying to get used to the idea of death so immediate. Then I dragged my gaze away from him and back to Drusilla.

"Then do you think it's true that the Ahwahneeches haunt the valley they were forced to leave?" I asked her.

She rocked for a while, then spoke. "You can hear singing and dancing up there in their caves." She paused. "But there's nobody there."

My teeth were chattering slightly when I said, "We saw the . . . what looked like the phantom horse. Didn't we, Christian?"

Drusilla did not look at him, but Christian tossed his head. "It might have been. Who can tell? The light can play tricks on you as well."

Drusilla mumbled something unintelligible, and I was surprised to see her cross herself.

Fearful thoughts plagued me. If my father had come here, was he still alive? Would we ever see him again?

I summoned up the courage to ask another question. "Do you think Father is following his map?"

A trace of irony, or was it amusement, crossed Christian's face. "Perhaps."

An idea occurred to me for the first time. "Do you remember what the map looked like? You said you saw it when it was in your possession."

He glanced at me quickly, and I thought his eyes narrowed. "Did I say that? It was a brief glance only. As you know, the next day the map had disappeared from my possession."

"I see," I said. "But then if you don't remember the map very well, how are you so sure Father is on Widow's Mountain."

The challenge in my voice seemed to annoy him, but then he covered his reaction with the nonchalance that was so much a part of his character. He shrugged, lifted his flask, and nodded to me.

"Call it a hunch. After all, I know the mountains. I know Gaspar. You will have to leave it to me to figure out where he might be."

Then more seriously he said, "I warned you this

125

undertaking was foolish. It might take many days for me to track him. If I hadn't known I could persuade Drusilla and Franz to keep you, I would never have brought you here."

I felt like a four-year-old put in her place. I sat back in my chair. Fanny continued with her knitting, but she dropped several stitches, and I saw the crease in her brow.

Thinking of Fanny made me worry. Her temperament was unstable in normal circumstances. It did not brook well to think that Yosemite Valley could have bad effects on one's mental capacities. One more pang of guilt for me to bear. But as I had gone over the subject a thousand times already, what else could I have done?

Chapter 9

We retired upstairs and undressed by the light of candles we had carried up. I placed mine on my bench. To my surprise, Christian began to hum a tune to himself as he prepared for bed. I felt awkward enough in the close quarters without listening to his lighthearted ditty right next to me.

On the trail we had all slept in a circle near the fire. But being inside the hotel with nothing but sheets between us seemed rather risqué. I self-consciously put my nightdress over my head before I removed my underthings. It was rather like undressing in a tent. Then I sat on the bench and brushed out my hair before setting the candle next to the small bed and crawling into it.

The sheets were a coarse linen, but I was thankful for them, and I pulled the blanket up under my chin. I blew out my candle and lay my head on my pillow. Then turning on my side, I drew in a breath at what I found myself looking at.

Silhouetted on the sheet that served as divider between "rooms," was Christian's figure as he moved about his sleeping area. Fanny's and my candles were out, and his light threw his nearly naked shadow on the sheet.

My reaction was instantaneous, and I pulled the blanket farther over my chin. I shouldn't look, I told myself, but I could not draw my eyes away. He was shaving, using a razor and a bowl of water sitting on top of the old chest that was in his quarters. I had wondered why Christian had gotten the room with the only piece of furniture in it, but now I knew why. Drusilla must have known he wanted to shave. Apparently Bertha Johns was not the only room keeper who was used to providing for his wants.

He finished shaving and threw the water out the window. I watched him arrange things and realized he was getting ready for an early start tomorrow. He must be totally unaware that I was watching him, which further increased my embarrassment. But so fascinated was I by the masculine figure that, perversely, I could not stop myself.

I reminded myself of Fanny, captivated by one of her chapbooks, for watching Christian thus was fantasy for certain. I imagined his strong arms around me as I stared at the profile of the muscles of his chest. The ends of my fingers tingled as I contemplated sinfully running them through his thick hair.

His movements were lithe and sensuous, and the sight of him set my body to tingling until I thought he would hear my heartbeat and become aware of my breathing. I shut my eyes, hoping that he would blow out his candle. When he stopped humming I opened my eyes again. But I positively gritted my teeth when I saw the shadow figure remove his trousers. For a brief instant the full figure of his manhood was silhouetted against the sheet, and I drew in my breath.

Then I clamped my lips together and lay very still.

Had he heard me gasp? He bent slowly and blew out his candle, and then I heard him crawl between his sheets.

The wind still moaned outside, but within the room I felt intensely aware of the sound of my breathing and found that I listened for his. I tried to wrench my thoughts away from Christian. On my other side I listened for sounds of Fanny and heard her turn over and sigh. I lay flat on my back, certain that sleep would not come, afraid to move for fear Christian would realize I was not awake and speak to me.

I think I must have wanted him to speak to me, but I don't know what I expected him to say. I was both glad and not glad that the two of us were not alone in the room that night.

When he turned over in his bed, I heard every sound. But I made myself lie still and breathe evenly. Still my thoughts were a jumble of weird tales and frightening precipices in Yosemite Valley. I thought of Christian, too, but I was so distracted by his obvious masculinity that it was very late indeed when a question arose in my half-sleep state.

Why had Christian been willing to bring us here if he believed, if only by half, the many threats of Yosemite Valley? Obviously, if he did not believe them he could travel here unafraid. But he was never quick to deny them. Therefore, he must believe in some of the dangers at least.

It followed then that he had a stronger reason to come here and to bring us as well, and something made me think it was not the money I was paying him. Did he, too, want to find Gaspar as badly as we did? Was there another reason? Or, and more dreadfully, did he refrain from denying the threats of the valley because he wanted us to be frightened?

That thought made me come wide awake again, and I almost sat up on my bed to wake him and ask him. Did he want us to be frightened? And if so, why?

I never got to ask him, for when I awoke the next morning, Christian had gone. I should have been glad he was doing what he said he would do, but I felt vaguely unsettled.

Drusilla served hot cereal to Fanny and me at the dining room table, and I saw right away that things did not bode well with my sister.

"This isn't too bad," I said, tasting the cereal.

Fanny made a face. "I could make better myself."

She sighed and put down her spoon, glancing around the crude dining room.

"What an awful place. I simply cannot believe we are here."

I didn't have a very big appetite myself, so I gave up on the cereal after a few bites and contented myself with coffee.

"I have difficulty believing it myself," I said. "But we might as well make the best of it until we've news of Father."

Fanny tossed her hair, which she had left loose over her shoulders.

"We could have stayed in Mariposa and sent this guide of ours here alone. I'm sure he would have made better progress without us, and he could have sent word or brought Father down to us, if he really is here. And we would have been so much more comfortable."

I had thought that some of the events on the trail had awakened her to some sort of maturity, but I saw now that I was wrong. Here was her complaining temperament again, just like before.

"So we might have," I replied without patience. "I suppose I was so anxious to see Father I would have chafed at the bit to have to sit in Mariposa. As it is, we've seen an unusual place if nothing else. Why is it you fight everything so, Fanny? Why can you not take what life gives you and meet the challenge head on?"

I squeezed my napkin as I thumped my fist on the table. She and I glared at each other, but I was not about to back down. Fanny's eyes crackled, but she finally dropped her gaze to the cereal, in which she stirred her spoon idly.

"Life has not given us the things I thought it would," she said. "I don't have your backbone, Hilary. You're the stronger. You always have been. I . . . I," she gestured futilely. "I'm not like you."

Tears formed at the corners of her eyes, and I felt bad.

"Fanny, I don't mean to be harsh with you. I wish we hadn't had to come here. I don't understand why life is so unfair."

"Neither do I." And she started to cry.

I sighed and went around the table to pat her shoulders. "Please don't cry, Fanny. Crying won't do any good. Try to look on the good side of things. We have a roof over our heads at least, and Christian is trying to find Father."

"If he's still alive." She only sobbed harder. "When . . . Mr. Reyeult . . . comes back," she said between sobs, "he must take us down. We simply can't stay in this godforsaken place with all the awful tales of people who've died here and Indians who try to scare people. It's a horrid place."

She scooted off the end of her bench and ran from the room, presumably to throw herself on the small bed upstairs. I had the urge to follow and try to comfort her, but as I was half out of my seat, I sat down again. What else could I say? I was having enough

131

difficulty keeping my own spirits bolstered, much less trying to bolster hers.

I drummed my fingers on the table, wondering what to do next. I couldn't sit idle all day. Perhaps I would offer to help Drusilla in the kitchen. But that might seem a bit odd, since I was a paying guest. I could go exploring, but the idea of venturing into the woods alone was not appealing. The hotel itself offered possibilities.

I got up and wandered into the lobby. Spying a door under the stairs I had not noticed before, I walked over to it and opened it. It was a small cubbyhole used for storage and held a couple of crates. To my pleasant surprise, the one on top held books.

Blowing the dust off the items on top, I saw that the books were old, and some looked like they had been damaged from water. Well, here was something to look into. I might even find something worth reading.

The crate was too heavy to lift down, so I satisfied myself with taking an armful and carrying them to the parlor. I set them on the hand-hewn coffee table, and pulled a chair near to look them over. They were so dirty that I decided the first item of business would be to clean them off, so I went in search of Drusilla to ask for a rag.

Drusilla was not in the kitchen, and I opened the door that let onto the steep stairs descending to the ground outside. Holding on to the railing, I carefully made my way down and then saw a lean-to built against the wall that extended to the ground on this side. Drusilla came out of the lean-to carrying a basket of vegetables. When she saw me, she stopped and eyed me.

"I was looking for you," I said. "I wondered if you might have a rag I could borrow. I decided to look through those old books you keep under the stairs. There might be something worth reading there."

She didn't acknowledge me, but took a few steps toward the stairs. When she reached for the railing and hoisted one foot onto the steps I forgot all about my request, so concerned was I as to how she was going to be able to climb the steep stairs with her shuffling step, her bent figure, and the heavy basket of vegetables.

"Can I help you carry that basket?" I asked, following close behind.

I did not stop to think that she must do this very often and must be used to it. To me, the venture looked quite precarious.

Again she refrained from answering, but suddenly she swung the basket behind her and held it in my direction. I took it from her while she made the climb. I followed, trying not to look through the open steps to the steeply receding hillside below us.

Once in the kitchen, I set the basket down on the table and Drusilla opened a cupboard and extracted a rag. She turned to face me and held the rag in her hand for a moment, her weird gaze fixed in my general direction.

"Here's a rag," she finally said. "Folks leave those books here. I got no use fer 'em, but Franz says other folks might want to read so to keep 'em here. Your pa left some of 'em hisself."

I brightened on this last note. "He did?"

She didn't bother to answer, but the idea that I might be looking at books my father had had in his possession was exciting to me. I thanked her for the rag and returned to the parlor.

I lost all sense of time as I brushed the dust off the volumes and eagerly opened each one. Some did indeed have water stains and a few pages were stuck together. But I pressed out bent pages and did what I could to put the books to rights.

There was a volume of Shakespeare, poetry by Lord Byron, Keats and Shelley, tales of horror by Walpole, Mrs. Radcliffe, and Matthew Gregory Lewis. Someone had a taste for the chills, I thought, though why anyone would want to read such fiction while in such a spooky place, I could not imagine.

I set the books in a row and went back to the crate for more. Now I was not so much paying attention to the titles as looking for markings on the inside that would identify the owners. I went through another stack and was on the third before I found what I was looking for.

My father's name was inscribed on the marble end-papers of a small book about explorers. I paged through the volume carefully and saw where he had underlined occasionally. There were notes and jottings in some of the margins, and I recognized the handwriting.

Just seeing it brought me closer to him, and I rose and walked to the small windows that overlooked the hillside opposite. I felt the urge to follow in Christian's footsteps to see what he had learned. My imagination ran away with me for a moment, and I envisioned my reunion with my father and tried to picture his surprise at seeing us here.

I smiled to myself. Would he recognize us? It had been twelve years. Would he think we were cut of the same cloth, after all, to have come all this way to find him?

Then the fantasy dissolved, and I returned to my task. There were several other volumes that had my father's signature on the endpapers. I did not know he was such a reader. But at the back of the last volume

I brought from the crate below stairs, I hit on something that made my blood race.

On the blank flyleaves at the back of the book my father had drawn several diagrams. There were a few notes like "North 100 feet" and "Indian canyon," but I could not tell what they meant. The longer I stared at the diagrams, the more they began to look like maps.

Could my father have left a clue here? Were these notes he had made on his search for the Indian treasure? He had the map with him. Had he no need of these notes and therefore left them behind? Had he simply been sketching more detail than the map contained, giving himself directions as to where to search?

My mind leapt ahead with the possibilities, and I spent the rest of the morning combing through the rest of the books for more clues and coming back again and again to the diagrams. Late in the morning Fanny came down, and I showed her the diagrams.

She had quit crying, but her mouth was turned down. I was so excited, however, that her bad mood did not dampen my spirits.

"Look, Fanny," I said, making her take a seat beside me. "Father left a number of books here. This one seems to have some drawings and notes in it. I believe he was thinking out where to search for the gold and made notes about it. If we can figure out what this means, we may be able to help Christian find him."

"Or the gold," she said absently, taking the book from my hand.

I blinked. Her comment made me stop and think. Was that why Christian really wanted to find Gaspar? For the gold? I shivered as I contemplated the fact that Neville might have been right, and that Christian had ulterior motives. I had been so anxious for him to find

Gaspar. What if I was only hastening my own father's demise?

Fanny left, but my thoughts made me stand up and walk to the windows again, though the scene outside hadn't changed except for the sun that had finally crept over the high ridge above us, sending golden streaks into the forest.

If I had showed Christian the book, he might be able to discern what the location meant. But if it was the gold he was after and not Gaspar, wouldn't that be helping him achieve his ends and threatening our own? The thought gave me something to ponder.

I went through the second crate of books, absently sorting them. But there were no more notes penned in my father's hand. I set the books along the baseboard at the side of the room opposite the tree, there being no shelf upon which to put them. I didn't know if Drusilla would approve of my efforts. I suppose it was an attempt to civilize the place, though now I was so distracted by my own dilemma that I was no longer interested in reading.

Feeling stifled by the room after a while, I decided to go out. I went upstairs to get my jacket. When I got to the landing I heard Fanny humming and found her arranging her hair. She had borrowed the mirror Christian had used for shaving, had propped it on her bench, and was sitting on the bed. I was glad to see her take an interest in her appearance, though I'm not sure what inspired her to do so.

"I think I'll go out for a walk, Fanny. Would you like to come?"

She cocked her head and looked at me with a question in her eyes. "Where would we go?"

"Not far. Just a little way into the woods. The sun

is bright now. I don't think there'll be any danger. Some fresh air might do you good."

She shrugged. "I suppose. There's nothing else to do."

"There are the books downstairs," I said while she finished pinning her hair. "You might find something you'd like to read. In fact, maybe we can figure out where the gold is."

"Gold," she said disdainfully as she laced up her boots. "Surely you don't think there's really any gold. It's just like all the rest of his stupid dreams. Nothing will come of it."

"Don't say that, Fanny. How can you know for certain?"

She tossed me a skeptical look and reached for her other boot. "Because it hasn't up till now."

Now who was being the practical sister? We seemed to have reversed roles. Always before I thought Fanny lived in her dream world, waiting for a handsome prince to carry her away. Now I was the one chasing rainbows. But I wasn't ready to give up so easily.

"We'll just have to see," I said.

We donned our jackets and went back downstairs. Then we crossed the precarious porch and took the steep stairs. Once on the ground I felt better. The scent of pine accented the crisp fall morning, and the clear air was invigorating. A little path led to the woods, but once there, it was impossible to see which way the trail went. We followed the way that looked like the easiest walking, our heels sinking into the pine needles underfoot.

There were many things to look at, and the quiet forest was so enticing I began to relax. But when I turned around, I couldn't see the edge of the trees anymore, and I knew we needed to prevent ourselves from getting lost.

"We'd better leave some kind of a trail," I said, "so we can find our way back."

I piled a group of small rocks together and set a twig pointing in the direction from which we'd come.

"There, that ought to help."

Fanny had wandered off to look at a bird's nest. I found a flat rock and sat down to enjoy the tranquil surroundings. Then I thought I heard some sort of humming in the distance. Thinking it could be the wind, I leaned back against a tree trunk and closed my eyes. I began to distinguish the sounds around me. The soughing wind had its own murmuring that gently rose and fell. But that was not the only sound that came to me from a great distance.

The music floated to my ears, and then I could not hear it, and I strained to listen. Once or twice I even imagined I heard a drumbeat and a rattle carried on the wind. I opened my eyes.

"Do you hear anything?" I asked Fanny.

She cocked her head to listen and said, "Just that bird call and the wind in the trees. Is that what you mean?"

I shook my head and frowned. "No. It sounds like singing. Let's walk a little further."

We made our way through the trees a little farther and stopped.

"There, do you hear it?"

A faint chanting sound that I was sure sounded like voices on the wind. Fanny frowned and looked about as if trying to decide where the sound might be coming from.

"I think I hear it, too," she said. "What is it?"

My pulse quickened, but I kept my speculations to

myself. The woods grew deeper, but I could not resist following the sound. Was this the Indians' chanting? Did human voices sing plaintively from some hidden camp? Or were these sounds the echoes of spirits? I wanted to find out.

I was not unaware of the danger. If we came unexpected and uninvited upon an Indian camp, we would surely anger them, but if I could determine that the singing was real, I could put an end to the fantasy that these mountains were haunted. Whatever the reasoning, the haunting sound drew me on as it became stronger. But Fanny was not so adventurous.

"I'm not sure we should go any farther, Hilary," she said.

I stood by a large boulder, uncertain. I, too, was torn between finding out where the sound came from and retreating to the shelter of the hotel.

I could see nothing from where I stood, and the slopes rose to a high ridge, which would take most of the afternoon to climb. And my stomach told me it was near noon. But I remained where I was, listening to the rising and falling of distant voices, which seemed to come from several directions.

"The wind is playing tricks on us," I said. "But I suppose you're right. We're unprepared for exploring."

"Let's go, Hil. I don't like it up here."

She looked apprehensively at the thickened undergrowth and the branches that laced closer together in the thick forest.

"All right."

We retraced our steps to the place where I had piled the small rocks.

"You see?" Our marker shows us the way."

No sooner had I made my proud statement than

another sound behind us made us whirl around. A crashing of branches above us told us that something was coming in our direction. Whatever it was made the hairs on the back of my neck stand on end.

Fanny grasped my arm, her fingers digging into my skin. "Something's following us," she said, her voice rising in fright.

We turned and fled down the slope. I turned my head once or twice when I heard the crush of branches and undergrowth. I saw some movement, but continued to run, my heart pounding, unable to tell what it was.

Fleeting thoughts of the phantom horse crossed my mind and I ran faster, unsure of which I was more afraid—a spectre, or the very real hooves of a wild horse that could kill or injure with one blow.

Fanny screamed and stumbled, and I halted to help her up. Then, holding her hand in mine, we fled. Our pursuer thundered on behind us, crashing through timber and scattering rocks before it.

We came out of the trees and crossed the small clearing in front of the hotel. Then we flew up the rickety stairs and in the door Drusilla held open for us. We collapsed against the wall just as a rifle exploded in our ears, and I nearly jumped out of my skin.

Outside a loud, painful roar erupted, and I heard the sound of crunching wood as the entire front of the hotel shook. Only then did I see Franz pick up a second muzzle-loading rifle for another shot out an open window. The shot rang out, and the gun smoked. There was another painful roar, and then Franz drew the rifle inward. He turned slowly around, looking at us with his impassive face.

"Bear," he said.

Chapter 10

Fanny and I were shaken but not hurt, and after gathering my wits I went to look out the front. Slumped on the ground between the steps to the hotel and the trees was a great mound of bear, the largest I had ever seen. I crossed the porch and saw where the bear had pulled down the lower part of the railing on the stairs.

"Grizzly," said Drusilla, who had crept up noiselessly behind me, making me jump. "Not the biggest I've seen, but big enough. Never seen one this far down though. They keep to the higher ridges mostly."

Now that it was all over, I was quaking from head to toe, and I leaned on the porch railing. Then, remembering that the railing was none too sturdy, I stepped back, catching my heel in a crack between split planks. The whole experience was almost too much for me, and I dove toward the doorway again, wanting to sit down before I fainted.

A bear had been chasing us in the woods. My head swam with the possibilities of what might have happened had we been a few seconds slower. With those mighty paws and those long claws, he could have torn us limb from limb.

Drusilla came into the parlor where Fanny and I were recovering from the incident, and she took a seat in her rocking chair. She rocked thoughtfully, though I could not tell if her expression conveyed sympathy or not. Still, she seemed disposed to talk about the bear.

"Wouldn't be surprised if there's cubs," she said. "Maybe you got close to her den, and she came after you. She-bears do that."

"We . . . we heard something and ran," I said, my heart still racing and my teeth still chattering. "I don't know what it was."

"Just lucky then. Franz's a sure shot with that rifle."

"Yes, thank goodness." Then I looked at her. "How did he know we were being chased?"

"Franz can smell a bear a mile away. Always has his rifles loaded and ready. Heard you scream, too."

"Yes," said Fanny, her eyes still round as she sat wringing her hands. "That was me. I nearly fell. Oh, Hilary, if you hadn't pulled me up . . ."

"Shh," I said. "Don't think about it. It's done now. We were very lucky."

I stared at the window through which Franz had shot.

"You say the bears don't usually come here?"

Drusilla moved her head slowly from side to side. "Never seen one this near here."

"I'm sure you would have warned us not to walk in the woods if you'd been aware of any danger," I said.

My words were a challenge, but Drusilla did not seem to react either way.

"Hard to say where there's danger. That's the way of the mountains."

I suppose she had a point. Men and women who explored territory like this took their chances. Most, of course, were prepared with weapons when they ven-

142

tured into the woods. It was foolish of me to want to walk in the woods without someone who could wield a weapon should the need arise. I would remember that in the future. I resolved that from now on we would stay near the hotel unless we had protection.

Fanny took a seat in the other rocker and began to rock back and forth while staring at the cold fireplace. Drusilla continued her rocking, and soon the squeaks of the two rocking chairs going at different rates was enough to drive me to distraction.

I searched among the books for something to read. Franz came in to build a fire.

"Got to skin that bear," he said when he got the fire going and left again.

And so we sat until shadows lengthened. My mind was only half on the book I was reading, however, for I wondered about many things.

Christian had not said how long he might be gone. Of course, how could he? Being at the hotel was setting my nerves on edge, and I felt more a prisoner than ever. Drusilla and Fanny were hardly going to be conversationalists, and I felt my patience wear. I simply had to find something else to do.

"Are there any more books?" I finally asked Drusilla, breaking the silence. "Perhaps I could organize them for you. I'm afraid I'm not used to being idle. I need something to do."

Drusilla stopped her rocker, but Fanny continued, like an instrument that continues to play after the rest of the ensemble has quit.

"Can ye' shuck corn?" asked Drusilla.

"Me? Of course. Would you like me to help you in the kitchen?"

I no longer cared that I was paying her to cook and

serve me. If I didn't find something to occupy my mind and hands, I would go mad.

We left Fanny and went into the kitchen where Drusilla gave me a stool to sit on and a large pot in which to put the ears of corn. I applied myself diligently to the work and had shucks piled at my feet in no time.

Once I felt the hackles on my neck rise and turned my head to see Franz watching me from his position by the door. I had not heard him come in. It occurred to me that Franz and Drusilla's brand of hospitality might do more to turn guests away than draw them here, and I wondered again why they chose the hotel business when their natures seemed so at odds with liking people.

His hands were bloody. Then I remembered that he was skinning and butchering the bear. He came into the kitchen, pumped water from the pump into the dry sink, and washed the blood off. Then he went outside.

I needed to stretch my legs, and I was curious about the butchering, so I stepped out to watch the proceedings. I saw that Duignan was helping Franz. They were laying long, thin strips of bear meat across a frame above a small fire for drying the meat. I did not look at the butchered bear carcass, unsure if I could stomach it.

Back inside, Drusilla commented, "The fat and some of the jerky'll make good pemmican. Skin'll be a good rug."

She was busy stirring something that bubbled in a pot over the hot stove. I saw that she also had a tin of muffins ready to go into the oven.

"I've finished the corn," I said. "May I help you with something else?"

"You can stir this if you want," she said, wiping her

144

hands on a dirty apron. I'll be needed to cook that bear fat in a while."

I took her place at the iron cookstove, and she shuffled over to the cupboard. When I saw her get down custard cups, I looked at the thick, yellow substance I was stirring, and I realized that she was making dessert. She poured custard into six cups. Then we arranged the cups on a tray, set them outside on the porch, and covered them to cool.

I smiled to myself. Perhaps I was winning her over after all. Undoubtedly the bear kill created a great deal of extra work, but there would be meat and a new rug for the winter, so she could hardly resent it.

I must have been right because later, before supper, Drusilla brought small glasses of brandy to Fanny and me in the parlor. The sweet, warm liquid had a soothing effect on me, and when we sat down to the smell of roasted bear meat, sweet corn, potatoes, and gravy, I was in a better mood. I helped Drusilla serve the custard for dessert, which we ate with fresh cream. Perhaps Drusilla wasn't so bad after all if one took the trouble to remember that under her odd exterior, she too, had a human, feeling heart.

After supper Fanny sat in the parlor and took an interest in reading. I helped Drusilla clear the dishes. When Franz took himself off to the porch to light up his pipe, Drusilla surprised me. She glanced about, making sure we were alone.

"Ye ought to leave here," she said.

"What do you mean leave? Where would we go?"

"The valley I mean. Ye oughtn'ta come here."

I sank onto the stool by the work table in the center of the room.

"I'm beginning to agree. It was just that I was so anxious about my father."

"No tellin' where he's off to. This valley's cursed all right, whether it be Indians or no."

I did not disagree. Whether there was a specific Indian curse or not, there seemed to be a great deal of hardship and bad luck associated with the place. Drusilla pressed her point.

"Can ye not see with yer own eyes what this place's done to the likes of us?"

Her question was so pointed that I could not think of an answer. Did she mean that living here had made the two of them so suspicious, odd, and withdrawn? I continued to stare at her, opening my mouth to reply, and then shutting it again.

She cast a wary eye toward the window. Then seeing that Franz was still settled there in the dark with his pipe and an oil lantern burning beside him, she beckoned to me.

Surprised, I followed her from the kitchen into a bedroom where evidently she and Franz lived. She lifted the glass on a lantern sitting on an old, scratched dresser and lit the wick. The flicker illuminated the simple surroundings.

A double bed stood with its headboard against one wall. I tried to envision the dresser being carried up here on the back of a mule. Two cane-seated chairs and a long bench completed the furniture in the room. Faded print curtains framed the small window, which looked out on the hill in back of the hotel.

She slid open the top dresser drawer and rummaged about in it. Finally she found a small portrait. The tintype was encased in a leather frame. She handed it to me.

As she did so, a folded piece of paper fell out. I bent to pick it up and handed it back to her, but not before I noticed some writing that looked nonsensical to me.

I stared at the face of a young, serious-looking woman in the portrait. I admired the creamy, youthful countenance and then glanced at Drusilla in question.

"I thought you'd not be able to see the resemblance," she said.

My mouth dropped open in surprise. Was she saying that this was she?

As if understanding my question she gave a jerky nod.

"I met yer father back then. He's seen the years change me."

My astonishment was great. At the same time I had the thought that if the years had changed Drusilla so much, what might they have done to my father? I had seen him twelve years ago, and he had looked much the same in the picture from the newspaper he had sent us. Of course he would have aged since then, but the thought of my father looking old and worn was shocking.

"I see," I finally said, handing her back the portrait.

She put it away again and picked up the lantern by its handle to return to the kitchen. Then the rest of her words sank in.

She had known my father then? Something made me wonder if she had been in love with him. How and where had they known each other, and what happened? I was determined to find out more.

The next day followed much the same routine. Fanny spoke little but worked on her needlework or read or arranged and rearranged her hair while I found little jobs to do about the hotel.

By late morning a light snow started. As I watched the silvery flakes float downward to dust everything with feathery white, I remembered Christian's warning that at the first snowfall we must turn back, and I despaired of our situation.

I paced back and forth, watching out the windows for any sign of Christian's return, but I saw no rider coming down from the mountains above us and no sign to make me hope for his return. The snow was moist, and the only thing that gave me hope was the thought that wet snow would not stick.

When I went to stand on the porch and to look up the small cut that seemed to be the direction Christian had taken, I scanned the ridges and even the snowy peaks of the High Sierras visible in the distance through the cut. I seldom looked down the valley along the trail by which we had come, not expecting Christian to return that way.

After lunch, I went out to the barn once to visit the horses, and I came upon Duignan, who was kneeling on a little pallet in a traditional silk robe, his pigtail flowing down his back.

"Oh," I said, startled.

He bowed once to the candle then turned his moon face toward me.

"I'm sorry," I said. "I didn't mean to interrupt."

"Is all right. No interruption."

I didn't know exactly what else to say, so I moved over to Gabrielle's stall.

"I just came to visit the horse."

"Horses good company," he said. "Good animals to talk to."

I wondered if he spent much time talking to them, but did not ask. After feeding Gabrielle some sugar I went out again, leaving Duignan to his meditations.

The snow stopped, and the sun came out. I decided to wash our clothes. I supposed that I would have to wash out our laundry in the same tub in which we had bathed. I remembered seeing Drusilla use a washboard and went to get it to begin the work.

Housework helped me spend my pent-up energy, and I actually enjoyed hanging the clothes out on clotheslines strung behind the hotel. A few hours of sun remained, and I hoped the clothes would dry.

As evening approached and I turned to go in for the twentieth time that day, a speck of movement across the meadow below caught my eye. I drew closer to the door, thinking it might be another bear. I almost called out for Franz to get his rifle ready, but I paused a moment. The speck grew larger, and I saw that it was a horse and rider.

I walked to the railing to watch then. The horse was dark, not like Christian's palomino, and the rider wore dark clothing. Beyond that I could not tell who it was. Curious, I went to find Drusilla.

"Looks like a rider's coming up the valley," I said when I found her washing out clothing in the wooden tub in the kitchen.

She grunted. " 'Nother mouth to feed. Not usually this much business so late in the year."

She said it grudgingly as if she did not welcome the business. Well perhaps she and Franz had expected to shut the hotel for the winter and go down to Mariposa, as Christian said they would. Under those circumstances she could hardly be blamed for resenting the intrusions.

I went back to the porch to watch the arrival more out of curiosity than anything else. The snow was coming down again, and the chilly flakes tingled on my face. As the rider cantered over the meadow, I brushed snow from my eyelashes and looked closer. The figure looked familiar, and I blinked, wondering if my suspicions could be correct.

For as a shaft of sunlight from the dying sun spilled through the cut and illuminated the trail below, I recognized the face of Thomas Neville.

It was several more minutes before he came to the forest, and I remembered that the trail wound through the trees before coming out at the foot of the steps to the hotel.

"Great Scott," I said to myself. "What is he doing here?"

I went back inside, unsure as to how to announce the news. Most likely it meant no difference to Drusilla. A guest was a guest to her. But he was obviously following us, or looking for my father or both. I thought he had gone to San Francisco. He had warned us against coming here, but now he was here himself. The reasons were beyond me, but his appearance confirmed my suspicions that there was more than met the eye about our circumstances and my father's presence or lack of in Yosemite Valley. And I was sure it all had something to do with that Indian map.

However, there was no time for speculation now. I walked to where Fanny sat reading by fire and candlelight.

"Fanny, we are about to have another guest at this establishment."

She put down her book and looked up inquiringly. "Oh?"

"I am afraid Thomas Neville is on his way here on horseback."

Her eyes widened and she rose, glancing at the window. "Neville here?"

"Apparently so. I saw him cross the meadow."

I followed her to the window, and we waited for him to emerge from the trees. In a few minutes, he walked his horse slowly out of the trees and drew rein. He dismounted and looked about him, then spying the barn, he led his horse there.

Franz appeared from somewhere, and he and Neville exchanged a few words, then Franz led the horse in. Neville followed him and a few moments later reappeared carrying his saddlebags.

Fanny rushed to the porch and called out to him, and he waved back to her. I waited inside, but as he climbed the stairs I could hear Fanny's excited chatter, and it annoyed me that she was so glad to see him.

Of course she had been so bored here she might be expected to be excited to see the arrival of anyone. It was just unfortunate that it had to be Neville.

The door creaked open, and he stepped in.

"This is the lobby," chirped Fanny. "Only the proprietress isn't here." She lowered her voice. "She's an odd bird, glass eye and hunchbacked."

"Well," said Neville, getting his bearings. "An interesting place." Then he saw me.

"Well, and how are you Hilary?"

He dropped his saddlebags on a rough-hewn bench and crossed to take my hand. I let him bend over it, but moved it slightly so that his lips kissed the air above it.

"I'm so glad to see both of you reached this outpost," he said.

"It is quite a surprise to see you here," I returned. "I thought you went to San Francisco."

"And so I started out to do. But at Modesto I received word that the ship I was waiting for containing spices I had ordered from the East was delayed leaving Hong Kong. There is no need for me to arrive in San Francisco for another month. Thus, naturally, my attention returned to you ladies and the predicament you have found yourselves in.

"And," he lowered his voice and frowned in concern, "I had not forgiven myself for leaving you in the hands of Christian Reyeult. I was concerned about the outcome should he find Gaspar before you did." He smiled. "And so, I was free to follow you here."

"How did you know where we would be?" I asked, raising my brows in a challenge.

He gave me an easy look, which nevertheless set my nerves on edge. "Why there is as yet only one hotel in Yosemite, though I have heard there are plans to build another, lower down, next spring. Naturally, I came here."

"Naturally," I replied.

The tension crackled between us, but Fanny laid a hand on Neville's arm. "The accommodations are not luxurious," she said. "But it is nice to have someone here to help relieve our boredom. There's frightfully little to do. I'm sure Thomas can help entertain us, Hilary."

"Yes," I replied testily. "I'm sure he can."

Drusilla Earley shuffled in and looked the new guest over. Then she named the price of her bed and board.

"Of course," replied Neville reaching for his wallet to extract some bills, which he handed her. "This should take care of a week."

"How do you know you will be here for a week?" I said.

"I don't," he replied. "But how long we remain here depends on what happens, does it not?"

Fanny gave Neville a shy smile. "I am sure we are both very glad you are here. This is a queer place, but perhaps we can do something to make it more amusing."

His look softened as he gazed at her. "That would be most enchanting."

He lifted his gaze to the surroundings. "So this is the first establishment of its kind in this famous valley. Simple, but welcome to the traveler after the trials of the trail."

We all wandered toward the parlor, Fanny on Neville's arm, and Neville looked curiously at the tree growing through the room and out the ceiling.

"Most unusual. I suppose having a tree in the parlor makes a good conversation piece."

"I long to be back in civilization," Fanny said with a slight swoon.

He patted the hand that was tucked into the curve of his elbow. "And so I would like to see you so," he said. "As soon as this curious search for your father is over, we shall see you ensconced back in more comfort, I assure you, my dear."

I lifted my brows. So, their flirtation was to continue, was it? I still did not like Neville's attentions to my sister. I had always been protective of her, and knew she did not know how to deal with a man of Neville's worldliness. He was altogether the wrong sort to court her. But I did not know how to stop them from mooning over each other.

He handed her into a rough-hewn seat and then took a seat himself in a straight-back chair.

"So tell me, where is that fellow, Christian Reyeult?" he asked.

"He's not here," I said. "He's gone into the mountains after Father."

Neville frowned in concern. "He has gone alone?"

"Well yes," I answered. "You did not expect us to follow him beyond this point, did you? As you said, the trail this far was rough enough for those not used to the outdoor way of life. It made more sense for Mr.

Reyeult to track Father from here alone, unhindered by us."

I watched Neville's reaction carefully. I hated to admit to him that I thought my father was a thief, but if he did not steal the map back from Christian, it was possible that Neville himself did. I must find a way to learn the truth.

"Christian told a different story about what happened the night of the poker game," I finally began slowly.

Neville looked at me in a distracted manner as if he had not quite heard what I'd said.

"He did?"

I nodded, smoothing my skirt. "Christian said that he won the hand that night. He accepted the Indian map as payment, but that the next morning when he awoke, the map was gone."

I watched Neville's eyes, looking for any change in them. But the only expression he displayed was disbelief.

"That's ridiculous." He shook his head, his look darkening. "I am glad I came here. I am most concerned for the welfare of both of you." He slapped his knee. "I tell you, Christian Reyeult is not to be trusted. Such lies. But then what can you expect of a foreigner?"

He expelled a breath. "I'm sorry. I do not mean to worry you two lovely young ladies. But being inexperienced in the ways of the world, I am afraid you have placed yourselves in the hands of an unreliable man. And it concerns me that he has now gone after your father. Gaspar may be in grave danger."

His tone of voice made me shiver. I did not like Thomas Neville, but neither did I know what to believe.

"Well, what do you expect us to do?" I asked.

He drew down his brows. "Nothing at present," he said. "But I shall go after Christian Reyeult in the morning."

Chapter 11

"You can't leave again so soon after you've arrived," pleaded Fanny. "You promised us some diversion."

He reached over and patted her hand in a most confidential way.

"And so I will do my best to divert you, my dear. After all, we have this evening and part of tomorrow, for I do not intend to leave early. I need a good night's rest. I trust supper is to be had in this establishment?"

"Such as it is," I replied testily. "Drusilla is a good cook of course, but you must understand that aside from the food that nature provides, supplies must be brought up from Mariposa by mule train. Thus you cannot expect a great deal of choice."

I suppose I sounded as if I were trying to persuade him to check out of this hotel and try the one in the next valley. But of course I knew we were not to be rid of him so easily. In fact when he did leave, if he did as he proposed, he would be going after Christian and possibly my father. Already an idea was forming in the back of my mind, though I was not ready to put words to it.

"Then after supper," Neville said, "we shall entertain ourselves in front of a fire in this very room, if this is the best that is to be had. Perhaps even a game of cards?"

He made the suggestion to be social, I am sure, but at the mention of a card game, I arched a brow. He caught my look, and his smile wilted. Inevitably, both of us were reminded of that unfortunate card game that had begun the dissolution of the former partnership between the three men and stirred up my curiosity.

"Well." He cleared his throat and his eye fell on the books I had lined up against the wall. "I see there are at least books to be had. Perhaps we can take turns reading aloud."

"Why yes," said Fanny, "that would be charming."

Neville rubbed his hands together and prepared to rise. "I must see about the lodgings and wash for supper. After two days' ride I am hardly presentable."

"Drusilla will acquaint you with the accommodations," I said with irony. "You may be surprised indeed."

He nodded and rose. Then he strode to the entry area. Franz was flipping a rag across the dining room table in the next room and eyed Neville. Then perceiving that the guest was looking for the hostess to show him to his room, Drusilla's husband went through the door to the kitchen. In a moment, the proprietress appeared with her hobbling gate.

She jerked her head toward the stairs and Neville bent to pick up his saddlebags to follow. As they climbed the stairs, I pulled my mouth into a wry expression. I wondered if he, too, would demand a bath or if he would be satisfied with the bar of soap, the towel, and the directions to the hot springs.

Evidently the latter, for in a few moments I heard

them on the stairs again. Neville followed her through the front to the dining room, and I could only guess that they were going to the kitchen from whence he would set out for his "bath."

For myself, I pumped water from the kitchen pump into a pitcher and took the porcelain bowl up to my elegant chamber to wash myself off with a cloth in preparation to dine.

Supper was a quiet affair, but Neville carried the evening off as if he were at the finest hotel. He had managed to shave and wore a clean shirt and frock coat to dinner. Fanny dressed in a clean blouse and the only gored skirt she'd had room to bring, and I was similarly attired.

After supper we sat about the parlor. Fanny worked on needlework. I stared at the notations my father had made in the book and Neville read aloud to us from *Moby Dick,* a novel that had been published a few years ago. I found the dark undertones disturbing and didn't wonder that the book was not popular.

All evening, he and Fanny exchanged coy glances, and every time they did my stomach twisted. In another circumstance I would have left her alone to flirt with her chosen conquest. She would interpret my acid temper as jealousy. I was the older sister. I should have a beau first. But that was not why I objected to her flirtation with Neville.

At that thought, my mind turned to the all-too attractive Christian Reyeult. His advances toward me left me in no doubt as to his feelings for me. But that could hardly be called courting. Being the unconventional man that he was, I could guess that his courting habits were equally as unconventional. All the more reason I must not fall under his spell. But he was not here, and so that was not my immediate problem.

As the night darkened around us like a cloak being drawn around the isolated refuge, I began to yawn. I hoped Neville would take the hint and suggest we go up, for I was determined not to leave Fanny alone with him.

The candles by which we had been working burned low, and finally, Neville began to fade. He stifled a yawn and put down the book.

"I don't know about you ladies, but I am fairly well done in. That saddle did not make a very good pillow the last two nights."

"Yes," I said, setting my little volume aside. "We should go up." I stood, picked up a candle holder, and smiled expectantly at them.

They stood also, and Neville offered his arm to Fanny as if he were going to escort her to her bedroom door. And so he did.

We climbed the stairs and then Neville asked in his most debonair tone, "And which chamber is yours, dear girl?"

She giggled and pointed to the flap of sheet that served as her door.

"Ah," he said with mock gallantry. "I hope your furnishings are as quaint as are mine."

He bowed as she swept into her chamber and then he winked at me.

"And yours?" he said to me.

I pointed, nodded to him, and went in, calling, "Good night."

And then I heard his footsteps taking him to the end of the row of partitioned sleeping areas on the end opposite the place where Christian had slept.

Our mock privacy was ridiculous since we could hear every move each other made. But as we all moved about preparing for bed, not another word was spoken as we all pretended that the sheets were walls separating us.

As I blew out my candle I remembered the shameful way I had stared at Christian's body through the sheets and tried to banish the shameful thought from my mind. The other two blew out their candles, and we were all in darkness except for the stars I could see glimmering through openings in the ceiling.

I tried to find a comfortable position, and eventually I fell asleep.

The next morning to my surprise Fanny was up and dressed before I was. When I went downstairs, following the smell of coffee, Fanny and Neville were nowhere to be seen. I went into the kitchen to find Drusilla putting a loaf of bread in the oven in the side of the cookstove.

"Good morning," I said.

She straightened as well as she could and gave me a lift of the lips that I now recognized as a smile.

"Have you seen my sister?" I asked.

She motioned with one shoulder. "Went out for a walk with that Mr. Neville. Said they'd be back for breakfast. I wasn't gonna fix no breakfast till there was someone here to fix it for."

"I see." I frowned. Gone for a walk, had they? "I'd like a cup of that coffee."

Drusilla handed me a porcelain mug and poured coffee from a kettle sitting on the stove. The coffee was strong and slightly gritty, but it tasted good and helped my brain start to work.

·"I hope they're not gone too long," I said. "I should like to eat breakfast at a reasonable time."

Then I turned and went back through the dining room and out to the porch. The coffee steamed in the chill, and I noticed the dew had not dried. The snow

160

had gone, leaving only moist droplets that sparkled on the small tufts of grass growing between here and the edge of the trees. I strained my eyes, but I could see no sign of where Fanny and Neville had gone.

I wondered if I should follow them. This was exactly the sort of thing I was worried about. Neville probably had no scruples when it came to women. Why, he might even rape her.

Remembering the terrifying experience she had had at the hands of the thieves who had broken into our home in Brooklyn, I set the coffee cup down on the windowsill and headed for the ladder. Fanny might think the worst of me, but I was not going to take the chance of leaving her in the hands of a man she hardly knew.

"Hallo," came a cry, and I looked up to see the very couple I was thinking about emerge on the path from the woods.

I arrested my flight down the stairs, my hand on the splintery railing. Fanny waved at me and came trotting down the path a smile gleaming on her flushed face. I glanced at Neville and caught his eye. He touched his hat brim in a salute to me, but I did not miss the pleased look in his eye.

Fanny came clamoring breathlessly up the stairs and I backed away, fearful of the way the stairs shook as she climbed upward.

"Oh, Hilary, there you are. I'm so glad. I have news."

She panted from her excitement or from the exertion, or both. She whirled to look at Neville, who was taking the stairs at a more leisurely pace.

"That is we have news," she amended.

"What is it?" I asked.

She put her hand to her face. "Well, perhaps I should wait so we can tell you together."

I did not like what I was hearing, but I picked up my coffee mug. "Let us go back indoors. We'll catch a chill out here without proper wraps."

I marched into the hotel and led the way to the dining room. Then I waited for them to join me.

"Good morning, Hilary," said Neville as soon as he had caught up. "I trust you slept well."

"As well as I might under the circumstances," I said. I smoothed the front of my ruched blouse and straightened my back, waiting.

Fanny glanced shyly at Neville, who seemed to give her an encouraging smile. Whereas before she was bursting with news, now she seemed unable to get the words out.

"Thomas has proposed to me," she finally said. "We're going to be married."

I stared stonily at them, unable to think of what to say. Neville's smooth tone picked up the thread, covering my discomposure.

"I'm afraid my heart has been lost," he said. "As soon as we find Gaspar, we will ask his blessing. And I hope you will give us yours as well."

Honey couldn't flow from a jar more smoothly than his words. I could hardly show pleasure, but I would wait until I had Fanny alone to give her my opinion.

"Well," I said. "This is a surprise. Of course you'll want to ask Father's opinion."

She wrinkled her nose. "What has he got to say about it? He hasn't even seen me in twelve years."

"It's a courtesy, Fanny," I said, trying to stall.

I managed to give a civil smile. "Well, now that we're all gathered, shall we ask for breakfast?"

Neville rubbed his stomach. "Sounds like a capital

idea. I am just beginning to catch up on decent meals since being on the trail. My cold meals could hardly be called appetizing."

Something about his words stirred something in the corners of my mind, but I could not quite grasp the thought. In any case, I let Drusilla know that we were ready for breakfast, and she brought in steaming bowls of porridge, more hot coffee, and rolls.

We said little. I did not inquire as to where the couple would live. If I could make Fanny see sensibly, there would be no wedding. At least we were safe for now. They would have to delay until this all-consuming search for our father was over. By the time we were all back down the trail Fanny might reconsider. However, from the silly looks the two of them kept giving one another, I began to wonder if that would happen.

"Well," said Neville, wiping his mouth with a faded linen napkin. "Now that I have Miss Fanny to think of, I am even more anxious to set off after old Gaspar. As I said, I think I need to be there to protect Christian Reyeult and Gaspar Fenton from each other."

And I shall be there to protect them from you, I thought, so certainly that I was sure Fanny and Neville must have heard my thoughts.

Aloud, I said, "I believe I shall accompany you up the mountain."

I was far more composed now, and I gave him a gracious smile. He returned my look with incredulity.

"Surely you don't mean to take to the trail again. It is far too dangerous."

"I believe I've heard that phrase several times before, and we've made it this far. Yes. I have determined not to wait any longer. I hate idleness with a passion. I shall accompany you, and we can bring Duignan along to cook."

163

I actually wanted Duignan along for my own protection. A third person would at least deter Neville
from any underhanded tricks if there were two pairs of
eyes watching him. I knew the idea was reckless, but I
could no longer sit here and waste away at this hotel
while the three erstwhile partners fought it out on the
top of some mountain. At least I wanted to be there to
see who won. They had the answers I wanted to know,
and the only way I would get them would be to go
along.

Neville looked as if he were going to reject the idea
outright, but then he threw up his hands.

"Of course I cannot prevent you from doing as you
wish. I only say I discourage it."

I put down my napkin on the rough table. "I have
decided. I can be ready at a moment's notice."

Luckily I had washed all my clothing yesterday and
had only to fetch it off the clothesline in back of the
hotel. I had forgotten all about it, so distracted was I
with Neville's appearance yesterday. I hoped our
clothes were not now frozen or wet with dew.

Neville slid his eyes to Fanny who watched us both
in fascination.

"Well then, I will take care of a few things and make
my goodbyes. Shall we say we will depart in one hour?
I will tell Mr. Earley to have the horses ready."

I nodded and stood up. I left Fanny talking to Neville and went to the kitchen where I found Duignan
slicing vegetables. I informed him of my plans and
asked if he would accompany us.

"Yes ma'am," he said, bowing in his Oriental way.
"Duignan go on trail with ma'am. Master not want
me to let ma'am out of sight."

I did not mention the fact that he would have me in
his sight but not Fanny and felt momentary pleasure

164

that Christian might have instructed Duignan to keep special watch over me. But of course that was ridiculous. Fanny's and my safety were equally important, and our guide would not have conveyed anything otherwise to his helper. I made my way upstairs to get the laundry, to pack my things in my saddlebags, and to change into the split skirt for riding.

I went out the little back door to the small porch from whence our laundry was strung up the hill. Our white clothing flapped in the breeze. I began loosening the pins that held it and gathered it in my arms.

At the far end of the line was a camisole on which black spots flashed. At first I thought that dirt or soot had gotten on it, or perhaps birds had left droppings.

But when I walked down the line and reached for the cotton camisole, I stopped short. A playing card had been pinned over the left part of the bodice. It was the ace of spades, and as I stared at it the meaning sank in.

The card was pinned where the heart would be on the wearer. Spades in cards stood for death. My own heart lurched suddenly. Either this was a very poor joke or someone was threatening me. Or, perhaps, warning me.

I looked up the hill as if expecting to see the perpetrator hiding behind a tree, watching me, but except for the boughs that danced in the wind, nothing moved.

Holding the laundry against me, I took it back inside and deposited it on my bed to sort. I unpinned the card and tucked it into my saddlebag. I would not mention this to anyone, nor did I want anyone to know I had found it.

Rather than being frightened I was actually glad I had decided upon a course of action. I would keep

Neville in my sight, being very careful, of course. And maybe I would ascertain what he was really up to.

Fanny came to watch me get ready. Luckily Neville was down at the barn seeing to the horses, so I had a few minutes alone with her. She stood in my "room" wringing her hands.

"How can you do this, Hilary? You're leaving me all alone."

"You won't be alone. Drusilla and Franz will be here. And we might miss Christian on the trail. If he returns here, you'll need to explain what happened."

"I don't care," she pleaded. "I think you're doing the wrong thing. And you're being selfish, taking Thomas away from here. It's not fair."

I straightened up from where I was bending over the saddlebags and faced her squarely.

"And I think you're doing the wrong thing by marrying Thomas Neville."

"Why? How can you say that? He is just the sort of man who can provide for me. And besides he adores me."

"I wouldn't be so sure it isn't something else about you he adores," I said.

"Whatever are you talking about?"

"I think he smells gold. Maybe it's something to do with that mysterious map." I put down the blanket I had been folding. "Look, Fanny, it's just that I don't trust him."

She took on her martyred look. "You're just jealous."

I continued to pack the saddlebag.

"I believe we've had this discussion before. However, I still believe it will be better to put off all discussions of marriage until we find Father and learn the nature of the relationship between his former partners

166

and him. When things are a bit more settled then we can talk about it."

Her lower lip protruded in an expression that told me she didn't like what I had said.

"You'll be all right here," I said. My words held more conviction than I truly had, but I was trying to convince myself as much as Fanny. "In a few days we'll have found out what's happened to Father and everything will be settled."

I turned to go down the stairs. If only it were that simple. Somehow I doubted it. I did not like leaving Fanny alone here, but I was tired of sitting idle myself. She would have to show spunk enough to take care of herself if anything happened. It was a risk, but I was bent on my purpose now, and nothing would make me reconsider.

Drusilla was on the porch watching the proceedings below. Duignan had packed an amazing number of parcels on one burro in a short time. His poncho and slouched hat made him look more Mexican than Oriental, except for his long braid. Neville wore the same dark suit, black hat, and sturdy high-topped boots.

I stepped out to join Drusilla and inform her of my plans.

"I have decided to accompany Mr. Neville on his search up the trail for my father," I said.

She grunted. "Makes little difference to me if you all want to run around that mountain. Gettin' mighty cold at night."

"I know. But I feel I must go. Fanny will stay here. Try to keep an eye on her, will you, Drusilla? She will get bored, but I don't want her to do anything stupid."

The brim of Drusilla's bonnet hid her face from me, so I could not see her expression. Last-minute anxiety about Fanny almost caused me to change my mind.

But as I watched Neville pull the cinch tight on his horse, I straightened my spine and climbed down the rickety stairs.

I slung my saddlebags on my horse and secured it tightly. Then I turned to wave at Drusilla and Fanny, standing on the porch high above us, the stilts below making them look as if they balanced on toothpicks.

I led my horse to a mounting block and managed to get into the saddle unaided. I was proud that I had become a western woman so easily and attributed it to my flexibility. I had had to meet many circumstances in my life, this was simply another one of them.

Neville's horse danced sideways as if a day's rest had made it frisky.

"We'll follow the marked trail to start," he said. "Then I suppose we'll let your guide's friend tell us which way he thinks his worthy employer has gone."

"Can you do that?" I asked Duignan. "Can you track Christian?"

He nodded, the hat brim flopping over his slant-eyed face. "Yes, ma'am. Can track good."

"Very well. Then we've nothing else holding us back."

Neville considered me for a moment. "No," he said. "I suppose we don't."

He wheeled his horse and threw a kiss to Fanny. She returned the gesture, making my stomach turn. Then Neville led off, I followed, and Duignan brought up the rear, riding one mule and leading the burro.

Could Fanny be right? Was I jealous? My trek up the mountain with Neville was half mad. If I examined my heart carefully, was it only because I wanted to hasten seeing Christian again? I felt ashamed of the way I so looked forward to setting eyes on the man. I felt like a character out of one of Fanny's romantic chapbooks.

I pressed my lips together, directing my thoughts away from Christian and to the matters at hand.

The sun was high as we rode up the trail and away from the hotel. The trail passed among the trees and then began a steep incline. Granite walls rose straight beside us as in no time the trail narrowed. Scarlet and brown vines and mosses crept out of the crevices beside us as they had by the falls below. I settled into the familiar rhythm of the horse, and soon we were turning on switchbacks like the ones we had traversed to get to the hotel.

From the side of the mountain I looked down at the hotel that was surprisingly far below us in no time. Soon the wind picked up, and it seemed to echo off the mountaintops. Fleecy clouds drifted across the sun and I hoped I had brought enough warm clothing for cold nights I was sure lay ahead. I said a silent prayer that we would find Christian soon, if for no other reason than to ease our hardships. For Christian would no doubt know where the best camps were.

As we climbed, the clouds seemed to reach down and touch us again. Then as I came out of a drifting cloud I spied a jutting precipice above and ahead of us. I recognized Devil's Point from Drusilla's description, and my spine tingled. I unconsciously held tighter to the saddle horn as we approached the rock which pointed upward and outward.

I glanced back at Duignan, who was scanning the ground beside us. Then Gabrielle took the turn and lurched upward. Here the trail narrowed along a ledge approaching Devil's Point, and I reached out to my left to touch the wall of rock beside me. In a few more steps the trail widened as the cliff hung over air below.

169

But we passed onto a curve where the trail narrowed again.

Then an odd sensation overcame me as I felt my horse's sides contract, and she expelled air. I felt myself, saddle and all, begin to slip, and I clawed the air in front of me.

"Kick free, kick free," Duignan shouted behind me.

I swung my feet out of the stirrups and grasped Gabrielle's mane as the saddle slipped around the horse. I went with it, letting go of the mane and clutching at stubs of bushes, my feet sliding down gravel. Out of sheer willpower I pinned myself to the side of the mountain. I could feel air beneath my perch and dared not look down.

When I stopped sliding and rested in my precarious hold, the real fear sent my heart right out of my body. Above me, hooves slid in the other direction, and I closed my eyes, not wanting to see Gabrielle go over the edge either.

"Hang on," a voice cried.

Slowly, slowly I dared move my chin upward until I peered at the edge of the trail. Duignan's face hovered several feet above me.

Chapter 12

I held my breath while Duignan snaked a rope down to me. I grasped it with one hand but was still too frozen to move. Time stopped and I thought I would surely be pinned to the mountain and turned to stone like some of the weird configurations that rose from the mountain walls.

"Easy, go easy," came Duignan's voice. "Pull up. Rope will hold."

I made sure I had a solid grasp on the rope with one hand before I dared try to move my position. Then I tentatively moved one foot until I had a foothold on a clump of brush. My heart stopped beating as I let go with the other hand and clung to the rope.

Then as I pushed with my feet the rope pulled me up and a pair of arms reached to pull me over the edge of the drop-off. Finally my heart started to beat again, and when it did, it raced as I realized how close I had come to perishing.

"Thank goodness." Neville hauled me to my feet.

I still felt like I was standing dangerously near the edge and had to move around him. Only then did I begin to take in the scene of the party perched on the narrow trail.

Duignan was examining the cinch that had come loose and Neville turned and let go a string of curse words.

"You should have checked that this morning. It's a little late now."

He obviously thought it was the Chinaman's fault that the cinch had come loose.

But Duignan paused in his work readjusting the saddle and turned slowly to face Neville. His narrow eyes seemed to narrow even more and he did not give his little bow. Instead he stared at Neville for a long moment and then finished tightening the saddle.

"It's all right," I said, though my legs shook as I walked toward Gabrielle. "I should have gotten off to walk."

I gave Duignan a shaky smile and took the reins. Then I ducked under the mare's head to walk next to the mountainside.

Neville cursed again under his breath, but we all took our positions again and got under way. I did not look down as we continued around the mountain. To avoid looking over the steep drop-offs I found myself looking up, examining the rocks above for any chance of a rock slide.

We finally came out to another high meadow. The yellow grass spread like a carpet up a gentle slope, and low evergreen bushes dotted the hillside. A little farther up, the white birch stood like an enclosure of a dark forest.

The sun had gone behind the high peaks when Neville headed for the trees.

"We'll make camp there," he said.

I looked at Duignan, but the cook seemed to have

172

no objection. We found a spot with nothing but rich dirt for a floor and then Duignan pointed to something I had not noticed. A ring of rocks around a depression in the earth indicated that someone else had made camp here and recently.

My pulse quickened. We must be on the right trail then. Christian must have come this way—or Father. I looked deeper into the forest, trying to see where either man might have gone. But it was too dark, and of course we could not travel any further tonight.

As we made camp, I tried to look for other signs that Christian had been here. Of course it was foolish to think that I knew anything at all about tracking. But I watched Duignan, and while he was going through the motions of gathering firewood and then coaxing the kindling, it seemed to me that his eyes passed over many small details. But his inscrutable face gave away nothing. I wished that Neville were not here so that I could ask Duignan questions about what he saw.

"Are you feeling better, my dear?" Neville asked as he spread a blanket on the ground, presumably for us to sit upon.

"Yes, thank you."

He shook his head. "I warned you against such dangers. That was why I did not recommend your coming this far."

I shrugged nonchalantly, not giving away the way my mind replayed the scene. And with every replaying I altered the ending, seeing myself go all the way over the edge and adding to the number of deaths that occurred at Devil's Point.

I sat on the blanket, leaning against a log Neville drew over to form a low back rest.

"It was a risk I decided to take."

"Hmm," said Neville, taking a seat beside me. He stretched one leg out before him and bent the other one, which he hooked with his elbow as we watched Duignan make preparations for our supper.

"I do not like such risks," said Neville. "This country is full of them."

I turned to study his profile. "Then after you settle your debt with my father, you will return to city life?" I asked. "That is, you and Fanny?"

He blinked, and for a moment I imagined he had forgotten he had just proposed to my sister. But then he slid on his mask of geniality.

"Why yes. I rather thought she might fancy San Francisco."

"She might."

I felt strained. It seemed silly to make idle conversation, so I simply watched the darkness gather around us and listened to the sounds of insects and birds settling down for the night. I strained my ears to listen for the strange chanting. I had not heard it since the day the bear chased us in the woods, and I heard nothing now except the soft soughing of the tall trees around us. But something made me shiver. I decided that there was something odd about Yosemite and its surroundings, and I still did not know if the strangeness were human or supernatural.

After a modest meal of roast bear meat, which we had packed in with us, we stretched out on our blankets near the fire. Duignan took our tin plates to a nearby stream to wash them, and then in his efficient routine, put everything away. Then he sat cross-legged in front of the fire, staring at the dancing flames, occasionally poking a piece of wood to make sparks fly up, or feeding it new wood.

I heard a wolf howl, and I shivered. Fires were

supposed to keep wild animals away from camps. I hoped it was true.

Finally, I slid deeper into my blanket, wiggled until I fit myself into the lumps and slopes of the ground, and closed my eyes on my saddle for a pillow. I was becoming rather expert at sleeping on the ground.

The next morning we rose, breakfasted, and took to the trail. Silver firs towered above us with branches pinnated like ferns, and sugar pines with their feathery arms stretched out as if the trees were addressing the lower scrub. We came through a pass and out onto another high meadow with yellow-green plumelike foliage. To my surprise I spied a shack a little way ahead, and to my further surprise, smoke curled out of the stone chimney.

We all drew rein to stare at it and then to glance at each other. Duignan nodded to himself as if in satisfaction.

"Do you think your employer is there?" I asked him, hardly daring to believe it.

He nodded with more certainty then. "Boss there."

Neville urged his horse forward, and I did the same. We rode straight across the little meadow and into the clearing in front of the cabin. Only then did the door open and Christian did indeed come out.

His moustache needed trimming and he had a few days' growth of beard. But other than that I thought he looked wonderful. My heart turned over in excitement at seeing his broad shoulders and firm gait as he strode forward, thumbs hooked into the belt loops of his trousers. His yoked white shirt was open at the neck, exposing small tufts of blond hair on his muscular chest. He faced Neville, saying nothing.

My attention was so fixed on the two of them that I almost failed to notice a small, wiry man emerge from the cabin and remove a pipe from his mouth. He was wearing a gray flannel shirt over another red one. His brown striped trousers were loosely tucked into wide-mouthed boot tops. A battered, wide-brimmed hat shaded face and neck. But the droopy moustache and perplexed expression were as familiar to me as if I'd seen him yesterday.

"Father!" I uttered it in loud surprise as if I never expected to find him here.

He had started toward us, but at my exclamation, he stopped and raised his hand to settle his hat back on his head so he could take a better look at me. Then he turned his head to look at Neville and Duignan and then looked back at me as if he had never seen any of us before.

All the pent-up tension, worry about our future, and anger over our circumstances came pouring out at that moment, and I threw myself off my horse and ran up the slope toward him, shouting as I went. My own wrath had set a charge under me.

"For heaven's sake, Father, what are you doing here? How long has this man been with you?"

I threw out an arm to point at Christian, who stood by, watching, but I did not pause in my tirade.

"Fanny and I have traveled thousands of miles to find you, only to learn from your . . . your friends that you were wandering around in this dangerous valley on some ridiculous search for an Indian treasure.

"Didn't you know that the Staffords died, and Fanny and I have nowhere to go? And here you sit in this out-of-the-way place tucked into your cozy cabin while we've been sleeping on the ground, eating off the land, and generally suffering to find you. I don't suppose it's going to do any good either. Don't you know you've got two grown-up daughters who would circle the earth to see you?"

I had reached him, and he still stood in stupefaction, but I saw the colors change in his eyes, and he raised his arms to catch me as I began to cry and threw myself at him.

"Oh, Father," I sniveled into his flannel shoulder. "I thought we'd never find you, and then what would we do? We don't have any place to go."

I sobbed loud and long, not caring how I appeared to any of them.

He raised his arms to encircle me, rocking me from side to side, and then he grasped my shoulders to hold me away from him. We were on eye level, and he squinted his small, dark eyes to examine my face.

"Can this be my own Hilary?" he said in a voice of wonder.

I nodded, not yet finding my voice again.

"Well, saints be praised. Reyeult, you don't lie," he said over his shoulder. "When my friend here said he had brought my daughters into the valley I thought he had partaken of some plant the Indians use for dreams and visions. But the fact that he knew your names convinced me."

My exasperation and relief returned together. "Oh, Father, you just don't know what we've been through. And I left Fanny at the hotel all alone, and I'm worried about her."

He raised a hand. "Now calm yourself, my dear. One thing at a time. I'm sure Fanny will be all right with Drusilla and Franz to look after her. It's you I'm worried about, for you seem a mite upset."

I stamped the ground, my hands on my hips, glaring

at all three of the men who watched me in varying degrees of amusement.

"And so would you be if you were I."

Gaspar put a hand on my shoulder. "All right, darlin', don't start in again. Why don't you jes' bring yourself into my cabin and take a load off your feet. We'll pour some nice fresh coffee down you. You're here now, girl, so stop fretting."

He started for the cabin, so I followed him. I hadn't even said hello to Christian, and he watched me, rubbing his chin. Neville dismounted and handed the reins to Duignan, who seemed to mumble something the moment Neville turned his back.

I faced a wood-slatted door that hung on cowhide hinges of skin with the hair on and a leather strap for a handle. I pushed open the door and stepped into the earthen-floor cabin. It was simple, but seemed at first glance to have everything a prospector would need. Several hand-hewn chairs with low backs sat around the room. Two had been drawn up to a rude stone fireplace where a fire crackled. Two more chairs had straight backs that rose to a normal height.

Two small beds graced either side of the room, and a hand-hewn table big enough for two people sat under a canvas-covered window. There was the smell of cedar about it all.

Lanterns sat on shelves built into the wall, and there were jars and boxes of supplies stacked helter-skelter. Blankets were stacked on a crate in one corner. It looked as if my father had made good preparations to stay here all winter.

I was still not over my initial emotional upheaval at seeing my father again, but I found I was curious to see the place he called home.

"How long have you been here?" I asked as I took a few tentative steps about the room.

"Been workin' on this place for two summers."

"Since . . ." I started to say since he'd left his erstwhile partners, but the door creaked behind me and I turned as Neville stepped in.

His eyes flitted around the cabin, taking in the fireplace, the beds, table, and then he looked upward to a loft above our heads at one end of the room, where more supplies were stored. He lifted a brow.

"Very tidy, Gaspar. I commend your enterprise."

Gaspar made a rumbling sound in his throat. "It does for an old widower like me."

"Yes," said Neville, stepping farther into the room and dropping his hat on one of the little chairs. "I can see you weren't expecting guests. Or were you?"

His eyes went from one neatly made bed to the other. My father's tone seemed to meet the covert challenge in Neville's voice.

"You never know when the odd explorer might come through. I was prudent to prepare for more than just myself to sleep here, though you are right, I never expected so big a party."

He turned his eyes on me and they lit up with amused pride. "I especially did not expect one of my daughters to come calling."

"Oh, Father," I said, expelling a breath of air in affectionate impatience.

I felt my heart lift. Now that I was here I wanted to sit down with him and begin talking. I resented the fact that there were so many people here as well, which prevented a fitting reunion between us.

"Well, now," said Gaspar, lifting his arms. "Now you've seen it. I suppose we'd better do something about victuals."

179

"You forget," said Neville. "We've brought a cook. That is, we've brought Reyeult's cook."

"Hmm," said Gaspar.

I went to the door, which was open a crack. Outside, Christian was listening with bowed head to Duignan, who was speaking rapidly and making many gestures. Christian must have felt my gaze, for he looked up at me and narrowed his eyes while still listening to Duignan and nodding.

I wondered if Duignan was telling Christian about my narrow escape, for I saw Christian's eyes widen and his nostrils flare. A moment later, he frowned. Finally he turned and issued some instructions to the cook, who gave his little bow and began to unpack the mules.

Inside, Neville had drawn his chair up near the fireplace where Father was stoking the fire. I shut the door and went toward the fire to warm my hands.

"What can I do to help you, Father?" I asked.

"Why nothing, Hilary. You rest your bones while I put on a pot of strong coffee to warm you."

The door slammed and Christian entered. With the three men in the room I immediately felt the tension. None of them said anything, nor did they look at each other. Well, I thought. We're going to have a confrontation at last.

But instead, each man seemed to be busy concentrating on his own thoughts. Christian took a chair. Once seated, he leaned forward, his elbow on his thigh, and frowned at the fire. Neville examined his fingernails, and my father took a kettle out front to get water from a well he had dug. I heard the bucket bang against the stone wall of the well on its way down.

Neville finally broke the silence. He stretched his

arms over his head and recrossed his legs in front of him.

"So," he said to Christian. "Have you and Gaspar been having a good chat about old times?"

"Maybe," Christian said. He kept his head lowered, but raised his eyes to Neville.

Neville sighed and laced his fingers over his abdomen. "Did you manage to settle that little matter that came between you before?"

Christian straightened. I saw his body tense, and his eyes took on the same angry glint I had seen in them when he had met Neville in the hotel dining room in Mariposa.

"And what matter would that be?" Christian asked, drawing his words out slowly.

"Why, the card game, of course. The one the night before the fire. There was a matter of money owed, as I recall."

"As a matter of fact there was."

Christian sat up and leaned both elbows on the low back rest behind him. He had a casual pose, but I knew better. It was from just such a pose that a quick man could spring. I knew, I'm not sure how, that at that moment Christian was acutely aware of the weapons he had about him. Even though his rifle was out of reach, there was a very long knife in a leather scabbard at his waist, and one in his boot, for I could see its hilt.

But Neville paid him no mind at all. He continued his talk as if they had nothing better to do than visit before the fire.

At that moment my father came back and crossed between them. I thought at the time he was ignorant as to what the other two had been talking about, but he could have heard them from outside the door. He set the kettle on a grate he had stuck between the stones in the fireplace so that the fire would heat the water.

"Well now," said Neville, "here's the man that might be able to settle it for us. Gaspar, my man. We were talking about the card game the night before the fire."

Gaspar sat back on his heels, poking among the coals, but I could see that the muscles in his neck stiffened.

"What of it?" he said.

"Surely you remember," said Neville. "Reyeult here, accused you of cheating."

My father spun and stood so fast I blinked. I found myself backing out of the circle, for here now was the altercation I had expected all along.

"Who said I was cheating?" my father said. "I'll slit the throat of the man who calls me a cheat."

The motion of his fingers across his own throat emphasized his words.

Christian was on his feet. "I never said that," he said with a snarl at Neville, who got to his feet more slowly.

"Why," said Neville, shaking his head. "I could swear I can recall a dozen instances when you addressed Gaspar by the words, 'you old cheat.' "

Christian raised his voice. "I don't think you can prove that, my man. I would watch my words if I were you. In fact, if I recall correctly, it is you who owe me a little money still. I was willing to forget it at the time. But since it appears you've done so well since, then why I believe I'd like to collect."

"Why, my good man," Neville protested. "I owe you nothing. It is Gaspar here I've come to repay."

"Well then," said my father. "Hand it over."

Neville raised his hands. "Now, not so fast. I have a few questions first. Surely you'll satisfy me about

182

your success with that map you brought out as stakes that night."

"That's none of your business," said Christian.

"Why I believe you wanted to get your hands on that map yourself," said Neville.

"I did," replied Christian. "I won it. Or don't you remember that?"

"No, I don't," said Neville.

Then the three of them were all arguing so loudly I could hardly distinguish who was saying what.

"Wait a minute," I shouted.

I stamped my foot in the dirt, trying to make them stop arguing, for I was becoming more and more confused about what had actually occurred during that card game. I had thought that with the three of them together I could at last arrive at the truth. But no one was listening to me.

In fact the verbal abuse had turned into something more. Neville said something that particularly angered Christian, and Christian had pushed Neville back a step.

Neville looked at the spot on his chest as if it had been soiled. Then with a menace in his eye, he clenched a fist.

"No one talks like that to me."

But my father stepped in. "Well, Mr. Neville. I don't particularly like what you said to me a moment ago, either."

"Keep out of this, Gaspar," said Christian, and he shoved my father aside, so that he stumbled and landed on a chair that rocked backward with his weight.

"Now just a minute here."

And my father was back on his feet and into the fray.

Neville took a swing at Christian, who ducked. But the blow struck my father on his jaw instead. Gaspar reeled. Christian caught him and pushed him. Then Neville knocked him aside to get at Christian. All three of them were entangled, and I clasped my hands to my head.

"Stop it," I yelled. But of course no one took any notice.

I did the next best thing. I circled around the edge of the tussle and opened the door.

Christian picked up a chair and swung it at Neville, who ducked. Neville swung his fist and hit Christian on the jaw this time and Christian fell backward out the door. Neville started after him, but my father started after Neville, catching him around the middle and pulling him to the ground just outside the cabin. They wrestled in the dirt, then my father got his arm around Neville's neck. But Neville broke free and got to his knees just as Christian came for him again.

Metal flashed and I screamed.

"Look out, he's got a knife."

But Christian saw the knife in Neville's hand, and he grasped his wrist. For a moment they balanced, their strength matched, their faces grimacing with the effort. But slowly Christian forced Neville's hand downward as I held my breath. Then Neville grunted and his hand opened. The knife fell to the ground.

Christian wrenched Neville's arm around his back and held him in a painful grip.

"That will teach you to try something like that, my erstwhile partner," Christian spat out.

But still Neville struggled. Suddenly he bent forward and threw Christian over his shoulders. Christian landed with a thud, and my heart lurched to my throat. I impulsively ran toward him, but my father caught me and held me still.

"Christian," I cried out.

He lurched to his feet, but Neville was upon him. Christian kicked, and Neville fell. Then the two men grappled and rolled dangerously near the cliff. Finally Christian got free and hauled back to plow his right fist into Neville's jaw.

Neville bucked backward, grabbed his jaw, and stumbled to his feet. In his stupor he staggered sideways.

A cry stuck in my throat. Christian was pulling himself to his feet. Time seemed to stop. I saw Neville's foot go down on the loose rock, saw the ground give way. Then with a cry that reverberated from peak to peak, he fell backward into space.

Chapter 13

Christian straightened and stared ahead of him. Then we all ran to the edge. Rocks had slid down the steep drop following Neville's body as it bumped against the rocks, turning over and over. I thought I saw him land. But then he slid farther and was hidden by rock outcroppings.

"Oh my God," I said on a breath.

We all stood and looked at each other. I heard Christian's heavy breathing, my father's breath slightly rasping in his throat. The wind howled up the canyon. I don't know how long we stood there. It seemed a very long time.

Finally Christian wiped his hands on his trousers and looked over the edge of the cliff once again.

"Now you know why they call it Widow's Mountain," he said. "I'd better go see what's left of him," he said.

"No," I said, grasping his sleeve. "It's too dangerous."

Blood ran from the corner of his mouth and dirt covered him from head to toe. He looked down at me with his intense blue eyes.

"Not as dangerous for me as it was for him," he said.

Even in the situation we found ourselves, his voice seemed to caress the words, but my heart turned over. Had I found this man who had touched my heart only to lose him again to the mountains so soon?

"No," I said, reaching up to pull back the hair that had blown loose and blew around my face.

He faced me squarely and laughed. Grasping my shoulders he looked at my face.

"I see the lady cares," he teased. Then he said over his shoulder to Gaspar, who was examining the cliff where it had fallen in, "I told you your daughter had many compelling qualities," he said. "You raised her to be an adventurer, if her presence here proves anything. But she would not let an experienced mountain man descend to find out what happened to a rival."

I faced him determinedly, my face displaying a rainbow of emotions, I am sure.

My father came up beside us. "I cannot take the credit for raising her, I'm sorry to say. But she has a level head, Reyeult. Perhaps you should listen to her."

Christian dropped his hands.

"It is unlikely he survived the fall, but we must see. I don't like the man, but I can't let him lie there if there's anything we can do about it."

Then to me he said in a gentler voice. "Don't worry. I won't take any chances."

Not taking any chances consisted of fetching a stout rope from the cabin, tying it around a tree, and trailing it over the edge, while my father sat on the edge and held it securely. Then Christian backed down the scrabble, looking for footholds among brush and rocks.

I didn't want to watch, but I couldn't tear myself

away either. I lay flat on my stomach and watched him descend. It seemed at one point that he came to a small ledge. There he rested. But then I saw the rope in my father's hands grow taut again as he kept inching downward.

He became a tiny spot so that we could hardly see him. Finally he reached the bottom of the ravine.

"I think he's hit bottom," said Gaspar.

I sighed in relief and got to my knees. I didn't need to watch him walk around on flat ground.

Father got up, too, and coiled the loose rope once on itself.

"We'll see when the rope grows taut," he said. "It'll mean he's on his way back up. Let's go in, Daughter."

He was right. We might as well let Christian make his search. Back inside the cabin we discovered that Duignan had begun to rustle up a meal.

"Smells good, whatever it is, my good man," said my father.

Gaspar sat down by the little table and I took the other seat. Duignan poured mugs of coffee and brought them to us, for which we thanked him gratefully.

Then father and daughter sat in companionable silence. I looked at him, looked at the cabin, and sipped the coffee. The afternoon was drawing on, and the shadows gathered outside the cabin.

"It's been a long time, Father," I said. "So much has happened."

"That it has." He shook his head. "I regretted not spending more time with my children. I'm sorry for that."

He made a gesture that I thought was meant to reach for my hand, but then he drew it back. I thought I understood his embarrassment.

I took another sip from the mug as Duignan began to shell peas into a bucket.

"I suppose I should have written you when Gunther Stafford died," I said. "But Sarah became ill and there was little time. Then when she passed on, it seemed more expedient to come than to send a letter."

He cocked his head, and I thought I saw moisture in his eyes.

"I'm glad you did, my girl. Glad you did." He made a futile gesture at the simple surroundings. "Though there isn't much here for you, I'm afraid."

I sighed. "No, I know that. I suppose I hoped we could make a home together. In Mariposa, if you like it here so much. At least it would be a place to call our own."

"Hmm." He scratched his beard.

I set my cup down. "Father, I deserve to know more about your life. I mean if we're going to live together we have some catching up to do. There are," I lifted a hand hopelessly, "so many things I don't know about you."

He shrugged sheepishly and scratched his head. "Not much to know, I reckon," he said. "But you're welcome to it, whatever it is."

"Like that card game," I said. "Why is there such an argument surrounding it? Why can't the three of you get along? Is it the card game that caused the falling out? And for heaven's sake, who won?"

I leaned forward on the last question, startling him. He looked at me, then he laughed a silent laugh and leaned back in his chair, hooking his thumbs through his belt loops.

"Well now I reckon we've got to get you straight on a few things. Not that I'd swear by my memory, now. But I'll tell it to you as rightly as I remember it."

189

"Well, that will do for a start."

I rose to pour myself more coffee. Duignan had the meal well underway, for which I was thankful. For now that I was reminiscing with my father, I didn't want to stop. I resettled myself.

"All right," I said. "What happened?"

He grunted and got up. Crossing the room, he reached up to a shelf and got down a tin of tobacco. Then he located his pipe and took his time filling it.

Whatever Duignan was stirring in the pot over the fire was beginning to make my stomach rumble, and I was not sure which I was most concerned about, my hunger or my curiosity. As it turned out, neither became first priority.

Gaspar lowered his pipe as he looked out the one glass pane window at the front of the cabin. The pipe clattered to the shelf beside him.

"The rope's taut," he said.

We both rushed out of the cabin and toward the cliff. A gentle evening breeze blew, and the sun had departed behind the high peaks. Father knelt on the edge, but I dropped to my knees some feet from it and crawled up. I was startled to see Christian climbing upward, pausing to gain toe and handholds on the steep scrabbly incline. Only the rope would save him should he fall.

Christian looked up. Gaspar waved, but of course Christian could not let go to wave back.

Slowly he came, and I think I held my breath until he reached the top. Then Father reached down to grasp his arm and haul him over the edge. Both tumbled in a heap beside me.

I expelled a breath and sat up. "Thank God," I said.

Christian got to his knees and brushed his hands.

"Well?" said Gaspar. "Any sign of him?"

Christian shook his head as we all got to our feet.

"Just his hat. Looks like the river took him. Nothing to bury."

I felt a little sick.

"Hmph," said Gaspar. "He'll go over the falls that way. Be broken to bits. Well, that's that."

Both men started for the cabin, but I gazed at the dizzying depths. The small silver ribbon below sent back gold flecks of dying sun. I imagined Neville's body being tossed and turned on the sharp rocks that jutted out from the riverbank and then going over those treacherous falls we had so deftly managed to walk behind. I stepped back from the cliff and went inside.

Duignan had dished up food on the plates, and the three of them sat down to eat. I took my plate and sat at the place left for me at the little table, but I had difficulty getting down the first bite.

"So he's dead," I said in a sort of daze.

"Hmm," murmured Christian between greedy bites. "Looks like. Saw where he'd bumped against the brush. Did all I could do."

I put my fork down. How could they eat so ravenously when we were talking about a dead man.

My father noticed my pallor and gestured toward my plate.

"Eat up, girl. This is better grub than you'll get from me."

I tried to do as he said and did manage to eat most of the meal. As Duignan cleaned up, Gaspar finished lighting his pipe and then took a seat before the crackling fire, tilting back his chair and balancing his feet on a crate. Christian spread a bearskin rug on the floor and sat on that, his back against the bed at the side of the room. I joined them, still feeling unsettled.

We watched the fire for a while and then I sighed.

"Well," I said slowly, "I guess there's nothing we can do about Neville. He had a father in New York. He should be notified."

Christian gave a small grunt of agreement. "We can send a letter from Mariposa."

I guess I would have to live with that. Gradually my thoughts returned to the subject we were about to discuss before Christian's return. I searched the faces of the two men who sat with me.

"The card game, Father. You were about to tell me about that."

"Ah yes," he said, drawing on his pipe. He rocked on the chair until I thought he might lose his balance and land on his back, but he brought it up straight and planted his feet on the dirt floor.

"We played a lot of card games," he said. Then the sheepish shrug. "But I remember that one. It was when I lost my map."

He glanced sidelong at Christian, but Christian didn't look up. His gaze was fixed on the fire. Gaspar continued.

"I'd traded for that map from some Indians. They said they'd located a valley of gold somewhere out here on the slopes of the Sierra Nevada. I didn't know if it was true, but I kept that map with me, didn't dare part with it. Well, I ran out of money all right, that night stakes were high. Had nothing to bet with but my map. So I put it up for stakes."

I looked at Christian for confirmation of the story. This time he glanced at Gaspar and me and nodded.

"Well," said Father. "Christian here won the hand. I had to give him the map."

He chuckled and smacked his lips. "But I couldn't sleep, no sirree, couldn't sleep at all. The Indians

192

meant for me to have that map. They trusted me. Knew I'd just take what I could use and not bring in hoards of men to exploit them. I could hardly let it slip from my hands, could I now? I meant to pay my good man, Christian Reyeult, back, but I had to have the map. So I took it when he was asleep."

"So," I sat back, "you did steal it."

"Well now," he chided. "I wouldn't call it stealing. I'd call it borrowing it back. I meant to pay him when I'd found the gold."

"And have you?" I asked.

His eyes twinkled with reflected firelight. "Well now, not the kind you're thinking of."

Then his look turned more serious again. "See here, I discovered there's a code goes with the map. Indians told me it. They'd put it in English, which they knew from the missionaries."

He shrugged and worked his lips together.

"Well," I said. "Did you write it down?"

"I did . . . I did write it down. But not till I'd forgot part of it. Then I lost that, too."

My brows crossed. "Then you don't know what it is?"

"Not exactly."

I expelled a breath of air in exasperation. "What did the code mean?"

"Must've marked the exact location of the gold far as I can tell, once you get to where the map leads you."

"Then the map is no good without the code?" I questioned.

Gaspar shook his head.

"Then when you put it up as stakes you knew no one could use it without the code."

"Well," said Gaspar, "they didn't know that, now did they?"

193

I looked at Christian, who was picking his teeth with a long splinter. He removed the piece of wood from his mouth and looked at me in amusement as if he would expect just as much from my father.

I shook my head. Then I looked up at them again.

"So what was Neville's part in all this? Did he really owe you money? Is that why he came here?"

"Owed Christian here some money, as I recollect. Ain't that so, Reyeult?"

Christian scratched his head. "I believe he owed us both a little money. Hard to believe he came all the way here just to pay it back, eh, Gaspar? I think perhaps he had something else in mind, no?"

My father grunted. "Most like. Prob'ly been obsessed with the map ever since he seen it. Prob'ly came to see if there was any gold. Always was a greedy son of a bitch."

I hated to hear them speak ill of the dead, but perhaps they were right. And now we would never know.

We were silent for a while, Father smoking his pipe and Christian cleaning his teeth. Then I thought of something.

"Father," I said, "I believe I've seen that code you spoke of. At least I might have."

"Well, speak up, girl. Where?"

"At Drusilla's."

I half smiled at the remembrance. "She showed me a picture of herself as a young girl. Said you knew her then."

I looked at him only long enough to see the reaction in his face, and his bright eyes gave him away, but I continued.

"A piece of paper with strange writing on it fell out of the frame when she was showing me the picture. It had letters in small groupings on it. I noticed it be-

194

cause it wasn't regular writing. I mean it didn't mean anything. Could that be it?"

"Could be. I'd know if you wrote down the letters."

He got up and searched in a tin can for a stub of pencil and then produced a pad of grainy paper, which he handed to me. I took it back to the table and sat and thought. My memory was quite visual and after recalling the scene when I had looked at the paper, I managed to remember most of the letters, which I wrote down. I pondered them for a moment, made a few changes, and then handed it back to my father.

It came out something like, "Mouth walk between daylight two humps never goes."

He squinted at the paper, holding it nearer the lantern and turning it this way and that. Finally he shook his head.

"I don't have such a good memory for that sort of thing," he finally admitted. "But that looks like it to me. Maybe something else to it. I can't remember."

"Well then," I said, growing excited, "if you put this with the map, you ought to be able to find the gold."

He scratched his chin. "Got to know what it means first."

"Oh." I sank back in the chair. "You mean you never deciphered it."

"Never did know what it meant." He slapped his thighs with his hands. "Got to bring in some more firewood."

"Duignan can help you,". said Christian.

Duignan got up from his seat in the corner. The Chinaman had been so quiet I'd forgotten he was there. Now the two of them left, leaving Christian and me alone.

I got up to shut the door, which the wind had blown open, and when I turned around, Christian was standing by the fireplace, one boot resting on the stones in front of the fire. Half of his face was in the light, half in shadow. He moved toward me, and I stopped in front of him in the center of the room.

"So, you found your father," he said.

His lips had a gentle curve and I remembered how worried I had been about him when he was fighting with Neville. Thinking of Neville made me shiver, and I stepped closer to the fire. Christian turned, and I felt his finger touch my cheek.

"Yes, I found him," I said. "Or rather you did."

I looked at Christian with a question in my eyes. "How long had you been here?"

"Only since midday. Smoke from his chimney guided me. Once I told him I had left his daughters at the Earleys' hotel, he began to make preparations to go back with me. It took me the better part of two hours to persuade him that I was telling the truth and had not made the story up in order to get him to come out of the mountains for the winter."

Christian chuckled and resumed running his fingers over my face. I had to look away. When he touched me I felt myself coming under his spell, something that I warned myself was truly dangerous. I moved away, stretching my hands out over the fire.

"But he finally believed you?" I said.

"He could not deny I had met you after a great deal of quizzing. He had just about made up his mind to go see for himself when you appeared."

"Yes, I simply could not sit by at that hotel waiting any longer."

"Oh no?"

I hugged myself. It was on the tip of my tongue to tell him how much he had been in my thoughts and how much I had wanted to see him again.

"I'm afraid patience is not one of my virtues," I said.

He moved his head nearer, so near I could feel his breath fanning my cheeks.

"And what, my lovely, are your virtues?"

The door flew open and Father and Duignan came in. They deposited their armloads of wood near the door and Christian and I moved apart.

"There," said Father, dusting his hands on his trousers.

He walked to the center of the room. He looked at the two of us, and suddenly I felt awkward. It was getting late and we would have to turn in soon.

As if reading my thoughts, Christian said, "The lady will be wanting to prepare for bed. Duignan and I will sleep outside."

"Nonsense, my friend," said Gaspar. "This cabin ain't a fancy hotel, but you can spread your bedrolls in front of the fire."

Duignan slid his eyes to Gaspar and bowed. "Many thanks, but Duignan prefer to sleep outdoors."

Christian winked at me. "Never seen him in a bed. The sky's blanket enough for him. The floor here's fine for me."

"We've plenty of blankets," said Gaspar.

"Then all I need is my bedroll for my head," said Christian and he followed the Chinaman outdoors.

"You can sleep there." Father pointed to the bed nearest the table.

I was surprised when he pulled down a sheet and handed it to me together with a blanket. I pulled the quilt off that covered the thin mattress and made the bed.

"You've brought a lot of things up here," I observed as he was undoing his suspenders and pulling off his boots. "You must have been serious about living here. Why?"

"It grows on you, it does," he said.

He unbuttoned his outer shirt and peeled it off. "Guess I got attached to the idea of lookin' for that valley o' gold. Reckon it's gonna take a while, and unlike that Chinaman, I like my comforts. I'm gettin' to the age where the ground's a might hard to lie on all the time."

I smiled at him. "Father, Fanny and I want to make a home for you, only I'm not sure this is the place."

I sat down on the edge of the bed. "Do you think you would be happy in town part of the year?"

"Well now, can't say. I'm used to the mountains. Just can't say."

I picked up the lantern from the table and went outside to take care of certain necessities out of sight of the cabin. I passed Christian and Duignan who were deep in discussion in front of the cabin. When I returned I saw that Duignan had rolled himself into his blanket by the cabin door.

I stepped inside and found that the other lanterns had been extinguished. Only the dying fire showed me Christian's form under a blanket, his back to the bed in which I would be sleeping. My father had tucked himself into the other bed.

I quietly made my preparations for bed, getting under the blanket and then undressing down to my undergarments. The stuffed mattress on the rope springs was surprisingly comfortable, and I leaned over to extinguish the lantern I had placed on the table.

I heard Christian turn over and as I slid down into my bed, the glimmer from the fire allowed our eyes to meet.

"Good night," I whispered.

He lifted his chin in acknowledgment. I forced myself to close my eyes and turn facing the wall, then I opened them again and stared at the dark logs. I was thankful that my father was in the room, for I still felt drawn to Christian, and while I longed for the privacy to explore those notions, I was afraid of them.

In the morning after breakfast I spoke to my father and Christian about Fanny. It was decided that Duignan would return to the hotel to tell her that Father had been found and that we would all return in a few days. On the way, Duignan would look for any further sign of Neville's remains, going by a different route than the straight descent Christian had taken.

"I've seen sign of bear," Gaspar explained. "Might be worth a chance to try and get a good bearskin. Need good bearskin rugs for the winters here."

I wanted to remain with Father and Christian of course, but I felt better about Duignan's taking the news back to Fanny. He would also break the news that Neville had been lost. I knew how she chafed under the boredom and thought I should be there when she learned of Neville's fall. I was truly torn.

But I had never believed that Neville had been the right match for her, and I believed she would get over that disappointment in time. To be honest, I could not tear myself from my father's side now that I had found him. I suppose I simply would not admit that I longed for a bit of time with Christian as well.

Just what I expected out of the budding romance with Christian Reyeult I could not explain. I knew in my heart that what we felt for each other was not the sort of thing that would last. Perhaps, unlike Fanny, I had suppressed my fantasies for so long that I was allowing them flight in the magical wilderness of Yosemite. I kept telling myself that our little adventure would be over one day soon, but I was stretching it out for as long as possible.

We would all return to Mariposa and decide where to live. Christian would kiss my hand and bid me a fond adieu, perhaps alluding to meeting again. Then he would turn his back and stride away, the fringe on his hunting jacket swinging against his strong limbs.

But for me, at the time, there was no future, only the present, only the winds of the canyons, sunsets bouncing off snow-covered peaks, the weird rock formations about which Christian told us many Indian legends around the fire, and I was savoring it.

After Duignan left with one mule, we packed a picnic lunch, for Father offered to take us to see the view from the top of a magnificent waterfall, and he planned to look for the bear's den on the way.

My heart was light as I helped with preparations, packing dried meat, nuts, and berries Father had gathered from the forest, and bread Drusilla had made just before we had left the hotel. While I looked to the food, Father cleaned his rifle and pistol and tested the sharpness of his knives. Finally Christian saddled our horses, and we prepared to leave.

We headed up the long meadow and then rode through trees, climbing upward. Mint gave us the gift of its fragrance as we brushed it in passing, and wild purple asters and goldeneye swayed in the breeze. It was a glorious day, the air crisp with the feeling of autumn, but when I looked at the mighty snow-covered mansions of the High Sierra, I tasted the threat of winter soon to wrap these mountains in its blanket of snow.

We stopped for lunch by a mirror-bright alpine lake, surrounded by granite debris left by glaciers from another time. Alpine chipmunks scampered over boulders, and marmots sat bolt upright, watching.

We took to the trees again, and we were not alone. The impertinent, raucous Steller's jay marked our passing. Onward we went until we entered a small ravine with slopes densely covered with manzanita and huckleberry oak. Our horses suddenly snorted and danced sideways, refusing to go on. Father succeeded in turning his horse and we followed him back out of the ravine.

"Bear," he said, explaining to me. "The horses don't like the scent."

Christian peered ahead, his sharp eyes marking signs of bear, I was sure. Finally he pointed.

"There."

Squinting, I followed his line of vision to a large heap of fresh earth.

"Ahhh," Father sighed and I could see the spark in his eyes.

"What is it?" I asked.

"The bear den," he replied, his hand automatically going to the rifle that rested in its scabbard under his knee.

Remembering the bear that had chased Fanny and me to the hotel, I shrank back, but then tried to calm myself so that my horse would not become more nervous. My father leaned forward in the saddle, and I could see how much he wanted to stalk the bear, yet my instant reaction was fear for his safety. I forgot, of course, that hunting was second nature to him.

"Then we must go back," I said. "It'll be dangerous."

"Nonsense, girl," he said. "I'll camp on that ridge

201

up there where I can watch the den. If the bear comes out, I'll have a clear shot."

"You may need some help," said Christian, and I sensed in his voice the same excitement of the hunt.

Was I then to be thrust into a bear hunt, camping on a ridge in the wilderness? It seemed for a moment that I might, but my father looked from Christian to me and then back to Christian again.

"I can manage. You take Hilary back to the cabin. I've been waiting for this chance for weeks. I daren't let it go."

Then to me he said, "Don't worry, girl. I've caught bear before. I'll stay here and Christian can return tomorrow to help me pack in the meat. If the bear hasn't come out by then, we'll lure her out and get her."

I didn't even want to think about them baiting a bear and grimaced. But looking at the two of them I saw I didn't have any choice at all.

I gave one last hopeless look at my determined father and my heart sank. It was more than just letting him remain alone in the wilds to catch a bear. I saw then and there that I would never be able to tame him. My hopes of a happy domestic scene with my sister and me caring for our father were dashed away as I gazed at the look of excitement on his weathered face.

"Very well," said Christian, rocking forward in his saddle. "I will go back with Hilary and return tomorrow."

He looked around him, marking the spot, and then with a nod of the head at Gaspar, he turned downhill. I cast a despairing glance at my father and wished him good luck.

"Then I'll see you when you return to the cabin tomorrow," I said to him.

He grinned. "Roast bear is mighty good eatin'."

I shook my head and waved affectionately, then I turned my horse to follow Christian. We spoke little on the way down, and I tried to console myself by looking at the rioting gold of the leaves, and wondered if this was the gold the Indians had spoken of.

It was the kind of beauty that many never saw, I was sure, having come from a crowded city where most people never saw cliffs higher than the palisades of New Jersey. And to the Indian people who drew my father's map, the wonders of nature would have been even more valuable than the gold in the rocks that the white man craved.

We passed the mirror lake and kept to our descent as twilight hovered over us, quickly drawing on toward night. I rode beside Christian when we came out to the broad meadows, and we heard a coyote pouring out his soul.

"Why does the coyote sound so sad?" I murmured. I was surprised that Christian heard me.

"Maybe he isn't," replied Christian, who rode close to me now. "Maybe he is happy. It sounds sad to us because we hear it with human ears."

Darkness fell, and the moon hung low over the granite profiles across the cut from the cabin site. Though I would have happily followed Christian all night, I was glad when we reined in.

I went inside the cabin, the coyote's cry echoing in my heart, and I listened to the sounds of Christian unsaddling the horses and hobbling them where they could graze.

I stirred the ashes and coaxed the fire to life. Then I lit the lantern that sat on the little table. As I was blowing out the match, Christian pushed open the door and entered the cabin. The lantern flickered between us as his eyes sought mine. My heart hammered in my chest, and as he crossed the room toward me, I knew the moment had come.

Chapter 14

I dropped the match on the floor, a sense of wonder in my heart as he crossed the room and took me in his arms. I held him to me, thrilling in his strength. His lips sought my ear and dropped deft kisses there. I swooned against him as he moved his face around to touch my lips with his.

His moustache tickled, but I joyously returned his kiss. Thrill after thrill danced up me, and I knew we were moving much too fast. His grasp tightened, and as my bosom pushed against him, he lowered his mouth to kiss my chin, my throat.

Then he pulled away, taking my hand and leading me to the little bed. He removed his buckskin jacket, tossing it on a chair.

My hand went protectively to my chest.

"Christian, we shouldn't . . . ," I began.

But his smile and the gentle pressure he exerted on my hand won. I sat down beside him, but the break in our embrace had given me a chance to gather my wits. That I was strongly attracted to him there was no doubt, but that I could compromise myself beyond a kiss was out of the question.

"Christian . . . ," I tried again.

"Now why waste the evening talking," he teased, and he reached for my chin, bringing my face around to his.

When he looked at me his expression seemed to soften, and I heard his intake of breath. He gathered me to him again and bent his head across mine for another kiss.

"Hilary Fenton," he breathed against my ear as his hands brushed across my bodice, "I want to make you mine. I have wanted that since I saw you."

He chuckled as he shifted me around so that I leaned across his lap facing him.

"Your father told me of his daughters long ago. Perhaps it is our destiny, no? You come to Yosemite looking for Gaspar. Instead, maybe you find love, no?"

Love? Did he speak of love? But his kiss on my brow made it hard to think. I was busy exploring the muscles of his chest and shoulders through the soft muslin of his yoked shirt.

His fingers found the mother-of-pearl buttons at my neck, and before I knew what he was doing, he had my high-necked blouse open and pushed back on my shoulders.

"Ah," he sighed as his fingers danced over my skin. "Just as I expected," he said, smiling into my eyes again. "Your skin is like the finest porcelain."

My heart quickened its flutter. I had never been spoken to like that. What woman wouldn't melt at such romantic talk? I yearned for more, and as if reading my thoughts he reached for the pins in my hair and pulled them out, letting my hair fall about my shoulders.

His eyes spoke more than his words and I shared the

desire I saw there. I unconsciously leaned toward him for another kiss, and as one of his hands cupped my bosom he took my mouth in his. Then just as suddenly he pushed me away.

"Ah, it is not fair, is it?" he said.

My head reeled for a moment. "What isn't?"

"I wait for a chance to get you alone, and now that I have you, I cannot take you."

I blinked. Quickly I sat straighter and pulled my blouse together. Only then did I realize how close I had come to being ravaged, for wasn't I a willing subject just a moment ago? Even if the small part that remained of my rational mind told me that wasn't thinkable.

He strode over to the fire and kicked one of the rocks there. I heard him inhale a deep breath, and then he turned around and gazed at me.

"And just tell me why I should not take advantage of you?" he challenged me.

"I . . . uh." I tried to think quickly, but the fire burning deep within me had not quite been doused. "Because you are an honorable man," I finally said, licking my dry lips and continuing to put my clothing back together.

"Honor be damned," he said, leaning against the side of the rock chimney. "You know very well why not. Your father."

"My father?"

Christian nodded. "He would know the moment he saw us tomorrow, and my life might be forfeit if I didn't have a chance to explain."

"Explain?"

I realized I sounded dull-witted, but I was having a hard time following Christian's train of thought.

He expelled a breath of exasperation. "You are

right. What would I explain? That I wanted to bed his daughter? I hardly think he would grant permission for that unless we were wed."

I blinked again and did not speak, but he shook his head. Then he cocked his head and looked at me.

"The idea of being wed has crossed my mind, now," he said. "But only if my bride-to-be understood my motives."

My head was beginning to clear.

"What motives? What are you talking about? Is there not only one motive for thinking of being wed?"

My face burned. He himself had mentioned love only a moment ago.

"No," he said.

My head jerked up. "What do you mean?"

"A daughter of Gaspar Fenton might think I was merely a fortune hunter."

"Fortune hunter?" I don't know what I expected him to say, but it wasn't that. "But there isn't any fortune!"

"No," he said slowly, scooting a chair in front of him and squatting so that he sat upon it backward. "But there is a map, and a code."

"Oh, for heaven's sake," I said, getting off the bed. I fetched the matches and lit the other lantern. "That map is probably meaningless, and anyway, we don't know what the code means. 'Mouth walk between daylight two humps never goes' means nothing."

Christian crossed his arms on the back of the chair and rubbed his chin. "Not yet."

I placed my hands on my hips and looked down at him. "Then you really believe there's something to that map?"

"I don't know," he said thoughtfully. "But Thomas Neville did."

"Neville?" I sat on a chair across from Christian. "What do you mean?"

"I've been thinking about it," he said. "It must have been the only reason he was here. He's not the sort of man to make a great effort to pay money back to men he owed it to. No. I'll wager that Thomas Neville was obsessed with Gaspar's Indian map ever since the night he first saw it. I wager he wasn't able to put it out of his mind."

Christian eyed me sternly. "My dear, I think he had the notion that Gaspar Fenton would be a rich man someday and decided to marry one of his daughters."

I drew in my breath. "I never favored the match between him and Fanny."

"Luckily you saw through him and he knew better than to waste his time trying to win you. Your younger sister is much more gullible."

I slumped forward. "I guess there's no more danger of her marrying him."

"No," Christian said. Then he returned the conversation to its original course. "So you see why I am hesitant to woo you, my dear."

"Oh."

I suppose my tone carried something of my disappointment for in an instant he was out of his chair and kneeling before me.

"Unless," he said softly, "you believe I do not want you for your future fortune."

His hands slid around my waist and his eyes drew me forward.

"I don't know," I said breathlessly. "It would depend on whether or not you behaved honorably."

He gave a sound that was half grunt, half chuckle

and worked his fingers up the back of my neck, pulling my face toward his for a kiss. My arms went around his neck and he kissed me deeply as he stood, pulling me up with him.

Then he held my head against his shoulder caressing my back. "I suppose you have given me your answer," he said in a half teasing, half caressing voice. "I have been ordered to prove my honor."

Another hour was spent in stealing kisses, in soft caresses, in whispering words of love, in snatches of conversation about the map, and about whether Gaspar would catch his bear. Christian finally stretched out on top of the coverlet on my bed and pulled me against him. I snuggled against the hardness of his body and watched the fire dance until my lids dropped shut. I heard Christian's deep even breathing before I gave way to a dreamy sleep.

Gaspar returned midmorning with the bear hide and several juicy cuts of bear meat. He placed the hide in a trough he had gouged out of a large tree and left it to soak in a bath that contained tannin from the bark of the same tree.

I volunteered to prepare a stew while Christian went back with my father to bring the rest, which Gaspar had buried lest the animals get to it. Before he left, Christian checked a pistol to see that it was loaded and handed it to me.

"Since you'll be alone, you'd best keep this near. We'll be back before nightfall, but I'll feel safer if you have a weapon."

I took it in my hand, which dropped with the weight.

"Here, let me show you how it works," he said.

He spent some time showing me how to put the powder in place, how the balls were seated in the chambers, and how to cap the loaded chambers. Then he rotated the chambers and eased the hammer down on the uncharged nipple of the one empty chamber. I practiced cocking the hammer, taking aim, holding and squeezing.

Outside I practiced a few shots. After the smoke cleared we looked to see where the bullets went. Christian reloaded, but I hoped I would not have to use the weapon. It felt so clumsy in my hands. I could see that Christian was averse to leaving me, but I assured both men, perhaps feeling more bravado than I should have, that I would be perfectly fine until they returned this evening.

While the stew was simmering, I occupied myself with tidying up the cabin. I shook out the bedding and remade the beds, then I swept the debris from the dirt floor using a homemade broom my father must have fashioned.

I had never made bear stew before, but I used the herbs and seasonings I found in the cabin, and as it simmered in a big pot hung from a hook in the fireplace, the smell was tantalizing.

At the sound of a whinny outside, I bolted up and reached for the pistol. I knew my father and Christian could not be back so soon, and while it might be an innocent visitor, I was taking no chances.

The knock on the door sent equal shivers of fear running up and down my spine, but I pointed the pistol at the door and called out, "Who's there?"

"Hilary, is that you?"

I started forward, hastily lowering the pistol. Yet, as I lay it on the table, I was just as startled to hear Fanny's voice.

"Hello," I called. Then I was at the door and swung it open.

My sister stood before me in her riding skirt and jacket, her face ruddy from the brisk air, her hair under a wide-brimmed felt hat. Behind her Duignan was beginning to unload her horse and his mule. I grasped Fanny's hands and pulled her in.

"Fanny, my goodness. Whatever are you doing here?"

She untied the cords that secured her hat and pulled it off.

"You didn't expect me to stay in that dreary hotel all by myself," she said. "And then this Chinaman shows up and tells me some story about Thomas going over a cliff. Well naturally I had to come find out what has happened. I could have rotted down there with that weird Drusilla and Franz eyeing me all the time."

"I'm sorry, Fanny. Things have not gone as I had planned. I thought we would be returning today, but Father insisted on catching a bear."

She threw her hands in the air and walked around the small cabin, glancing at its meager furniture.

"A mother bear, is it? And where is he now?"

"Bringing back the meat. Oh, Fanny, do sit down. I'm sorry things have turned out this way. It was rather horrible about Neville. But at least we've found Father."

She stopped her pacing and confronted me. "So he really did go over a cliff? Is he really . . . dead?"

I nodded, pressing my lips together. "I'm afraid so. He seems to have fallen into the river. Christian climbed down to look for him, but he only saw the signs where he had fallen and entered the river. It's rather mean just there. I'm sorry, Fanny, really I am."

She pursed her lips and sat down slowly on one of

the little chairs. I waited for some sign of grief, for I knew I ought to comfort her, but she appeared bewildered rather than grief-stricken.

"You're sure," she finally said, her lips trembling a little.

"I saw it with my own eyes, Fanny. He and Christian and Father got in a row. No one pushed him over, he stumbled after Christian got a knife away from him."

Her shoulders drooped and her lips quivered. Then she looked away.

"I'm a widow before I'm even married," she finally said.

"No you're not," I said, finding my old impatience with the whole situation returning.

I rose to stir the stew. "I'm sorry Neville died, but I don't think he would have made a very good husband, Fanny. After all, you hardly knew him."

She twisted so that she crossed her legs and rested her arm on the back of the chair.

"But I would have been married after all. And Neville would have taken me to San Francisco."

I was relieved that her loss was more material than personal, but it troubled me that because she was willing to marry for money and security she might have thrown her life away on a man unworthy of her. I was harsh in my judgments of Thomas Neville, but I had always had a habit of judging a person based on first impressions. And it was remarkable that I had most often been right.

"Well," I said. "It is too bad that will not occur, at least not with Neville. But at least we have found Father."

"When will he return?"

"By this evening. I'm making a stew that should feed us all."

She jerked her chin. "I'm sick of bear meat. Was this bear so much more important than seeing his daughters?"

I hesitated in my answer. I did not want to admit that my reaction had been much the same. Instead I found a way of defending him.

"He was of course very anxious to see you, but men like Father live off the land. A bear kill means meat for the winter and a warm skin to sleep under. Once he spotted the den, it was essential that he hunt the bear."

"Was he really anxious to see me?"

"Of course."

We were interrupted by Duignan, who brought in things from the horses. I cleared off a shelf for Fanny to use and we spent some time arranging her things. Duignan approved of the progress I had made with the stew and left to see to the horses. Now all we had to do was wait for the hunters to return.

To distract Fanny I brought out the pad on which I'd written the code as I remembered it, telling her what Father had told me about the map.

"The code marks the exact location, you see. At least that's what Father thinks."

She had been examining the code with an air of cynicism, but the longer we looked at it, the more she seemed unable to resist the puzzle. The turned-down corners of her mouth softened as her lips pursed with interest. The bored look in her eye became one of curiosity as she bent over the code.

"Well," she finally said, sitting up. "Where is the map?"

I looked stupidly at her. "I'm afraid I don't know."

"Well, it has to be here somewhere," she said. "Let's look for it."

Pleased at her interest, I joined her in the search. It didn't take long. Fanny opened a small leather-bound chest, saw a large folded piece of paper and opened it.

"Look, Hilary. This has to be it."

I looked at it and from the markings on it, I agreed. We smiled at each other.

Taking the map to the table, we carefully spread it out, and Fanny drew her chair near so that the two of us pored over it.

After studying the markings for a while, I began to recognize locations.

"See, here is the hotel. This is the trail to where Father built the cabin. He must have built here because it's near the center of this area. This must be the vicinity of the gold."

I pointed out the natural landmarks I recognized. There were ridges, creeks, lakes, and Indian trails, but stare as hard as we might we gained no other clue as to the exact location of the gold.

Fanny sat back and picked up the paper with the code words on it and read them out.

"Gold," she said. Her eyes rounded as she looked at me. "If there really is gold, then we will be rich."

I didn't like what I saw in her enthusiasm. I could not understand how Fanny had grown to be so greedy. There was no other word for it. She had had no advantages as a child, yet we had been fortunate to live with people who were kind to us and welcomed us into the bosom of their family, being childless themselves.

I, too, longed for the comfort of home and family, but I had to say I was different from Fanny in that I did not expect the world to open its coffers to me, nor did I expect a white knight to rescue me. Or did I?

Guilty thoughts of Christian assailed me, but I put them from my mind.

My agitation made me rise and pace the dirt floor. "We mustn't get our hopes up, Fanny. This Indian map may mean nothing. It could be something they simply pawned off on Father in exchange for liquor or trinkets. Is all you ever think about money?"

I regretted my last words, but it was too late. Now I was afraid we were in for an argument.

"What do you mean?" she demanded, the color tinging her cheeks.

"I just mean that you seem to think money is the answer to everything. There are other things worth living for, Fanny."

"Oh really? I suppose it's all right for you to remain as poor as a church mouse, but not me. I don't want to work my fingers to the bone in some sweat shop or clean other people's houses. We'll die young if we do that. Father hasn't anything unless this map is telling him the truth, so the only other hope for us is a good marriage."

"Marriage is important, I agree," I said, feeling the knot in my stomach. I simply was not in the mood for this discussion. "But you should not sell yourself to some man just for money. And if Father's dream of finding gold doesn't materialize, you ought to be satisfied that we can at least make a home for him."

"Where? Not here."

She looked aghast at me, and I truly felt that we were completely alien to each other, even though we had always been sisters. It was difficult to comprehend.

"Oh please, Fanny, let's not talk about it."

"You started it. All I said was that if Father finds his gold, we'll be rich. And we will."

I sat down again. "Yes, I suppose we will."

I tried another tack. "Fanny, I don't mean to speak ill of the dead, but did you ever think that Neville might have wanted to marry you because he believed in that gold?"

She shrugged. "I don't know. I don't care, why?"

I gave up. "Because if that were true, then he didn't love you."

She sniffed. "Many women don't love their husbands and vice versa when they are first married. Arranged marriages sometimes work out very well. You can learn to love your husband."

I sighed. "That's true. I just didn't want you to be exploited."

She gave a laugh. "Moot point now. But, my dear sister, I've noticed how your mountain man has been eyeing you. Couldn't you say the same thing about him? He must have known about the map if the three of them were partners. Seems they all had funny stories to tell about it. How do you know Mr. Reyeult isn't lying to you with that smooth French Canadian manner of his? Tell me that? Maybe he is the real fortune hunter."

I stood up, and we stared at each other. She had voiced what had only been marginally in my mind before, but of course it could be true. I wrung my hands together and went to stir the pot so I wouldn't have to look at her.

"I don't know. He might be," I finally admitted.

A wave of grief threatened, and I choked it back. I realized at that moment that the reason I had been so swept away by Christian's attentions was that it seemed so unlikely for a man of his robustness to pay any mind to a plain person like myself. I had never had the means for making myself attractive, nor had I even

217

developed the pretty airs that Fanny seemed to have learned, not that I approved of them. But I fancied that such prettiness and coyness was what most men liked, and I was not like that.

In fact, men had for the most part ignored me except for the stares I had sometimes gotten from delivery men on their wagons making the rounds in Brooklyn. No one had ever courted me, except for Johnny Doolittle. He was a neighbor boy we had practically grown up with. Sometimes he took me for a ride in his father's milk wagon and he always said he would someday marry me. But I expect it was because Johnny, like me, didn't know very many other girls.

In a word, I had been shy when it came to thinking about the opposite sex. When the Staffords died and I had had to take on more responsibility, I suppose I had truly grown up. Then when we came out West, I sensed a new flowering in my bosom, a release I couldn't help feeling in the immense space and the awesome beauty of nature I had seen.

But surely all this had blinded me to Christian's intentions. It was still not clear just why Christian and Thomas Neville had converged on Father at just this time, and Christian could be every bit the fortune hunter that he accused Neville of being. In fact, could not the accusation arise from his own thoughts, even if he was not fully aware of them?

It would be wise not to find myself alone with Christian again. Treasure or no treasure, I was too susceptible to his kisses, to his words and caresses to trust myself with him. I had been in danger of losing my heart and possibly something worse. I would have to make sure circumstances did not lead to that possibility again.

Chapter 15

As evening drew on and Gaspar and Christian did not return, I grew worried. Perhaps something had happened to them. I tried to tell myself that they were experienced woodsmen and surely could handle any threat, especially since they were together, but I could not help but worry.

I stood between the cabin and the cliff gazing up the trail for any sign for a long time, but finally I heeded Fanny's call to come back inside.

"Let's eat the stew, Hilary," she said. "We can save some for them, but just because they're not back yet is no reason to starve the rest of us."

I saw the logic in that and when Duignan dished up bowls of stew and handed them round I accepted mine. I had not done such a bad job of cooking, and even Duignan seemed to approve.

"Not enough pepper," was his only comment and he added some of that commodity to his dish.

I can say now that that was one of the most uncomfortable evenings of my life. Between guilt about my feelings for Christian gnawing at my conscience and concern for the two hunters' safety, I knew I would not get a wink of sleep. I tried to spend some time deciphering the code, rearranging the words as in a puzzle.

I came up with the possibilities, "never walk between two humps goes daylight," but that left out "mouth." Then I tried "daylight mouth walk never goes between two humps."

The puzzle befuddled my brain, and though I was still upset, my mind grew fuzzy. Had I remembered all the words? I thought not, but I could not remember what else I had seen on the paper.

Duignan bedded down in his corner and Fanny took Father's bed. I sat on my little bed, listening to the howl of some animal outside. I thought at first it was the same mournful coyote Christian and I had heard, and remembered with nostalgia how he had said the coyote was singing a happy song. But the howls increased in number and in my mind they became louder until I imagined a wolf pack getting closer.

The wind came up, and branches of the trees behind the cabin scraped across the roof, sending creepers up my spine. I began to imagine all sorts of dangers and reached several times for the pistol that lay on the table above my head. I caressed its wooden stock, careful not to put my finger on the trigger, lest my nervousness should make it go off.

The odd little Chinaman's passive presence did nothing to reassure me in the event that we would need protection.

Suddenly Fanny sat up in her bed. "What's that?"

"Just noises, Fanny," I said, though I was unable to sleep myself. "Go back to sleep."

She lay back on her pillow, but turned this way and that, trying to get comfortable. Then the wind brought a long mournful howl that seemed neither human nor animal, and Fanny sat up again.

"What is that dreadful sound?" she said, throwing the covers back and searching for her boots.

I recalled the Indian chanting we had heard above the hotel, and this sound had much the same quality. My own heart raced, and the hairs on the back of my neck stood on end. Had the spirits found us and were coming for us at last?

Fanny stumbled across the floor and crawled onto my bed. She huddled next to me and I welcomed her presence as much for my own comfort as for hers. We seemed to shrink into the rough cabin wall at our backs, and I found myself looking into every corner trying to decide if there was a safer place.

I preferred action to waiting, but what were we to do?

"I don't know what the sound is," I told Fanny. "Probably night prowlers. They won't harm us."

The one thing I could do was stoke up the fire, and I slid off the bed to do so. I was thankful there was enough wood in the cabin, for I didn't want to venture outside for more in the harrowing night.

But it was when I turned from the fire and saw a shadowy figure move past the glass window that my heart stopped. I was unable to make out what the figure was, but something or someone moved outside. I held my breath, the stick I had used to stoke the fire clutched tightly in my hand. I was paralyzed with fear, unable to move or speak.

Though I stared at the window for some time, nothing passed the window again, and I forced myself to move to the table and exchange the stick for the gun.

"What is it? What's wrong?" whimpered Fanny.

"I don't know," I said in a low, trembling voice. "I thought I saw something."

"Ssss . . . saw something?" she stammered.

"I don't know. It could have been a branch of the tree," I said, though I knew it was not.

For some moments we remained frozen in our positions, and then when a scrabbling noise began against the logs of the cabin, I nearly jumped out of my skin. I had the gun aimed at the door, and I nearly squeezed the trigger, making it go off, but I prevented that from happening by a hairsbreadth.

The scrabbling reoccurred, only this time the sound came from nearer the door. Surely it was an animal trying to get in. But what? Wolf? Bear? Mountain lion? And where were the horses? Had the prowling beast chased them off? My imagination ran away with the possibilities, and I was certain that death awaited in the next moment. My only hope was to keep the gun trained on the door, which was securely latched with a long stick for a bolt, and get off a reliable shot should the beast push through.

The scrabbling moved again, this time coming from the opposite corner, and I suspected that whatever the beast, it was looking for entrance. With all the commotion, Duignan awoke. When he saw me aiming the gun at the door, he jumped up and pulled a long, sharp knife out from under his bedding.

"What is attacking?" he hissed.

"I don't know," I said in a stage whisper. "It's circling the cabin."

The noise sounded like claws raking the bark off the sides of the logs that formed the cabin walls, and the sound stood my hair on end. Even Fanny had reached for the stick I had left on the table and sat with the blanket pulled around her knees, the stick by her side.

For some moments the scrabbling continued unevenly. Then it stopped. We all stared at the four walls, waiting. Even the silence set my nerves on edge, then the sound started up again.

Duignan crept up to the window and tried to peer out, but he could see nothing. I was afraid for him to be too close to the window in case a claw should reach in and swipe at him.

I strained my ears to try to hear footsteps or any other identifying sound, but there was nothing more except the wind. Sometimes the branches scraping against the roof sounded like the scrabbling and I was sure that the beast had climbed up on top of us.

Then as suddenly as it had begun, it left. We waited and listened for how long I don't know, but all we heard was the wind in the trees and once in a while the distant coyote.

When at last I moved, the pain from stiffened muscles proved how rigidly I had been holding myself. Duignan shuffled toward the door.

"Duignan go see," he said, starting for the door.

"No, Duignan," I said. "It might be out there waiting for you. I won't risk another life."

I took a deep breath and tried to relax, taking a seat by the fire, but facing the door.

"Whatever it was has gone. It probably smelled the food but discovered it couldn't get in and went elsewhere for its prey."

I worried for the horses but realized we could do nothing about them now.

Gradually we all took positions of rest again, though I am sure the other two remained as alert as I did. We didn't speak, and I leaned against the wall, the pistol on a crate by my side in case I should need it again.

The night drew on, the fire crackling in the fireplace. At last the wind outside died down, and fatigue finally overcame my fear. I drowsed against the wall, sitting in the chair.

Near the wee hours of the morning, something awoke me, and I sat up with a start. I grabbed the pistol and waved it in front of me as I fought away grogginess. But sleep fled when the latch on the door began to lift by itself. I stared at the gradual motion as I arose and backed up against the rough wall.

The latch fell back and the door moved slowly inward. I tried to stop my hand from trembling as I struggled to aim. The door opened wider and then I gave a gasp as Christian was silhouetted against a bright moon that had risen outside.

For a hair-raising moment we stared at each other, and then I dropped my arm and fell forward.

"My heavens, Christian, why didn't you call out?"

I slumped into the chair, the pistol clattering to the crate beside me. Then I began shaking so hard I could not control myself.

Christian entered and shut the door. He set his rifle down by the door and glanced at Duignan, sleeping soundly in his bedroll, and Fanny, whose light hair drifted over the blanket on my father's bed. She murmured, opened her eyes, and then turned over. Christian crossed to me.

"I didn't want to wake you. I used a stick to raise the latch from the outside. I'm sorry if I startled you. When did they get here?" he asked, motioning to Duignan who had opened one eye. Seeing it was his boss, the cook went back to sleep.

"Today," I replied, still trying to calm my nerves.

Christian reached for my shoulders and pulled me up to stand next to him. His arms around me did

224

something to stop my trembling, but I still felt uneasy.

"Where've you been?" I asked. "What's happened? Has there been an accident?"

He shook his head. "Nothing like that, but it took longer to butcher the bear than we thought. Then it was too dark to travel. We had to wait for the moon to rise to light our way. You're trembling."

"Well of course I'm trembling," I said.

I was angry now, angry that he had frightened me. "Don't you realize I almost killed you?"

He gave a chuckle deep in his throat. "If you had been able to hit me." He said it with mirth, which made me angrier that he could joke about it.

"We've been frightened out of our wits all night," I said. And I told him about the animal that had evidently been scrabbling around outside the cabin.

"Hmm," he murmured. I will check for tracks in the morning. "I should not have gone to help Gaspar. I was afraid something would come to bother you."

I was stiff though he tried to hold me in his arms. "It did more than bother us," I said.

He glanced at the other two soundly sleeping forms.

"At least everyone else found sleep, but not you, my little one?" he said in that maddeningly caressing voice.

"No, not me. I was too worried about being eaten alive. But where is Father?"

"He comes along. I hurried down the trail as soon as the moon lit my way."

I turned toward the fire and lifted another log onto it.

"There was something else," I said in a low voice as we stood warming our hands over the bright, crackling flames. "I actually saw something pass the window before all the scrabbling noise started."

225

"You saw it?"

"I'm not sure what I saw. It looked like a man. But it didn't sound like a man."

Recalling the events of the evening I realized how terrorized I had been. I hated to rely so on Christian, but I could feel myself relax now that he was here to protect us. Of course he had a rifle with which to do so, and we had been left in the cabin with nothing but a pistol good for short range and a few knives.

His expression looked serious in the light the fire cast on his face. He seemed to ponder my words grimly.

"A man, you say?" he finally said.

I hugged myself. "I can't be sure."

Neither of us spoke of the Indian curse, and I did not want to start accusing spirits of terrorizing us. But there was another possibility.

"Could any of the Indians have come back here?" I asked. "Perhaps they were prowling about. If they don't want strangers here, they might try to frighten us away."

"That is possible. But the Indians knew Gaspar. They would not bother his cabin," Gaspar said.

Deciding that further sleep would be impossible, I fetched the coffeepot and filled it with water from the bucket we had inside, adding coffee grounds. Then I set it on the fire to boil. I thought of showing Christian the pad on which Fanny and I had worked on the code, but decided I would wait until Father returned to show what we had done.

As dawn began to lighten the sky, Christian went to see to his horse. The other horses had wandered up the slope, but he was easily able to catch them. The mule was down by the stream.

After pouring myself a mug of coffee, I sat down

with the pad and stared at the code. I finally recalled two more words that fit, and that must have been on the paper I had seen at Drusilla's.

I wondered idly if Drusilla knew about the code that had been hidden in her picture. My mind was only semialert, but in the early morning dawn I began to make some connections that I had not done before.

Drusilla had not said when she had married Franz, but perhaps he knew of my father and Drusilla's courtship. Perhaps Franz's odd looks at the hotel really did bear us ill will. Had Franz and Drusilla known about the map? Perhaps Drusilla had been jilted by my father and wished revenge. No wonder she had not welcomed us to her establishment, but had been won over only after I had made the effort.

They would not know what the code meant. But perhaps they planned to follow us here and find a way to get the map.

Christian came back in, and I tucked my wandering thoughts into the back of my mind. I decided I was glad Fanny had not stayed at the hotel alone any longer than she had.

It was not long before Father appeared, his mule loaded down with huge cuts of meat, and he, Duignan, and Christian set about building fires outside to smoke it. They would make every effort to use as much of the bear as possible, smoking and drying meat for winter, as we could not possibly eat it all at once.

I cooked hot cereal for breakfast, and we went through several more pots of coffee before the morning's work was done. Toward the middle of the day I lay down on the bed fully dressed, and dozed. My sleep was filled with the words from the code combined with images from the hotel and the diagram of the map.

And when I awoke I believed I had the answer.

Chapter 16

It was midafternoon, and no one was about the cabin. I shook the cobwebs from my brain and got up. Locating the pad on which I had been working out the code, I sat down to write what I had come up with in my semisleep state.

Yes, that was it. The words I had not been able to remember before were "in big," and "where," and by adding them the sentence read "walk in big mouth between two humps where daylight never goes." Perhaps it would mean something to Father.

Between two humps might refer to rock formations or hills. Where daylight never goes would mean where it is dark, as in a cave. Maybe he knew of a cave between two humps.

As if sensing I had something to show him, he came in.

"Ah, there you are, my dear. Did you have a good rest?"

"I think my rest was profitable, Father," I said with a grin. "Look at this."

I held up the writing to him and he furrowed his brows over it. Then he tilted his head and tried the words on his tongue. But when the light shone in his eyes and he gave out a whoop and a holler I knew I had guessed right.

"That's it, that's it!" he said, and he grabbed me and danced me around the cabin.

We were both laughing so hard we failed to hear the door open and Fanny and Christian come in. They looked at us as if we had lost our minds.

"What causes this celebration?" Christian finally asked, reaching for a flask on the shelf and tilting it back for a drink.

Gaspar let go of me, and I panted for breath.

"Why my smart Hilary has deciphered the code that goes with the map. I do believe she's just pointed us to the gold. If that ain't cause for celebration, I don't know what is."

Retrieving the flask from Christian, Gaspar took a swig.

"Where is it?" asked Fanny. "What have you made it say?"

I showed her the paper, which she frowned over for a moment. "Well, it makes sense anyway," she said. "Which is more than it did before. I suppose Father knows where this cave between two humps is?"

"You're darned right I know where it is."

He got out the map and unfolded it on the table so we could all see.

"See here, this stream leads to the mirror lake. On the other side of the mirror lake is a series of caves. I've explored them a bit, not knowing I was nearly on top of the gold. By gum, I should have smelled it."

"Then two humps means two rocks or two small hills," I speculated.

Gaspar's eyes glinted at me. "Exactly. There's two

little shoulders that rise above one cave in particular. That must be it."

We all straightened and looked at each other.

"Well," said Gaspar, rubbing his hands. "It looks like an expedition is called for."

"But not this season, I'm afraid."

We turned to see Christian gazing out the window. Large snowflakes were drifting silently past outside.

I remembered the light snow that had drifted down while I had been at the hotel. That snow had not stuck, but these flakes were bigger and looked heavier. We all stepped outside to look.

The sky to the northeast was a heavy mass of thick, dark clouds. I could see that this snow was going to be more than the trifling dusting we had had earlier. Christian had walked out farther and was looking at the ominous sky as well.

"We'll have to leave tomorrow," he said.

"Now I'm not leavin' until I've had a look at those caves," my father said as he stepped over to join Christian. "I'll go by myself if I have to, but I've got to have a look."

"Now, Gaspar, you know that's not wise. You could be trapped up there," argued Christian.

"Nonsense, my boy. There's enough meat to last the winter now," he said.

Christian stretched his back and rested his hands on his hips.

"Enough meat to last one person through the winter. But you know that storm might bring drifts that would trap you in those caves. You wouldn't be able to get out if there's a blizzard. As for the rest of us, we'll have to start for the hotel in the morning and hope the drifts don't block us before we have a chance to get all the way down."

Gaspar grumbled, but from the set of Christian's chin I could see that the two men were fixed in their disagreement. Finally a compromise was reached.

"I'll go with you as far as the hotel," Gaspar said, "but no farther. Then if the storm lets up, I can make one more trip up here and see the caves."

With the plan established, we all began to pack for the trip down. We cooked and salted meat and wrapped it in cheesecloth. Father left a store of meat in a dry place in the cabin where it would remain cool until his return. Duignan went to look for edible plants and brought back a basketful of highbush cranberry, elderberry, reindeer moss, and a large collection of piñon nuts.

We packed our things, and Christian continued to try to persuade Gaspar to come all the way out of the valley with us, but he remained adamant.

"Father," I begged, "are we to be deprived of your company again so soon after so many years of not having a father? If the snow comes and anything happens, well . . ." I found myself choking with emotion.

He took me in his arms in a bear hug.

"Ah, now, Daughter, I would not trade you and Fanny for all the gold in the mountains, but there is no danger. You yourself talk of a fine house so you can wait on your old father hand and foot. But it takes money to build such an establishment. I reckon I'm lookin' for that gold for the likes of you two girls. How else am I to outfit you in fine clothes so you can catch rich husbands?"

He winked, but I still had difficulty with the lump in my throat.

"We can wait on you hand and foot in a modest house, and what need have we for fine dresses when we'd rather bring you back to town with us?"

He waggled a finger at me. "Now don't be soundin' like you have to make such a choice. You can have me and the gold both. But I have to find it first."

"Why?" I persisted with my pleading. "You can't bring it out of the mountains now."

"No, but if I find the vein, I can file a claim and make preparations for a real mining operation come spring. Then we can while away the winter making our plans."

"Oh, Father," I said, shaking my head. But it did no good. He would come to the hotel, but that was all.

That night we settled ourselves around the cabin, Fanny and I in the two small beds and the men on blankets on the floor. Though I was as comfortable as could be, I had a difficult time falling asleep. I felt as if something was wrong, though I could not name it.

The circumstances that had followed us here menaced my sleep. The Indian curse, the odd personalities of Franz and Drusilla, the rumor that staying in Yosemite to look for gold drove a person mad, and the natural threats from bears and howling beasts all combined to make me toss and turn.

In the morning I had the feeling I had done little more than doze all night. I forced my stiff limbs to rise and helped in the breakfast preparations. We ate hastily and gulped down Duignan's strong coffee, then with everything packed, we climbed on our mounts and fell in line.

Christian paused before leading off. He scrutinized the cabin, the cliff, and the mountains beyond with a strange look on his face, which I could not read. I almost asked him what he was looking for, but I felt, as his distant gaze passed over me without seeing me, too intimidated to intrude on his thoughts.

And perhaps I feared knowing what he was thinking. If he sensed danger, I did not necessarily want to know about it that morning, though I knew that was the fool's way of burying his head in the ground. For once I wanted someone else to guard against danger and let me concentrate on guiding Gabrielle along the trail, which was challenging enough.

The way down was made even more difficult because snow had drifted across the trail in the night. While the sun was bright, it glanced off the snow, threatening to blind us until we came within the shadow of the mountain. When the trail twisted steeply, I thought surely I would slide right over my horse's head and tumble beneath her feet.

Needless to say, there was little conversation until we came to the narrow canyon where sheer granite walls seemed to enclose us. Even then I avoided looking up, for fear that even my glance would start a rock slide or a small avalanche, for drifts rested precariously on overhanging cliffs at every turn.

We paused briefly for a cold lunch, but soon pressed on. Even so, darkness blanketed the canyons where we traveled before we reached the hotel. With the snow dusting on the trees' branches and pillows of snow in rocky crevices we passed, the terrain looked so unfamiliar I was certain I would never have found my way back had I been on my own.

I would have missed seeing the outline of the hotel set against the hill, except that as we approached, a solitary light in an upper window told us that someone must still be there.

"At last," I breathed in relief to myself as we traveled the remaining distance between ourselves and the barn below the hotel.

We dismounted, and the men took charge of the horses. Fanny and I pulled our saddlebags off our mounts and tumbled toward the stairs. We climbed wearily upward, hanging on to the shaky railing for support. Then we pushed the door inward to the darkened foyer.

"Hello," I called out. "It's Hilary Fenton. Is anyone here?"

We set our parcels down and I fumbled for matches in an attempt to light the lantern I found sitting on the small side table.

Then a glow began to emanate from the dining room, and a few moments more brought Drusilla carrying a candle in its holder. She wore a dressing gown and her hair fell straight about her crooked shoulders. In the weird candlelight, her face looked even more grotesque than in normal light, and I thought for a moment that she did not recognize us.

"Drusilla, it's Hilary Fenton. We've returned. Father is with us."

The sound of boots on the steps outside announced the men's arrival, and the door opened, sending in a cold wind.

Gaspar stepped into the light.

" 'Tis the truth. My own daughters tracked me down in the wilds and forced me to civilization. Are ye glad to see this weary old face, my darlin' Drusilla?"

And he grasped her free hand, lifting it to his lips. Her glass eye seemed to glare right through him.

"Never thought I'd see the front of you again," she said, retrieving her hand.

She held the light higher, and it fell on Christian's face.

"And so you've brought back this golden-haired devil as well. And what about the other one, that smooth-talking easterner?"

"If you mean Thomas Neville," answered Christian,

"I'm afraid to say we've seen the last of him. He met with an unfortunate accident."

"Ahhh . . ." her voice spun away like the echoing wind. She shook her head.

"And I suppose the rest of ye wants beds."

"We would be grateful," I said.

"Well, ye know the way. It's fearful cold up there now with no warming pans. Ye'd be better off spreadin' yer beddin' around the fire in there." She tipped her head toward the parlor. "I leave it to ye. Where's yer Chinaman?" she asked Christian.

"Most likely in the kitchen making a fire in your stove," he said. "He'll have gone up the backstairs after bedding down the horses."

"Hmmph." And thus ended our greeting.

She turned back toward the dining room, passing that way to her bedroom behind the kitchen. No doubt she would meet Duignan on the way.

We took her advice and climbed the stairs to take the bedding off the beds to combine with the blankets we had brought. Christian built a fire in the parlor, and soon we had beds spread around the floor and a fire toasting our faces and hands. It was too late for Drusilla to think of rustling up any supper, for she did not try to hide the notion that we had showed up at an inconvenient time, but I went to the kitchen to see if there was anything we could eat.

I found some bread, which I sliced, and there was a pitcher of milk chilling on the porch. I hesitated to use it for fear she might have planned to have it for breakfast. But a growling stomach often wins out over the best attempt to be a polite guest. The bread, which we tore off in chunks, and milk made a tasty supper, and we did not have to go to bed with our stomachs empty.

* * *

I had just drifted to sleep when I began to hear the eerie chanting that I had heard before. It drifted to us on the wind, broken by the gusts that slapped the eaves. I sat up, staring. I glanced across Gaspar's sleeping form to see Christian on one elbow, listening. His eyes met mine in the firelight, and I knew he heard it, too.

I pushed the blanket aside and stood, walking to the window. More snow drifted past, and my breath fogged the windowpane. Christian came noiselessly to stand beside me.

"What is it?" I whispered.

He listened for a moment as the chanting came again, sounding more like a wail in the night.

"I don't know," he finally said in a low whisper.

I unconsciously moved toward him and he slipped a hand around my waist. He pulled me in front of him so that I leaned against him, and his other arm went around my waist. He dropped a kiss on my ear, and I twisted my head aside.

"What's wrong, my little one?" he whispered into my ear.

"Not now, Christian," I said, "not when . . . ," but I could not explain.

Would he understand my feelings, too confused by the unsettled questions, the danger, and our strange circumstances to allow me to make rational judgments about my affections?

Perhaps because we were not alone, he did not do anything more than hold me gently against him as we listened to the wind and the weird music that came in snatches. The sound worked on my mind until I thought I would go mad. Finally I tore myself from

Christian's embrace and paced toward the other window, peering out at the white night.

"Why won't it go away?"

He followed me and rested a hand on the window frame.

"I don't know. But we cannot go see in the middle of the night."

I turned and faced him, the light from the moon reflecting off the snow into the window, giving a bluish tint to our faces.

"Tomorrow then," I said. "Tomorrow we must try to see what it is."

I recalled the last time Fanny and I had gone exploring, trying to trace the sound to its source, but we had not had a rifle and Christian had. My nerves were so on edge that I preferred to face a bear rather than remain tormented by the high whining.

Christian brushed my cheek with his finger. "All right. I will go into the mountains tomorrow. Now go back to bed."

Satisfied that we would do something about it in the morning, I retired to my blankets, but this time, even though I had a rug and blanket underneath me, and a pillow for my head, I could not find a comfortable position until dawn.

The morning brought worse problems. Gaspar was ill. I awoke from a doze to his moaning, and when I sat up to ask what was wrong, I saw the sweat beaded on his forehead.

"Father, what is it?"

"The cave, the cave," he mumbled to himself. "Got to get to the cave."

"Father, wake up," I said, shaking his arm.

But when he looked at me, his glazed eyes did not see me.

237

"He's ill," I said to the others with a sinking of my heart. "What could be wrong?"

I had to keep myself from breaking down altogether. From the pallor of my father's face and his feverish mutterings, I knew he was seriously ill. There was no doctor, and I doubted if anyone here could properly diagnose or treat him. It was the last straw, and it made me want to scream curses at the top of my lungs. We should have been out of the valley before the snow came, and now we had a sick man who would not be able to travel. Had the curse of the Ahwahneeches caught up with us for good?

Christian unbuttoned Gaspar's shirt and looked him over.

"I'll have Duignan look at him," said Christian. "His remedies have cured more than one sick man in a gold camp. Let's bring down one of the beds. We'll need water to bathe his face."

Fanny looked at him with horrified eyes. She wrung her hands in such a way that I feared for her sanity as well. Giving her something to do would be the best thing for her, so I asked her to come with me and pump fresh water into a bowl and take it in. I went along in search of Drusilla to ask for towels.

She was poking wood into the stove in the kitchen and talking to Duignan.

"I'm afraid Father's ill," I said, bursting in on them.

Duignan got down from the stool on which he was hunched.

"Mr. Fenton sick?" he said, shuffling toward me. He shook his head. "No good, no good. Duignan come look."

He shuffled past me while I stayed to ask Drusilla's advice. "I don't know what to do," I told her. "He's feverish and seems a bit out of his mind."

238

Her good eye seemed to darken. "It's the curse then finally got him. I warned him. He shouldn't be in the valley this time of year."

And she, too, brushed past me to go examine Gaspar. I was too rattled at the time to ponder her words. We all knew we should not be in the valley this time of year because of the snows, and yet Drusilla and Franz had remained here. Why? Surely not just because they expected us to return. And did the curse function only in the fall and early winter? My father had been here in all seasons, and yet Drusilla made it sound as if the curse was particularly dangerous now.

I handed Fanny a bowl, and she went to the pump.

"Bring the water in, Fanny," I said, then I took towels from a cupboard where I remembered Drusilla kept them.

I rushed back to find that Christian had carried down one of the beds, and we got Father into it. Then Duignan pulled back my father's eyelids to look at his eyes. Drusilla stood on the other side of the bed muttering to herself unintelligibly, but I did hear her say, "hyssop," and "cayenne," which names I recognized as herbs and presumed she was thinking of remedies she could make for him.

Sure enough, she raised her eyes to me and said, "He ought to take some hyssop for the fever, and I can give him a chicken broth with cayenne to make him sweat, but if you ask me it's a shaman you need not a doctor."

And with those comforting words she hurried off to the kitchen and left us surrounding Gaspar.

I looked at Duignan hopefully. Not that I could trust his medical knowledge any more than Drusilla's, but he seemed a resourceful man when it came to food

239

and sustenance, perhaps he knew home remedies that we could come up with here as well.

"What do you think, Duignan?" I asked. "Have you ever seen anyone like this?"

He tipped his head from side to side. "Not good, not good. Act like malaria, but no mosquitos here. Feed hot soup, make poultice, and wait."

He shrugged his shoulders and followed Drusilla to the kitchen.

I felt helpless, and the drawn look on Christian's face did nothing to reassure me. Then Fanny started to whimper.

"We'll all go crazy," she whined. "It's this cursed valley. We've got to get out of here."

Her eyes were wide and she looked wildly about. "Got to get out of here. Neville would have taken me away. Now he's gone. What'll I do?" And she rushed to the stairs and up.

Christian and I exchanged glances and I rushed after her.

"Fanny, where are you going?"

I found her in the sleeping quarters running from chamber to chamber and pressing her palms and her face to the glass windows.

"We have to leave. The curse will get us all."

"Fanny!" I spoke sharply and turned her around by the shoulders. "Fanny, get a hold of yourself. Father has caught a fever, that's all. He can't possibly travel. We'll just have to stay here for the moment."

Her eyes darted from side to side, and I felt her shoulders shake in my hands.

"We'll die here. That's what'll happen. We should have listened to the warnings. He dies who goes to Widow's Mountain. We came here. We came here, and we'll die."

Hearing the very words from the warning note come out of her mouth frightened me so that I let go of her suddenly, but I didn't like the wild light that came into her eyes, and she began to rave almost as nonsensically as Father was doing downstairs. Unable to stand it, I raised my hand and slapped her cheek.

"Fanny, stop it!"

She looked startled as if wondering why I had hit her. She raised her hand to her cheek and touched it, but her eyes cleared.

"Why did you slap me?" she asked in a more normal voice.

I exhaled a breath, feeling at my wits' end. "Because you were getting hysterical."

I drew another large breath and spoke slowly but firmly. "Fanny, we are not in the best of circumstances, and for whatever part of it is my fault I apologize. But we must all pull together and think what to do. Running about raving will not help. You *must* control yourself. Do you understand me, you must!"

I seemed to get through to her, for she gave a small frown, rubbed her cheek and nodded, but she looked better.

"That's better. Now, we will take turns sitting by Father and bathing his forehead. Drusilla is preparing some broth for him. More than that we cannot do except pray. As soon as he is better we'll see about returning to town. Now go and make yourself useful. Ask Drusilla if you can help her in the kitchen. There will be more than the normal amount of work to do with a crowd of hungry people to feed and a sick man to boot."

I stood with my hands on my hips until she got the message through her head and started slowly for the stairs.

Perhaps because Fanny was weak, I remained strong. But as I walked through the downstairs, looking at the snow coming down outside, I felt doomed. What else could go wrong that had not already? Even though I was worried about Father's state of health, I spared a thought for our own survival.

We had not planned to winter in the mountains. Would there be enough food? Would Christian abandon us to our fate? Surely he had not planned to tie himself to our party for so many months, and without his trusty rifle, how would we catch meat?

Of course Franz had proven himself an apt shot, but the thought of spending an entire winter with Franz and Drusilla gave me the shivers. Surely if we had to stay here that long we would all be shriveled and mad by spring.

And so with heavy laden steps I dragged myself to Father's bed. Christian had got him undressed down to his drawers and covered him with a sheet and blanket. His head was propped on pillows and Drusilla was spooning some broth into his mouth. His eyes still looked feverish and his forehead was hot.

When she was finished, I took a cloth and bathed his forehead and neck. Then Duignan brought a poultice of Echinacea root and wrapped it around his chest, saying it would help lower the fever. I sat beside the bed, trying to keep him comfortable. He murmured from time to time, but finally drowsed off.

I sat watching the silent snowflakes come down, and as they touched the ground I felt the great weight of the heavy snow as if it were piled on my chest.

Fanny came to relieve me, and I had to reassure myself that she was not in danger of another outburst before I would let her sit by Father. When I left them there, I heard her soft, high voice singing a song we had known as children. Perhaps that would have a soothing effect on Gaspar, and would bring back pleasant memories.

Chapter 17

Christian went out during the day to investigate the trail and see how much snow blocked our way. He also planned to keep his eye out for meat, for he must have been as aware as I was of the difficulty of feeding such a large number of people if we remained at the hotel for very long. The bear meat would do for a while, but we all longed for a change of diet.

When he returned he was noncommittal about the trail, saying it was hard to tell how the pass would be until we got there.

Fanny and I took turns sitting with Father, and Drusilla continued to get various broths and teas down him. I found myself listening to his ravings when he awoke from a slumber and talked in his sleep, but what he said made little sense, and I finally decided it was better not to listen to him at all. Instead I tried to knit. I thought ironically that I ought to knit faster, for if we were trapped here, we would all need more warm clothing.

Christian and Duignan played a game of backgammon after supper, and we had little conversation. Night was a welcome relief because I laid down in a bed that had been warmed with hot bricks, and closed my eyes thinking that perhaps in the morning everything would somehow be better.

I stretched my stiff muscles the next morning. When I tossed back the sheet partition between my room and Fanny's, I saw that her blanket had been thrown back, but she was not there. Thinking she must have gone downstairs to check on Father, I took my time visiting the little outhouse behind the hotel and then gathering fresh snow in a bowl to bring inside to melt and use to wash with.

I saw Drusilla bringing a tray into the kitchen with an empty bowl on it.

"How is my father this morning?" I asked her.

She gave me her dour, cross-eyed look, her face shuttered by the bonnet. "Hard to tell. Seems back in his head more'n yesterday."

With this hopeful news, I hurried into the parlor-turned-infirmary. Father had his face turned toward the window. His fever had broken, and he looked much better.

"Father, how are you?" I asked as I took a seat on the little bench beside his bed.

He moved his head slowly in my direction and tried to smile, but I could see it took an effort.

"Fair to middlin'," he answered. "What day is it?"

I thought for a moment. "Why, I'm not certain. I believe it is Thursday."

"Then we ought to have been in Mariposa by now."

I patted his hand. "We stayed here to see how you would fare."

He turned his head to the window again. "You should have gone on. Snow'll be blockin' the passes now."

"Don't you worry about that," I told him. "Chris-

245

tian has been to inspect the trail. We'll let him decide when we can travel. But first you must get well. There are plenty of provisions here for a while, and Christian will hunt. Why, we could stay here for months if we wanted to."

He turned back to me. "I'd planned to winter in my cabin, but I'll be doggoned if I'll stay under this roof once I'm on my feet. Wouldn't hear the end of Drusilla's naggin'."

His comments on Drusilla aroused my curiosity, and I wanted to know more about their earlier relationship.

"She was most attentive," I told him. "Giving you teas and broth until you got over your fever," I told him. "She seemed a very good nurse to me."

"Hmmph. Surprised she didn't poison me. What'd she feed me anyway?"

"Why chicken broth with cayenne and hyssop tea, I believe. And some good-smelling beef broth last night. I almost asked her to let me have it for supper."

I took another tack. "And why are you so anxious to leave this abode? Are there comforts to be had at your cabin not to be had here?"

He squirmed uncomfortably and wouldn't meet my gaze.

"I understand if you don't want to talk about it," I said. "I know you courted Drusilla a long time ago. But she's married to Franz now. Surely she doesn't hold a grudge any longer."

He gave me a perplexed look that I thought had nothing to do with his previous delirium.

"I wouldn't try to guess what was in that woman's mind if you paid me all the gold in these hills."

I pressed my lips together in smothered amusement. Apparently I was not going to learn more about his erstwhile courtship of Drusilla or why the love affair did not blossom into marriage.

Christian came in to greet Gaspar and roused him with cheerful manly talk. I left them and went to help Drusilla get breakfast. Later, Christian stuck his head in the kitchen to say he saw fresh tracks outside and wasn't going to lose any time following them for possible game. It was only after he had gone that I realized Fanny was missing.

I went to call her to breakfast, but she was nowhere to be found.

"Have you seen my sister this morning?" I asked Drusilla.

She shook her head. "Ain't been keepin' count of the guests."

Where could she be? I ran upstairs and flung on my coat and boots. Then going out the front, I scanned the trail and the far meadow.

"Fanny," I called. My voice echoed down the canyon.

I turned the other way and looked for signs that someone had gone up the trail toward Gaspar's cabin. "Fanny," I called again.

Where was Christian? Perhaps he might come upon her as he hunted for game. I stood on the porch for a long time, straining my eyes along all the possible pathways I could see from where I was. The door creaked open behind me.

"Ye'll catch yer death of cold out there," Drusilla said. "Best put something hot in yer stomach."

I went back in and followed Drusilla to the dining room where she served me some hot cereal. But I ate quickly, feeling the anxiety mount. I had yet to check the barn or the outhouse, but surely she would not stay in either place this long.

247

I saw to my father's comfort and helped Drusilla wash up after breakfast. Then I checked the outdoor locations around the hotel. Still no Fanny. Unwilling to wait until Christian returned and I could send him to look for Fanny, I decided I must go look myself. Fanny's emotional state had been so unstable, I feared the worst. If I didn't find her, something dire might result.

Upstairs I confirmed that her jacket and boots were missing, but I could see nothing else that she had taken with her. Had she simply decided to take a walk in the snow without telling anyone?

Donning another thick pair of stockings, split skirt for riding, boots, hooded jacket, and gloves, I prepared to go out, leaving word with Drusilla that when Christian returned to tell him I had gone to look for Fanny. I took care to take with me a skein of yarn from my knitting with which to mark my trail. I remembered getting lost when Fanny and I had been chased by the bear, and with the snow to hide landmarks it would be even easier to get lost. I did not plan to let that happen this time.

While my impulse was to run down the trail on foot, I knew that I would be better off on horseback, for if I found her, Gabrielle could carry us both.

I went to the barn, but Franz was nowhere to be found, so I went to the tack room and found Gabrielle's bridle. Back in the stall, I slipped the bridle over her head, guiding the bit into her mouth. Just as Christian had taught me, I slipped my thumb into the side of her mouth and pressed on her lower jaw so that she opened up to allow the bit to be put in place.

"Good girl," I said, patting her on the neck. Then I drew the top of the bridle over her ears and fastened the throat latch.

I returned to the tack room and lifted the saddle from the stand where it rested. Taking the saddle blanket with me, I heaved everything toward the stall again.

The saddle blanket was easy, then I flipped the right stirrup and cinches over the seat of the saddle and swung the saddle up onto Gabrielle's back. I shifted it around until it seemed to sit right. Then I did up the cinches, careful to see that she had not blown herself up with air, which would cause the cinch to loosen later as it had on my near disastrous fall.

"All right, old girl," I said when she was ready. "We've got an important mission. We must find Fanny. The poor girl has run away."

Then leading her to a crate, which I used for a mounting block, I climbed into the saddle. Gabrielle trotted out into the snow as if glad for the exercise. Duignan was chopping wood with Franz now.

Christian had still not returned. I would try not to go far, but I did not worry. Christian would be able to follow my tracks and assist me with the search when he got back.

I pulled the hood of my jacket over my head, as much to help block the bright sun as for warmth, for the sun had come out and was sending its blinding rays into our little valley.

"Fanny," I continued to call, stopping at the edge of the silent woods and turning to send my call in all four directions.

I was not unaware of the dangers, and shivered when I recalled the black bear that had come bounding after us before. But my anxiety for my sister outweighed concerns of safety for myself, and besides, this time I was mounted. I skirted the woods, stopping to look for signs that anyone had passed this way, but so far the blanket of snow lay unbroken.

Try to think, I told myself. Where would Fanny go if she came outside? My immediate reaction was that she had fled down the trail with some compelling notion to return to Mariposa. Since none of us had agreed to take her back until Father had recovered, she might have simply decided to take matters into her own hands, obsessed with getting out of the valley before winter progressed any further.

Tying yarn on branches every hundred yards, I skirted the woods and picked up the main trail where it led in the direction of the high canyon and the waterfall. On the other side of the meadow, the trail was clearer owing to the protection of canyon wall, and I could actually see fresh footprints in the mud. So she had gone this way.

I hurried Gabrielle along, following the footprints, hope rearing its head as I told myself she could not have gone far on foot. Surely I would catch up with her on horseback. I pushed Gabrielle along the trail as it turned and twisted. Each time I stopped I was careful to break off some yarn with my teeth and tie it around a branch or boulder to mark the way.

I finally dismounted and went off the trail a little way to investigate a clump of trees where I thought I heard the sound of water running. It looked like the footprints led that way, and I guessed Fanny had gone to get a drink of water.

I tied Gabrielle to a branch and proceeded where I thought the footprints led, walking carefully, aware that the snow might disguise a hole that could turn my ankle. I made my way down to the covert and had just bent over the tracks to examine them when something sharp assailed the back of my head.

Dizziness overcame me and my hands flailed out in front of me, trying to find support. But to no avail, for as my mind sank into darkness, my body slumped into the snow.

Hours later my consciousness stirred, but when I fluttered open my eyes I was surrounded by a mantle of white. My body seemed to be still asleep, and I was tempted to shut my eyes and float back into my cocoon. But the voice of survival said I didn't want to die, and so I struggled to sit up.

But when I sat up and still found myself covered in white, sudden terror impelled me to fight my way upward. Fortunately the snow had not buried me too deeply, and by clawing upward I made a hole through which I saw a gray, leaden sky.

A branch hit my face, and I turned to see that I had fallen near a low tree, which had kept the snow from suffocating me. Branches and trunk had formed a pocket of air behind my head, which in my panic I had not seen at first. But getting on top of the snow was another matter. It would not hold my weight, and I spent a long time struggling to get nearer the trees where the snow had not fallen so heavily, and I finally found solid ground.

By the time I crawled out on a little rise among a covering of junipers I was out of breath and simply lay on the ground, the back of my head throbbing more violently with the exertion. I reached my hand around to feel the welt, and drew my hand quickly away as the place where I had been hit was quite tender.

I pulled myself against a tree trunk and looked out over the rest of the valley. Snow lay everywhere, and if the heavy sky was any indication, there would be more snow soon. I sat there in a stupor, aware that I was growing colder, sitting there, no longer insulated by the snow, but I was too dazed to do anything about my situation. Gabrielle was no longer where I thought I had left her.

Thoughts seemed disconnected as I tried to remember what happened. Fanny was still missing. But now so was I. I had a moment of hysteria as I thought that one by one we were all beginning to disappear. And I had not seen Christian since before breakfast. Where was he?

Where was Gabrielle? Perhaps she had gotten loose and returned to the hotel. At least a riderless horse returning to the barn would alert anyone who looked that a mishap had occurred.

But who had hit me? As my slow-working brain pondered this, I stared harder at the ground around me. I should look for footprints. But the horrible truth penetrated the haze that surrounded me. The falling snow had wiped away all traces of footprints—Fanny's, mine, Gabrielle's, and my assailant's.

My assailant—surely human and not animal, for I was not torn limb from limb. An animal would attack only if it were hungry. Someone had deliberately knocked me out and left me in the snow to die! The enormity of it made me shiver even harder. But I forced myself to stand up. I must get back to the hotel.

Walking on unsteady feet, I kept to high ground, trying to discern where the trail lay. Now, with so much more snow, everything looked different. Not only was the landscape transformed, but every identifying mark was gone, and the snow must have covered the yarn I had tied around the branches to mark my way. I could not even see the sun through the iron gray clouds to verify my direction.

I heard a whinny, and then to my surprise, I saw Gabrielle some distance off. She had seen me and was making her way toward me.

"Gabrielle, come here, girl," I said.

Ears forward and nostrils flaring as she snorted and pawed her way through the snow, she came up to me. I reached up to pat her gratefully.

I thought of mounting, but to keep from freezing I knew I needed to keep active, so I took the reins and led the mare.

I remembered the granite walls I had traveled beside and started back in the direction that seemed to be the way I had come. Twenty inches or so of snow covered the trail, but I pressed on. Night was fast approaching, and I despaired of reaching the hotel, for I must have come farther than I had thought. I tried to call out, but my voice sounded weak and frail and I preserved my strength for pushing through the snow.

As I had predicted, the flakes began to fall again, settling on my eyelashes and blinding me. I completely lost my sense of direction, trying uphill and down. I stumbled and slid, catching myself until my gloves ripped on the sharp branches. Once I thought I heard someone, and thinking it might be Christian come to look for me, I called his name.

Stumbling around a rock, we came face to face with a large gray wildcat with mottled fur, its eyes narrowed to slits. Gabrielle let out a high whinny, reared, tore the reins from my hands and bolted. Stupidly, I turned and began to run, stumbling in the snow, screaming. But when I came to a stop, I saw the branches waving where the big cat had run back into the trees, equally frightened of us.

I got to my feet again, tasting blood on my face from a scratch and tried to ignore my bruised ribs. But I slipped again and slid down a slope. It was night now, and I was certain that my end had come. I hadn't the strength even to look for shelter.

I must have lost consciousness, for the next thing I remembered was someone calling my name from a great distance. I looked up at a starry sky and tried to move.

"Hilary, for God's sake."

Even in my semiconscious state I heard the fright in Christian's voice.

"Mother-in-heaven, let her be alive," he muttered.

I moaned, and he slid his arms around me, gently.

"Hilary," he coaxed softly. "Thank God, I've found you."

I sank against him as snow bit into my cheek. Then his hands quickly examined me. When he touched the welt on my head, I yelped.

"Did you fall?" he asked.

"Someone . . . ," I swallowed and gulped for breath. "Someone hit me."

What he muttered then doesn't bear repeating, but the anger and other strong emotions coursing through him conveyed themselves to me.

"Can you sit up?" he asked me. "I don't think you've broken anything."

I nodded. "Just bruised," I said weakly.

He touched my face. "You've scratched your face, but it's not deep."

"We saw a wildcat, big and gray. Gabrielle ran off."

"I know," he said. "I saw her an hour ago and caught her. The trail was blocked from an avalanche. I thought you were buried under it, but after using long poles to search, I gave up. But I finally found you."

I sighed, letting his strong arms lift me.

"If you can ride, we can get back faster. Do you think you can sit in the saddle? I'll sit behind you. My body warmth will help keep you warm."

"I can ride," I managed to say.

I saw then that Gabrielle was standing by, and I touched her nose briefly.

"Thanks for trying, old girl," I said.

I thought Christian looked relieved that I could talk. I had no idea how long I had been exposed to the cold or how long Christian had been looking for me, but already I could feel the blood flowing again in my veins. At least I would not die from frostbite.

He got me into the saddle on his palomino, and I hung on to the saddle horn as he climbed on behind me, his arms around me and the reins in his hands, leading Gabrielle behind.

I leaned against him, each step of the horse jolting through me. I still felt dizzy and cold, but Christian's soft clucking to the horses, urging them around snowdrifts, and his jaw against my temple went some distance to comfort me.

Around us the night was silent, and a half moon came out from behind fleeting clouds. The snowstorm was over and had left a sharp crispness and snowy beauty that belied its deadliness.

An hour or more passed before we saw the glimmering lights of the hotel, and Christian reined in at the foot of the stairs. He dismounted. Then reaching up to grasp my waist, he pulled me off into his arms and carried me around the horses.

"I can walk," I mumbled into his heavy sheepskin coat, but he only grunted as he took the stairs.

He kicked the door open with his foot and carried me into the parlor where a fire was licking logs in the fireplace. He placed me in a rocker near the fire and

255

then proceeded to pull off my wraps. I clumsily pulled off my gloves and spread my hands gratefully out to the fire as Christian struggled to unlace my boots. When my fingers thawed sufficiently, I bent to help him.

"You need this?" Drusilla appeared next to us out of nowhere holding out a long, brass shoe hook.

"Thank you," I muttered, taking the hook and applying it to my laces. When they were loose enough, Christian pulled off my boots so I could wiggle my toes in front of the fire.

"So you found her," said Drusilla.

"Thank heaven I did," said Christian.

"Well, you were gone long enough. I decided all of ye were doomed. In the meantime yer sister's turned up. Found her way back to the barn and been sleepin' in the hay. She's up with yer father now. He carried his bed back upstairs and asked for some bricks to warm it. I swear I'm beginnin' to think I run a looney bin, not a hotel."

And with that she turned and shuffled off toward the kitchen. "I've got some broth on the stove," she said over her shoulder. "I'll bring it to ye."

Christian paid her no mind. He was busy examining me more thoroughly, now that I was out of my heavy outerclothing.

"Can you move your arm like this?" he asked and had me test every joint and muscle of every limb.

Then he felt my ribs, making certain that none were broken. Only bruised. He examined the lump on the back of my head. It was still tender, but the snow had made the swelling go down some.

He cursed under his breath. "Who did this?" he asked.

"I don't know," I said. "I didn't hear anyone, and

then suddenly I felt the blow and everything went black."

"My poor Hilary," he said when he had finished, and he buried his face in my bosom, his arms gently around my waist.

I rested my face against his hair, brushing snow crystals out of it with my hands.

He turned his face upward and kissed my chin, then my lips. Then he pulled me toward him for a more ardent embrace, but the sound of Drusilla's shuffle returning, broke us apart, and I leaned back in the rocker again.

Drusilla set down a tray and handed me a mug of hot soup. The taste and smell of it helped revive me further, and I drank it down quickly, the heat warming my insides while Christian put more logs on the fire.

Fanny came downstairs, looking nervous and concerned.

"Hilary, are you all right? We were so worried about you."

She drew up a chair by my side. I leaned back in the rocker.

"I went looking for you. Where did you go?"

She looked guilty and wrung her hands. "Just for a walk. I couldn't stand being cooped up in here any longer. I wanted to get out."

The fire and the broth were making me drowsy, and I longed to lie down and sleep.

"Then you didn't try to go out of the valley by yourself?"

She shook her head. "It's too far to do that."

Christian knelt before me again. "You need to get some sleep."

He made a move to lift me into his arms, but I insisted I could walk upstairs. He helped me up and I leaned on his arm, feeling drowsy. Upstairs I looked in on my father, but he was sleeping. His color looked better, and I felt relieved. For all the dangers we had encountered, at least we were all back under the same roof again.

Christian took me to my chambers and helped me undress. I was feeling too hazy to care if it seemed improper, and in any case there was no one to watch. Fanny had remained downstairs.

Drusilla had put a warm brick in my bed so that when I slipped between the sheets, my sore muscles found comfort. Christian pulled the blanket up under my chin and bent to kiss my forehead.

"Sleep well," he said.

I murmured drowsily and dropped off to sleep.

Chapter 18

The next morning I felt better. After I rose and washed from a bowl of water Fanny brought up to me, I put on a fresh blouse and my gored skirt.

Downstairs I found Father sitting in one of the rockers and staring out the window. It was a bright morning, and sunlight sparkled like diamonds in the snow.

"Good morning, Father. How are you feeling?"

"Ah, fine, Hilary. And I might inquire the same as to yourself."

I drew a chair up next to him. "I'm feeling better."

In truth, my muscles were very sore, but I didn't want to mention it.

His leathery face looked at me in concern. "I'd've been out there myself yesterday lookin' for ye if I'd been able. I was worried."

I was touched by his fatherly concern. "I would have been able to find my way back if it hadn't snowed," I told him. "I marked the trail. But luckily Christian found me."

"Lucky for that."

We sat in silence for a little while, looking out the

window. I suppose we were both wondering how soon we could get on the trail. It looked like the snow had stopped, and it might be best to try to get out of the valley before another blizzard struck. Unless, of course, we were going to give up and actually winter here. I knew we would have to discuss that with Christian.

"Shouldn't have come here," my father said after a long bout of silence.

"The hotel?"

"Bad luck here," he continued.

"What sort of bad luck?" I asked.

"Hmph. Drusilla's never forgiven me for the way I treated her years ago."

"What happened?"

But instead of answering he twisted around in his chair. Then he leaned closer to me and whispered, "Walls have ears."

I gave up pestering him. It seemed I would never learn the story of their unrequited love, and something about it fascinated me. There was something I did need to ask him, however.

"Father, how did Drusilla get a copy of the code to the map? It was in the picture of herself that she showed me."

He frowned. "I never gave it to her."

"You only got the map two years ago. Did you stay here after you knew the code?"

"I came this way, sure enough, on my way last spring. It's true I stopped here thinking to make my peace with Drusilla. If we was to live in the same valley I thought we might treat each other like neighbors."

"In the spring you say?"

"That's right," he nodded with certainty. "I came

by, but she and Franz didn't look none too glad to see me, though she gave me a meal."

I could imagine the dour greeting he got. To the hotelkeepers' naturally off-putting personalities would have been added Franz's jealousy of Drusilla's old lover. For some reason the idea piqued my curiosity, and I wanted to know more about what had happened then.

"Did you tell Drusilla about your map?"

He hung his head sheepishly. "Well, I did mention it."

I sat back. "Bragging, I'll bet, that you were off to find your fortune."

His guilty look told me I had hit upon the truth. What he said started me to thinking, however. If he had bragged about his map, it was not so hard to figure out who might be threatening us. Perhaps Father's notion that he had been poisoned was not as ridiculous as it sounded. Maybe Franz had slipped something lethal into the brew Father had drunk.

I imagined the scenario thus: Father had shown up here in the spring seeking some private time with his erstwhile sweetheart. But the jealous recluse, Franz, was going to have none of it. He overheard Father talk about the code and jotted down what he said. Either he or Drusilla hid it in the picture. When we arrived here, Franz could have put the threatening note in the laundry. Then perhaps he followed us to Father's cabin.

Perhaps it was he who had tried to frighten us that night in the cabin. It could easily have been his shadow I had seen pass the window. Maybe he had been following us to see if we located the gold. Then he might have planned accidents for us, getting rid of all obstacles until the gold was his alone.

A grim thought, but a plausible one. If my logic was true, then it left little doubt as to who had followed me from the hotel and knocked me senseless. My only question was why hadn't he done away with me then and there? I surmised that he thought I would die from exposure to the elements, thus making my demise look like an accident. It might have looked like I had stumbled and fallen, hitting my head on a rock as I fell. No one to blame.

Either that, or he knew that Christian and Fanny were also about and feared they might see him, so he had to get away from the scene as quickly as possible.

As I thought about it, I grew more certain that I was right.

"Father," I said, pulling my chair closer and lowering my voice. "I agree that we are in danger here. We must be very careful until we can leave. I will speak to Christian about leaving tomorrow, if you think you will be well enough to travel."

He patted my hand. "I reckon I can ride, all right. But you're jes' tryin' to get me to go down to town, when you know durn well I said I was stayin' up here all winter."

"Oh, Father." I protested. "Surely you're not still considering that under the circumstances."

"What circumstances?"

I could see that he was determined to be stubborn.

"You've been ill. You need to see a doctor in Mariposa. Someone here may mean us harm. You can't search for your damned gold until spring no matter how badly you want to."

He gave a great sigh of resignation but didn't say anything. I would not press the point further until I had a chance to speak to Christian. So I set out in search of him and found him in the barn having a discussion with Duignan. They broke off when I entered.

Duignan gave his moonfaced smile and bowed. Christian strode toward me.

"We must talk," I said, at once all business.

He gave me a lazy smile, his eyes flitting over me. "Always a pleasure, I assure you. What would you like to talk about?"

"I was hoping we might be able to leave tomorrow. It's stopped snowing, and I wondered if you could tell if the trail might be clear enough."

His expression changed to one of doubt and exasperation. "I warned you we must be out of the valley before the snows came. Surely you have noticed the ground is white outside. In fact you had the misfortune to be covered up with it, I do believe."

I grew irritated. Now was no time to tease me with his cynicism.

"I am well aware that it has snowed. But today is clear. Perhaps if we don't get any more snow we might be able to make it."

I stepped nearer, lowering my voice. "Can't you see what has happened here? There's danger in this place. We must not stay here all winter or worse will happen than what's already befallen us. You must take us out of here."

I was afraid my voice had taken on a tone of desperation, but I had gained Christian's serious attention. He glanced over my shoulder as if to make sure no one was listening to us. Then he gestured to Duignan, who bowed and took the hint to make himself scarce. We were left alone in the barn.

"I don't like the notion of staying here any more than you do," he said. He sighed as if weighing the two evils. "But the going won't be easy. And if the pass at the southeast end of the valley is blocked, we'll have no choice but to turn back."

"I realize the risks," I said. "But perhaps action is better than merely sitting here awaiting our fate."

"And what fate is that?"

"I mean risk watching Fanny go crazy in the isolation, wait until whoever means us harm to find opportunities for each of us to have an 'accident.' And wait for our own tempers to endanger us of killing each other out of boredom and frustration."

"You do not paint a very pretty picture."

"That is how I see it."

His face softened, and he put his arms around me and pulled me against him.

"For you mademoiselle, I would brave the worst winters, climb the highest passes."

I grinned up at him. "And would you take me with you?"

"Humph."

Then he lowered his face for a kiss, but I turned my cheek, allowing him to brush my ear with his lips. I was still susceptible to his charms, but something told me I would have to keep him at arm's length. Except for that one night in the cabin, he had not mentioned love or marriage. He was most likely caught in the romance of the setting that had thrown us together. And seen in the strong light of real life when we reached civilization, his feelings would surely be diverted to the pleasures most men sought in such towns.

Thinking of it I almost reversed my decision to leave the enchanted valley. Once we were on the other side of the pass that separated us from the rest of civilization, Christian's mind would turn to whiskey, cards, and brothels, of which Mariposa had its fair share. He would probably head straight for an evening at the

Bull Whacker's Rest. I myself had been witness to the fact that he was well known there.

I pulled abruptly away. Better he be the villain of the piece so that my heart would not be in danger of being disappointed when things did not turn out as in one of Fanny's novels.

"Christian, this is not the time for . . ."

"For what, my love?"

I shook my head. "Don't call me that."

"Why not?"

I somehow found the courage to look him in the eye. "Because you don't really love me."

He blinked and for a brief moment we looked at each other, then I could stand it no longer, and picking up my skirt, I fled across the hay-strewn dirt floor of the barn, knocking over Duignan's candle holder as I went.

I ran up the stairs to the hotel and paused at the top. Glancing over my shoulder before I went in, I saw Christian staring at me.

My father saw me come in and got to his feet. I crossed to him.

"I believe Christian agrees that we must leave as soon as possible. We must pack for tomorrow. I believe he will take us. Now where is Fanny? I must tell her to start packing."

I found Fanny in the kitchen, peeling potatoes. She applied the knife so vigorously to the potatoes that the peelings were piling up all around her. Indeed, so engrossed was she in her task that it took several attempts to get her attention.

"Fanny," I said for the third time, grasping the arm that held the knife and forcing her to stop for a moment.

265

"We are leaving the valley tomorrow. We must get everything ready today."

Then I turned to Drusilla. "We're all going to leave, Drusilla. Perhaps when you have time, we can settle up the bill. We'll leave in the morning, that is, I think we will. I'll just have to confirm our plans with Mr. Reyeult."

She looked up from sweeping the potato peelings. "Best to go now," she said. "Winter's just the other side of that range to the east. If you don't watch out it'll follow you down anyway. More'n one's been buried in an avalanche, but I don't need to tell you that."

"No, you don't need to tell me that. When you have time I'll be ready to go over our bill with you."

I believe my determination to set the party in motion carried everyone along with me. Christian gave me no argument, and when I saw him checking the horse's hooves and examining the tack later, I knew that he was going to go.

Drusilla and I sat at the kitchen table while she added up figures from her ledger. I expected the sum to be overpriced, but to my surprise, it was reasonable. Father insisted on helping me pay for it, but when I pointed out that it was his money drawn from the bank that I was spending in any case, it did not seem to matter. Though Christian and I had agreed on his fee for the trip, he had asked me for no money at all, and so I did not begrudge paying his bed and board.

Drusilla had made a good profit after her expenses, I expected, seeing as how many of her supplies were for the taking right outside the door, and she was going to keep some of the bear meat we had brought.

Luck was with Christian that day as he spied an elk. I was in the barn with him going over the saddles when he grabbed his gun and slipped out into the forest.

I saw the movement among the trees and then saw the great animal leap forward, its magnificent seven-pronged antlers crowning its noble head.

Christian aimed and fired, and the animal staggered. I gasped, my hands to my cheeks, for though I knew we needed to eat game, I was not used to seeing an animal fall.

Christian reloaded in case he needed to make another shot, and I followed him a little way up the hill. He waited for the animal's death struggle, and when it looked as if it was dead, he took a step nearer.

Then suddenly the animal leaped up and sprang at him. I screamed as Christian aimed his rifle. But the elk's strength was short-lived. Even as the lethal hooves struck out, the animal fell dead.

I reached a tree and leaned on it in relief as Christian went to examine the kill. It had fallen dead as it had made that last terrible leap.

Gaspar and Duignan came to help butcher the animal, and Drusilla set about preparing the meat for supper. Christian brought back the seven-pronged antlers and presented them to Drusilla to hang up in her parlor.

With all the preparations for the trip taken care of, and everything well in hand in the kitchen, I found myself with little else to do. Then as I stood on the porch looking about, I heard, faintly at first, the Indian chanting. Perhaps it had been there all along, but I had been so busy, I had not noticed it.

Now the wind was still and I heard a rhythmical, high-pitched musical sound drifting to me from far away. I walked to the edge of the porch and listened hard. The sound was faint, but it was there. Christian was just coming up from the barn and I went down the stairs to him.

"Do you hear it?" I asked when I set my feet on the ground.

"Hear what?"

"The singing. The Indian chanting."

He followed my gaze and listened intently. The sound came again, and I thought surely he could not miss it.

He nodded. "I hear something," he said.

I looked at him. We had nothing more to do until supper. I had wanted to follow the sound before, and the bear had prevented us. What was to stop us now, with Christian's rifle for protection? I seized his arm.

"I must find out where it's coming from," I said. "You promised you would help me search."

"It might be dangerous, if the savages are angry," he said.

"But I must know if it's real or not."

He looked at me quizzically.

"I mean whether the sound comes from Indians or their spirits."

He frowned. "Surely not spirits."

I was determined. Perhaps because I was leaving the valley tomorrow I wanted to resolve the old superstitions surrounding it. Christian had promised the night we had heard it. Then with everything else, we had forgotten to look for its source. But now I was reminded. At least it might make it safer for other travelers to know whether they were dealing with vengeful flesh and blood or supernatural elements.

"Bring your weapons, Christian," I said with the authority I had been assuming all day. "We must settle this matter once and for all."

He rested his weight on one leg, his hands on his hips, gazing upward to the ridges above the trees.

"Some things best be left alone," he grumbled.

I turned to face him, my own hands on my hips. "Christian Reyeult, as a frontiersman of this territory, don't you feel it your duty to explore this phenomenon and be able to report to those who want to know from what source this weird sound comes? Surely you want to know if Indians have returned here to their original home or whether they have merely left their spirits behind."

Christian looked hesitant, an anomaly when one considered that he fearlessly withstood an attack from a charging elk and had killed bear and other wild beasts, but then I perceived the truth.

Christian had no trouble facing dangers he could see and fight on a physical plane. What he did not want to deal with was supernatural phenomenon for which he had no weapon. Seeing the uncertainty in his otherwise brave countenance, I thought I knew how to deal with it.

I gave a light, tinkling laugh. "Of course no one really believes in spirits, do they? Why, what nonsense. Of course maybe the sound is some phenomenon of the wind and the mountains. Nothing to be afraid of. But we must see, Christian, don't you agree?"

When my teasing about being afraid of something ethereal did not seem entirely to persuade him, I put the final straw on the argument by telling him I was going alone if he did not wish to accompany me. I started for the trees.

Christian uttered curses and words to the effect for me to wait until he had got his rifle and our mounts.

When he reappeared, leading the horses, the rifle in its scabbard, I felt reassured. Perhaps we could put an end to the Indian legend, for though angry Indians out to protect their former homelands would be dangerous to meet, I preferred knowing the enemy to being

269

haunted by their curse. Knowing that we would probably not be able to keep Father from returning here, it would make me feel better, as well, if we could trace the mysterious chanting to its source.

Christian left word with Duignan as to our quest so the others would not worry, and we mounted up. Christian led the way, winding in and out of trees. There was no trail, so we were forced to find the easiest path upward, stopping now and again to listen for the sound that we followed.

The shadowed glen with the occasional hooting of an owl and rustling of trees made me glad I had not come alone. The newly fallen snow cushioned our horses' feet, and we passed noiselessly through the silent forest, with only the occasional sound of chanting drifting down to us.

We passed between a narrow cut in the rocks, the granite rising steeply beside us, and then wound along the side of an evergreen-covered slope, coming at last to a view of ridges and gullies. Snow lay on the north face of the dome that rose above us, and jewels seemed to sparkle on the trees in crystalline spheres. The late-afternoon sun shed its light on the iridescence for a time, but as we rode up the canyon, the sun lowered behind pink clouds, leaving only shadows in its stead.

As the canyon narrowed, barren walls on one side rose in varied coloring a thousand feet above us, while on the other side, snowy robes covered all life forms. Still, we pressed on, for the chanting was with us for longer periods now. Christian scanned the sky for smoke. He raised a hand when we reached the edge of some trees.

"We'll wait here until nightfall. We'll be spotted if we go any closer now."

We dismounted and tied the horses, making a cold

camp. We gnawed on some jerky and waited as the fingers of sunlight faded from between the trees, taking the warmth and light with it. As we waited, Christian gathered me closer to him for warmth and we spoke softly of many things—of our early lives, of his parents, his son, Ceran, about whom I had grown curious. We compared how different our experiences had been.

Night fell, and Christian deemed it safe enough to make our move. We left the horses tied where they could munch leaves and grass and climbed upward, between and around boulders, passing a small lake where cold, inky mountains stood about, and stars twinkled above us in a clear sky.

There could be no mistake about the sound of the singing now, and we followed it toward a cut in the ridge from which emanated a glow of light. My heart raced from exertion and the nervous excitement about what we might find.

Christian had to wait for me several times, for my progress was slow, and often he took my hand to pull me over a steep incline to a more solid foothold, for we were off any trail now.

As we approached a cut between the rocks, we got down on our hands and knees to creep up on it. For the singing was loud now, and the drumbeats throbbed in our ears. From the cut we would surely be able to see something. But at such close range, whoever we watched would be able to see us as well.

Our hearts beating in time to the drums, we slithered quietly upward until we reached some protective boulders over which we peered. A flickering light danced from a bonfire below, and masked dancers, their bodies painted, waved feathered spears and chanted their spell.

I watched, breathless, transfixed by a sight such as I had never seen before. The feathered and painted dancers shook their rattles over leaping flames, the chanting rising and falling in wild passion. Women surrounded the male dancers in a circle, baskets raised above their heads, which they waved from side to side.

I trembled at the sight, pulling my head further down behind the boulders so that I watched between a small opening, for I was sure that if they discovered uninvited white intruders, our scalps would soon be lifted on spears above the fire.

Being unfamiliar with the Indians' ceremonies I could not tell if they were invoking the spirits to come to their aid, declaring war, casting a spell, or simply making offerings to their gods. Perhaps Christian knew their lore, and I glanced at him. His eyes were squinted as he gazed at the sight below, neither of us moving.

I looked back at the moving, chanting, fierce-looking warriors. From the sweat glistening off their bronze skin and from the human odor that drifted this way, I knew that these were very human Indians and not spirits. If all the Indians had supposedly been removed to a reservation, then they were not supposed to be here, at least according to the white man's way of thinking. They must have slipped back in, and perhaps their ceremonials were meant to frighten people such as ourselves away, and their chanting meant to create the rumor that the valley was haunted.

Haunted by other spirits this place might be, but not by these savages who most likely only wanted to remain in their homeland.

I glanced at Christian, who nodded that he had seen enough, and as quietly as we could, we slipped back down into the shadows and glided among the trees

272

until we again came to our horses. Lucky for us the Indians did not have a lookout, for if we had been spied, we would have been taken, and if our horses had been found they would have been stolen.

Still remaining quiet, we untied our horses, mounted, and rode away. I should have felt satisfied that I had finally traced the chanting to its source, but the shadowy canyon where we rode still left me feeling uneasy, even though I kept on Christian's horse's heels all the way back through the hills until we again saw the lights glimmering from the hotel windows.

Chapter 19

When we reached the hotel, there were only a few hours until dawn. We planned to tell the others we had found where the Indians were camped, but we agreed not to mention the ceremonial dancing and masked warriors, lest it cause further anxiety. I was particularly concerned for Fanny's state of mind, and until we got back to civilization, I did not want to say anything that would cause her undue upset.

My thoughts were filled with images of the feathered warriors, and I awoke several times from a light doze, thinking the hotel was under attack. But all I heard was the creak of the other beds and an occasional snore. Finally deciding I was too much on edge to sleep, I sat up and reached for my dressing gown and slippers. I tiptoed downstairs and went to the window to look out.

To my surprise I distinctly saw someone prowling at the edge of the woods. The sky was almost gray with dawn, and when the figure came out from between the trees, the silhouette appeared against the white snow. But it darted into the trees so quickly I could not tell who it was.

My heart beating quickly, I ran back upstairs to wake Christian. When I pulled back the sheet to his chamber and tiptoed in, nothing stirred.

"Christian," I whispered, but there was no response.

I crept closer to the bed and reached down in the still shadowed room to shake his shoulder only to find that he was not there. My hand fell on splintery wood and empty blankets.

So it must be he prowling about the woods. I went to the window at the end of the room to look out, but now I could see nothing.

My aggravation got the better of me, and needing something to do, I went into my chamber to put on my clothes. It would be dawn soon in any case, and there would be things to see to.

Downstairs in the kitchen, I put wood in the stove and started the fire, walking to the windows every few moments to watch for Christian to come in. When he did, it was from the barn.

He stamped up the backstairs and came into the kitchen. He stopped short, surprised to see me there, for a pink dawn was just creeping over the high ridges. Then he came to drop a feathery kiss on my brow.

"Hilary," he said, "you're up early."

"I saw someone in the woods," I said, carrying the tea kettle from the pump, where I had filled it, to the stove.

I set it down and turned to face him. "Were you out in the woods?"

He crossed again to shut the door behind him and came back into the room. "I saw the footprints while I was out checking the horses."

I got two cups down from the cupboard. "Then it must have been Franz or Duignan," I said, trying to sound unconcerned. I knew it hadn't been my father, for he had still been in bed when I had risen.

"Duignan was in the barn sleeping, until I went out," said Christian, standing before the window that looked out over the outbuildings and the edge of the woods where I had seen the shadowy figure.

"Franz then," I said.

In my own mind, I had another thought. A spirit would not leave footprints, but an angry Indian would.

There was no use speculating, and I was still determined to leave today. Together as a well-armed group we would be safe enough. We could not remain cowering in the isolated hotel all winter long.

Fortunately we had no more snow that night, so the morning was clear and crisp. As the others got up, I made sure everything got under way.

Christian inquired of Franz whether he and Drusilla planned to winter at the hotel. If not, whether they would like to travel to town with us? Franz replied that Drusilla did not like towns, and so they planned to winter here.

I could not help but hope, sardonically, that they would use the time to make improvements to the hotel. I was not, perhaps, off the mark, for Franz told Christian that they'd heard of another hotel being built down on the valley floor, so soon they would have competition. After our last hearty breakfast at Drusilla's table, we got into the saddle.

The sun shone brightly on the snowy valley when we began our descent on the trail. On the other side of the meadow I turned to see Drusilla standing stoically on the porch of the hotel that seemed to cling so precariously to the wooded slope. I waved, and she raised her hand in an odd little salute.

Then we rounded a pillarlike boulder and the path hugged the side of the mountain as we began the series of switchbacks that took us down to the waterfall.

The day passed without incident, and gradually the roar of the falls told us we were nearing it. We finally drew atop the ridge where we could look down on the falls, and the sight was so breathtaking that we dismounted to appreciate the view for a brief moment.

The river narrowed here to twenty yards, rushed over the steep ledge, and cascaded downward some several hundred feet into a small grotto between large boulders. The water swirled there in a deep pool until forced to roll over a slanting piece of granite and jump downward again another several hundred feet to the roiling waters below.

The rushing grandeur of the scene seemed to root us to the spot. Foaming, frothing spray rose high above the verge like a moist cloud, and a rainbow arched across the waters between the valley walls, painting the bare canyon walls where snow had caught only in crevices with rich reddish colors. Soon we would be walking behind the solid white curtain of the upper falls.

As if realizing that it would not speed our way if we remained there too long, we climbed back into our saddles and strung out again, Christian in the lead, followed by myself, my father, and Fanny. Duignan and the pack animals brought up the rear. As we continued downward, our party often strung out along three different switchbacks, one above the other.

The trail was muddy where the snow had melted, and once we had to stop when one of the mules decided to go no further. However, Duignan beat on the animal's hindquarters and uttered such a string of

Chinese curses that the unruly mule eventually fell in line.

We paused in a turnout some distance from the waterfall so that Christian could go ahead and make sure the ledge behind the falls was still passable. We sat in a little circle while we waited, and with the sun shining on us so brightly and the crystalline snow spread over the valley, I felt more peaceful than I had since we had entered the valley. My father seemed to have recovered from his fever, and Fanny looked about with interest. Indeed, I decided leaving the hotel was a healthy decision.

Christian returned up the trail with the good news that the ledge was passable.

"I was afraid it would be icy," he said with obvious relief. "But there's been enough sun to keep it melted. It's wet, but if we travel slowly, we'll have no problems. We'll lead the horses. Duignan will hold the mules on this side until we've crossed. When we get to the bottom of the trail before the falls, we'll dismount."

Following his instructions, we turned back onto the trail, which led along the side of the mountains. The roar of the falls became louder until we rounded a curve and stopped in wonder. What we had seen above now cascaded over our heads and plunged into the depths below. As it had before, the curtain of water arched far enough away from the chiseled rock wall to allow passage along the narrow ledge.

I had a moment of trepidation, wondering if there might be another way to the valley floor. But remembering that we had made it safely across with no mishap coming up, there should be no reason why we could not safely cross now.

We dismounted. Christian went along the line to

278

make sure all was secure. As he passed me, he gave my shoulder a reassuring squeeze and I looked into his face, hunting for any signs of misgiving, but there were none. As usual, he looked fully in control, able to command nature to do his bidding.

On foot, leading our mounts, we started under the falls, Christian leading us. I followed on his horse's heels, but far enough back that should the horse decide to misbehave I would be well out of the way. At this stage I knew of course that if any accident befell the animals, the thing to do would be to let them go and save ourselves by clinging to the rock wall at our side. Fanny came behind my horse, and Gaspar brought up the rear of our little train.

The mist sprayed us lightly, and I was glad that none of the slate surface beneath our feet had turned to ice. I was concentrating so hard on my steps and those of my horse that I was unprepared for the awful thing that happened next.

I heard shouting and looked up, thinking someone's voice must be bouncing off the rock walls. But when the shouting reached my ears in a frenzied pitch I looked around Christian's horse to see what I could see.

A crazed spectre came toward us from the far end of the ledge, emerging as if from out of the waterfall itself. The man's hair stuck half to a bloodied, mud-covered face and straggled about his head, the twisted locks bunched up wildly. The madman seemed to have four arms, which he waved about like a windmill, but wiping mist from my eyes I saw the extra pair of arms was really the tails of a coat that must have split up the back, leaving the cloth to flail about him in the wind.

"Get back, man," commanded Christian, taking a

step toward him, but onward came the spectre, fists raised, voice shouting.

That voice—a timbre I had heard before. I trembled where I stood, one hand braced on a jagged cut of the rock wall to my left, the other twisted in the reins of my horse. My horror was so great I thought I would turn into stone as I stood there and stared at the disheveled, crazed apparition. For at first I thought it was truly an apparition.

"I've been tricked," the apparition was yelling, over and over again even as Christian walked steadily toward him.

It was Thomas Neville come back to life. But a Thomas Neville such as I had never seen. Gone was the dapper, well-dressed conniver with meticulous moustache and starched collar. In its place was a wild man, clothes torn, mind obviously deranged, half dead. I clawed the rock wall by my side, fearful of what would happen next.

I risked a glance behind, but I could not see Father. Turning my head, I saw Christian moving ahead, trying to talk to Neville, and then I saw them disappear into the mist toward the other end of the ledge. I decided it best to follow, for the sooner we were across the ledge the better.

Step by step I moved along, Gabrielle snorting and tossing her head.

"Easy, girl," I said. "Not much farther now. Good girl."

As I approached the edge of the falls, I began to hear their voices again. Christian had gotten Neville onto the trail beyond the rocky ledge and roaring falls now and I came out, leading Gabrielle in a circle to make room for the others to follow.

"I came for gold, I'll have gold if it's the last thing

I do," raved Neville. And in the sunlight I could see that this was no apparition, it was Neville himself.

As Gaspar followed and led his horse to safety, he stared, incredulous.

"It's Neville," I said. "He's not dead."

Father went back to help Fanny step off the ledge, then we were all in the sunlight. Christian had backed Neville up a grassy slope and was trying to talk to him. My father joined them, which sent Neville into wilder ravings. Truly he had gone mad.

What had happened I wondered? The fall from the ledge by the cabin had not killed him, but he must have lain injured and exposed to the elements for a long time. He never really came to his senses then, and must have been wandering the mountains ever since. Why hadn't Christian found him? Had he gotten up and wandered off before Christian had made the descent to find him? Evidently so.

In a flash of understanding I realized who had been frightening us. It could have been Neville, not Franz, who prowled about our cabin the night we were so frightened. Why he did not knock I could not imagine, but if he was out of his mind, there was no explaining his actions.

He too could have been prowling about the hotel. I began to listen to what he said, hoping to gain a clue to other unexplainable events that had occurred since we had left Brooklyn. Neville must have looked us up in Brooklyn and escorted us here as an excuse for finding out what had happened to my father and the map.

"We were partners," he growled, tearing his tangled hair with one hand.

He lunged at Gaspar, but Christian held him back. Nevertheless he let go a spate of angry words.

281

"Not fair that you two were going to share the gold. I've worked just as hard as you. A third of it is mine."

"We never said we were going to share it," Christian said, but his words did not penetrate Neville's poor brain.

I moved toward Fanny, who was staring with round eyes. Here was her erstwhile fiancé, and I feared what she might do. But the defiant look on her face kept me from offering any sympathy. Neville went on.

"Tried to marry your daughter. Get at the gold that way," he snarled. "But you foiled me, Reyeult. If you hadn't been here, I might have gotten what was my due."

Neville suddenly pulled a knife from somewhere and charged at Christian. I screamed, and he sidestepped, bringing his hand down on Neville's arm. But Neville didn't drop the knife. The two men tangled in combat, and I held my breath as they rolled along the ground.

I ran toward them shouting, "No," but my father caught me and pulled me out of the way.

To my relief Christian finally grasped Neville's hand and knocked it against a rock, forcing him to drop the knife. In a swift move, Christian was on top of Neville, sitting on his back. He bent Neville's arm around so that Neville could not move.

Gaspar handed him a rope he had retrieved from the saddle, and they tied Neville up, pulling him to a sitting position. He still looked mad, but his raving had subsided a little. Mad or not mad, I was angry now that I figured out who had been causing us most of our grief. I didn't know if he could answer my questions, but I approached him when it was clear he could not hurt me.

"Was it you who had our house broken into in

Brooklyn?" I asked. "Were you searching for the map even then?"

He flashed me a guilty look and as Gaspar, Christian, and I exchanged looks I thought I knew the answer.

"Hired thugs, most likely," Gaspar said. He shouted at Neville as if he were deaf. "Was that it, did you hire thugs to look through that house?"

Then Gaspar laughed ironically. "Thought I would send the map home to my girls, did you? Place them in danger? I'm not that stupid."

Father went to Fanny and wrapped an arm around her shoulders for a hug.

"Tried to bring my girls here, did you? Let them track me here? I would never have given my permission for you to marry one of them if I'd known your intentions. Never trusted you, Neville, not even then." His last words died softly as if he realized the futility of them.

Neville gazed about, dazed. But then his eyes cleared and he looked at us with an expression of hatred.

"You can't prove a thing. Can't prove a thing. No proof, no proof at all," he whined.

I turned away in horror and disgust and felt Christian's arm on my shoulder.

"There isn't even any gold," I said. "Only gold fever, the evil that taints a man's mind."

I looked up at Christian as if in appeal that he at least had resisted the call of the gold stuff. His sanity, balanced nature, and his own values seemed to communicate to me even as Neville rocked from side to side, mumbling and shaking his head.

Gaspar stood comforting Fanny, and I was in Christian's arms. Duignan had brought the mules through and had them in a circle some distance off from us. None of us was looking when suddenly Neville flung himself forward. His arms were pinned to his sides by the rope, and his feet were tied, but he did a somersault on the ground and then rolled. Before any of us could stop him, he rolled over the edge of the precipice beside the falls.

I started that way, but Christian held me back. "It's better this way," he said.

Neville's cry bounded from wall to wall, echoing up the canyon as he fell, the sunlit mist seeming to carry it to our ears.

Then the cry faded even as his body must have been lost in the swirling water and the rocks below. This time there would be no escape.

"My God," I moaned and buried my face in Christian's shoulder.

No one moved for a long time, and then Christian gently left me and approached the precipice. When he returned to where the rest of us were standing he shook his head.

We stood for a moment, looking at each other and at the sunny surroundings, each of us trying to grasp what had happened. Neville had been our nemesis from the beginning. I saw it all clearly now. There would be much to talk over later, but there was no longer anything to do about it. We must get on down the trail.

That night we camped on the valley floor. The mighty Merced was beginning to freeze, but our crisp fire sent flickering light into the air, and our blankets in the small cavity we found near the canyon walls protected us from the chill wind. Duignan sat apart on his little blanket, mumbling his prayers over his candle.

We spoke little, and when we did it was of Neville. Fanny said nothing, just looked at the fire. But as I watched her carefully I felt relieved. Her eyes were clear and she was not hysterical. I knew she was thinking over all that had happened, weighing, reviewing, and I hoped, putting it all into perspective.

Finally she did speak in a calm voice, and I knew I had been right.

"I guess all he wanted was the gold," she said. "I believed him." Then she turned to me. "I'm sorry, Hilary. That's why I helped him. I thought he really was sincere and wanted to protect us. I guess I wanted to get married so badly I fell in love with him." She pressed her lips together to stop herself from crying.

"What do you mean you helped him?" I asked curiously.

"The note he gave me at the hotel. He told me to leave it for you the night you came back from your supper with Christian. He said it was a warning, but it might make you change your mind about going to Widow's Mountain. I didn't want to go, you see, because I thought he might take me with him to San Francisco."

The note! *He dies who goes to Widow's Mountain.*

"So you knew about the note," I said.

She nodded. "I didn't know what it said. In fact I forgot about it the next morning, I was so upset that he had gone and left me there. But I guessed he didn't want to take me with him until we were married." She gave a little shrug. "I was wrong, though, wasn't I? He never wanted to take me to San Francisco. All he wanted was the gold."

I scooted over to her blanket and took her hand. "It's all right, Fanny. You've learned now. You have to look deeper than the surface in a man."

285

She sniffed and nodded.

I shook my head. "But what about the warning in the laundry?" I said.

Everyone looked at me curiously. Finally Gaspar said, "What laundry?"

"Oh, the laundry at the hotel. I had hung it on the line in back of our room, and when I brought it in, there was another warning, a sign of sorts. It was a playing card—the ace of spades. For death.

We all frowned.

"Neville could have done that," Fanny said. "He could have put it there in the morning before we took our walk." She swallowed. "Before he proposed to me."

We were silent for a while. Then I spoke to my father.

"Then you don't think Drusilla was trying to frighten us and poison you?"

Gaspar laughed. "She's never forgiven me, that's for sure. I jes' wasn't the marryin' kind after your mother died. Got the wanderlust. I tried to tell her that. I know old Drusilla's become an odd one. But she's got a good soul."

He sucked on his pipe. "No sir, I don't believe she tried to poison me else she woulda succeeded when she was nursin' me back to health. And here I am fit as a fiddle to prove her nursin' worked, all right."

Neville, I thought. His greed turned into an obsession. He had been obsessed about that map ever since he had first set eyes on it, and our lives had been in danger because of it. He could have had the white horse that I had mistaken for a phantom horse. He must have watched us as we made our ascent up Widow's Mountain. He could have turned the white horse loose and ridden a second horse to the hotel.

Either that, or Yosemite Valley still had its phantom horse.

Well, now he was gone, and I hoped we were all the wiser for it.

That night as I rolled into my blanket between Gaspar and Fanny, I looked up at the velvet night dotted with diamond stars. No Indian chants haunted my dreams, nothing seemed to watch us from afar, and when the coyote sang, it sounded like a happy song.

Chapter 20

Though it was late autumn by now, as we passed through the Yosemite Valley, following the curves of the Merced River, we were delighted by the stands of oak, brilliantly colored with red and yellow leaves. The meadows on the north side were tawny and seared by autumn frosts, but the snow had not fallen there. On the riverbank, maple, willow, and dogwood glowed in shades of scarlet, crimson, yellow, gold, and amber.

Snow piled high in drifts lined the shadowy south side, and it occurred to me that the hotel builders who planned to compete with Drusilla and Franz would be wise to build on the north side of the valley floor.

Progress was slow as we began the ascent to the pass that would take us out of the valley, but we paced ourselves, stopping to lunch only on cold jerky, dried fruit, and bread. The pass was not too heavily blocked by snow, and a great weight seemed to lift from all of us as we topped the pass and began the descent on the other side.

I turned once to glance back at the brilliant sight of the lush and mystical valley. Alas, for the poor Indians who would be moved aside by the inevitable coming of the white man.

I thought as I turned toward civilization that it would not be the gold of the ground that would lure people here in the future, but gold of another kind.

The day warmed, and by the time we were on the lower slopes above the plains it felt like an Indian summer. We were tired, dusty, and hungry by the time we trailed past the miners' shacks and into the town of Mariposa, and I had to blink my eyes several times to get used to the bustle of the mining town. I had been isolated from humanity for so long, it was an adjustment to come face to face with it again.

However, after leaving the horses at the livery stable and making our way to the hotel, where we again ordered rooms, I found that the thought of a warm bath, a soft bed, and a change of clothes did something to improve my temper.

The hotel manager located the trunks we had left there and brought them to our rooms. A bath was drawn and I insisted Fanny be the first to bathe. It was such a luxury to pull the bellpull and have two Chinese servants come to toss the water out the window and bring fresh water for my bath. I laughed to think of Drusilla's establishment and her soap, towel, and directions to the hot springs and river.

After a long bath, I dressed my hair and rubbed lotion from the pharmacy into my skin. I took my time dressing in fresh underclothing, stockings, and finally putting on wide petticoats and high-necked gown with ribbons and ruched bodice.

When I was finished, I felt ready to go calling. I thought I might go see Bertha Johns to report the successful conclusion of our journey.

I stepped out onto the street to the stares of all the

males from one end of the street to the other. But I raised my parasol and ignored them as I made my way along the boardwalk.

I knocked on Bertha's screen and she came to the door, her thin lips curved into a smile.

"Well now, look who's here. But then I already heard that you're back in town, and with that devil, Gaspar, too. But come on in, dearie. I just gave your sister a spot of tea, you'll be wanting yours, too."

"My sister's been here?" I asked.

"Yes, she has. Told me everything, poor dear, including the madness and death of that fiancé of hers. She's better off without him, I can tell you. But come in, come in."

I took a seat on the same faded upholstered chair as I had when I first came here and waited for the rattle of the teacups to announce that the tea was ready. Bertha returned with a tray and served tea in her white crockery. After tea from camp kettles, I was delighted to be able to use silver tongs to drop sugar cubes into my cup and pour in a bit of cream.

How different things were now, I thought. We had found our father and succeeded in getting him out of the valley for the winter. Fanny was rid of poor Neville, and the rest of us had come through with life and limb intact. I chatted with Bertha about our journey, and she nodded and asked questions. By the time an hour had passed, I thought we had both been thoroughly entertained.

"Is Christian Reyeult staying here?" I asked, trying to sound offhand about it.

"That he is, the rogue."

She set her cup down on the little coffee table and peered at me through her spectacles.

"I take it you got to know your guide rather well on your adventure."

I could not help blushing, but I tried not to meet her gaze.

"He was a quite competent guide," I said.

She gave a little chuckle in the back of her throat. "Competent. Yes, I can see that. Brought you back alive, and healthy in mind and body."

I hastily took another sip of tea. Shortly after that I thanked her and left.

Back in our rooms at the hotel, I found Fanny sitting on the bed, her hair pulled back in a snood at the back of her head. She was surrounded by a pile of small bound books, and at first I thought she had somehow found a source for her favored chapbooks. But as I approached the bed I read the titles.

Gooday's Primer, ABC's and Numbers, and *Elementary Geography* among others, lay by her side.

"What are these, Fanny?" I asked.

She looked up from the book with large print she held in her hand.

"Oh, Hilary you'll never guess what. I went to see Bertha Johns, and she told me that the town council had decided to build a school. I guess they want to make this place decent for regular folks to live in. They need a teacher, and I've applied for the job. I know you'll insist on staying here with Father, and if I have to stay here, I might as well have something to do."

My eyes rounded. "You, a teacher?"

"Well why not? I can read, can't I? You know very well we both went farther with our schooling than most girls did. Oh I know they'll have to get someone who's been to a teacher's college eventually, but they can use me to start. It'll keep me busy this winter until they find someone permanent. I think I'd make a good teacher."

I could only stare.

"Well, perhaps that is a good idea. I hope they accept you. When will you find out?"

"Well, there's a meeting of the town council this Friday night. I'm going to be interviewed in front of them all."

"That's why you're reading these?"

She nodded, looking very serious. "Yes. I've got to know what I'm supposed to teach the students. Oh, and by the way, I gather not all the students are children. Some are grown men."

"I see."

Well, there was more than one way to meet a prospective husband.

"If you're sure you want to do this, I think it's a wonderful idea."

She looked at me steadily for a moment and then nodded. "I'm sure."

I was just starting to think of supper when there came a knock on our door. I went to open it and drew in my breath in pleasant surprise. Christian stood there, freshly shaved, dressed in frock coat, snowy white shirt, and black tie, felt hat in hand. His long blond hair had been washed and flowed about his collar.

"Good evening," he said, glancing past me into the room.

"Hello, Christian," I said, still feeling the flutter in my heart his appearance always caused me. "Come in."

He entered the room and gave it a turn. "I had hoped you would accompany me to supper," he said with a half smile.

"Supper? Oh, well, yes, I suppose. I am feeling a little hungry. Fanny and I . . ."

"Oh don't worry about me," said Fanny, who had come into the room. "I promised Father I would dine with him. I'm going to practice my teaching on him in preparation for the meeting Friday."

"Oh, I see," I said. Then turning to Christian I explained. "Fanny is applying for a job as school-teacher here in Mariposa," I said.

"Well, that is good news," he said. "Good luck, Fanny."

She gave a coy smile and turned to flit back into the bedroom, closing the door behind her.

"That leaves just us," Christian said, reaching for my arm and drawing me nearer, forcing me to look into his face.

"Yes," I said. "Just us." I swallowed. "I'll be ready in a moment."

"Hurry," he said.

We dined in the hotel dining room, but I scarcely realized what I put into my mouth. Christian poured more wine for me than I should have drunk, and I finally pushed my goblet away, lest I sway out of the dining room the way some of the miners swayed out of the bar next door.

After supper he sent me for my wrap because he wanted to take a walk through town. I did as I was bid and met him on the boardwalk in front of the hotel.

We walked along the boardwalk to the end of the block and then followed the next block until we ran out of town. A few houses dotted the landscape at the edge of town, and Christian headed up a slope that took us to a stand of trees. From here we looked back at the lights from oil lanterns, the sound of piano music tinkling from the bars in the crisp night air.

"This way," he said to me. "A little farther."

Curious, I followed him through the trees until we came out on a little knoll. A grassy meadow dipped on the other side and the land undulated upward toward the mountains. The moon rested low, illuminating the snowy peaks farther in the distance. A dark ring of trees encircled the spot where we stood.

"About here," he said, tucking his arm around my waist.

"What?" I asked.

"The house?"

I could tell he was teasing me, and I remained befuddled.

"What house?" I asked.

"Ours."

Before I could ask another question he turned me and planted his mouth over mine. His arms encircled me, and I gave no thought to resisting the demand of desire I felt rising between us. Finally he released my mouth and nuzzled my ear, his moustache tickling me. I nestled into his arms, trying not to think, trying only to enjoy what I wanted so much and what I had been prepared to have taken away from me.

"Marry me, Hilary. You want to stay here by your father, I know that. But he's an ornery cuss. Can't depend on him. You never know what he'll do. He's got to go look for that damned gold come spring."

My heart thrilled at his words. I could hardly believe he really wanted to marry me.

"So?" I felt lighthearted enough now to do a little teasing of my own. I pulled back and faced him, a challenge on my face. I wanted him to ask again. I wanted him to persuade me.

"So, you need a dependable man to look after you," he continued.

"You are calling yourself dependable?" I said.

He chuckled. "I should think you'd be able to judge that for yourself."

I smiled, but I was not hasty in accepting his proposal, still prolonging the moment. Instead I turned in his arms, looking out over the little scene where he planned to build our house.

"But you're a mountain man, too," I said. "You'd no sooner build me a house than you'd leave me in it alone and go wandering in the hills."

"Then I'll build you a house in the valley as well. Mountain man I may be, but there's plenty of mountain for me right here. The Indians are gone. Our kind are going to overrun this place in a quarter of a century. They'll need guides. I love this place, Hilary. I wouldn't mind knowing every rock and cranny from here to the site of Gaspar's cabin."

"And farther than that?" I asked.

He laughed. "That gold. That's his business. If he wants me to go with him next spring to see if it's really there, I'll go. But I want you to marry me now before you think I'm in love with you for your money."

"Bertha Johns says you're a rogue, Christian. Are you sure you really want to settle down?"

"Ceran needs a home—a mother if you're willing."

He took me in his arms again and gave me a look so full of love and longing that I questioned him no more.

"Rogue no more, my sweet Hilary. I'm yours forever if you'll have me. And we'll build a place where our children can thrive. After all, if your father does find that gold, he can pass it on to his grandchildren."

I could resist no more.

Epilogue

In the spring, Christian, Gaspar, and I climbed among the conifers and boulders that surrounded Mirror Lake. The lake was full from spring runoff, and the rocky summits were perfectly reflected in the cold depths of the glassy waters.

"Not much farther now," said Gaspar. One could not mistake the excitement in his voice.

We followed a trail pieced together from the Indian map and the deciphered code that would lead us to the caves Gaspar had dreamed about all winter long.

I stopped to catch my breath and turned to grin at Christian, who was bringing up the rear. We had left our horses hobbled by a stream at the bottom of this slope with the supplies we would need to set up camp.

I had not camped out in many months now and wondered if I would find it as much of an adventure as I had when we first penetrated these mountains, what seemed now to be so long ago. For I was used to sleeping in a comfortable bed now, nestled next to Christian in the house he and my father had built.

It was a grand house, the grandest in Mariposa, and though it would take time to decorate it the way I wanted to, I enjoyed every detail of it because it was ours. Ceran would be joining us this summer, and I looked forward to meeting the boy. Already, he had written me several letters, and I had made every preparation possible for his arrival.

The house was large enough to accommodate Christian and myself as well as Father and Fanny, who each had their own rooms. I was Mrs. Reyeult and held my head high as I walked down the streets of Mariposa, enjoying the respect of shopkeepers and businessmen.

Miners still stared, but now the ones who knew us tipped their hats with a, "Good morning, Mrs. Reyeult," and "How is your father, Gaspar?"

Fanny was thriving as a teacher. Keeping up with a room full of students from age six to twenty-six occupied her mind, and I had no more worries about the state of her emotions.

As I had predicted, she was being courted by several young men and seemed to favor the one who worked most diligently in her classroom. He had taken several meals at our table, and I liked him immensely. I hoped there would be a wedding soon.

Gaspar had bided his time, but as soon as he and Christian deemed the trail to be safe, they had organized our party. I, of course, refused to be left behind. I was not counting on finding any gold.

I had resisted the contagion of gold fever that spread through the region, telling myself that the wiser man would be the one who capitalized on the gold economy to perform services, thus building a steady business. But perhaps I had come along because something drew me, after all, back to Yosemite's grandeur.

We had stopped at Drusilla's and indeed found a few improvements. Franz had spent the winter hewing log planks, and now walls replaced the sheets that had separated the rooms upstairs.

At last we approached the caves my father had so long dreamed of exploring. A series of openings beckoned to us once we had scrabbled up the side of the mountain at the edge of the lake, and we stopped to view them. Father consulted the code, which we had recopied together with directions from the map.

" 'Walk in big mouth between two humps where daylight never goes,' it says," Gaspar said speculatively.

Christian pointed. "Then that is the one I would explore first."

Gaspar considered the surroundings. "I think you're right. There are the two humps."

Two small hills protected the opening to a cave. They rose like shoulders over a yawning mouth.

Gaspar looked toward me expectantly as if proving himself right.

"Father, remember we may find nothing," I said.

But he was not about to take my cautionary advice. "Nonsense girl. We'll find something, it's just a matter of how much there is and where in these rocks."

I shook my head but followed as we gained the plateau at the ingress to our chosen cave. We paused while Christian lit two lanterns and handed Gaspar one.

"Watch your step. It'll be dark. One misstep will send us plunging over the brink."

Christian led, holding the lantern high over his head. The going was not difficult to begin with, but the farther we went, the lower the ceiling came. Rocks jutted out in varying formations to the left and right.

We came to another room and Christian drew to a halt. He held the lantern out to the right, where the cave floor was smooth, leading away around a jutting

298

rock. When he moved the lantern to the left, darkness opened its maw, and I saw what Christian meant about false steps.

The men tied a rope around my waist and fastened it to themselves, but Christian assured me that the ledge around the jutting rock was wide enough to support us. He would lead the way, testing each step of the ground carefully before we proceeded further.

Gaspar was studying the ceiling and walls with great interest, and had to be jarred from his reverie when it was time to take to the ledge.

I had a horrible moment when I was reminded of the similar dangerous ledge under the waterfall, and half expected to see Neville's apparition rise up on the other side. But we passed safely and there were no threats of any kind.

We came into a small room and stopped.

"Ah," said my father. "It is as it was described."

"Described by whom?" I queried.

"By the Indians," he said. "They told me of this."

Gaspar had never mentioned what the Indians had described about the place where the gold lay hidden to all but he who possessed the code and the map.

We looked around for further passageways and then we saw it. As the lantern crossed an opening wide enough for two men to pass through, light bounced off the walls of the inner chamber.

Gaspar wasted no time in passing through the entrance to the sparkling vault. I heard his drawn breath even before we could follow, but as I stepped into the inner chamber and Christian added his light, we all stared in awestruck wonder.

The walls were streaked with gold.

"No telling how deep it goes," Gaspar said.

Christian shook his head, continually gazing from

wall to ceiling. "It's a rich yield, that's for sure," he said. "I guess those Indians knew what they were talking about."

Ironic that they hadn't taken it for themselves, but among most Indians gold had no value. It seemed my father had found his fortune after all.

"Well, Daughter," he finally said to me when we could strain our necks no longer to stare at the fascinating strata of gold alternating with layers of porphyry rock. "What do you think of it?"

"It is quite a sight," I said, hugging him as he came to grasp my waist in his exultation.

"There's one thing you must promise me though, Father."

"And what is that?"

"That you won't gamble away that map in any more card games."

He grinned widely as the two men set down their lanterns and we all hugged each other, dancing around in a little circle.

"We're rich," Gaspar kept shouting, his words echoing through the cavern. "We're rich."

We finally left the vault and retraced our steps, passing again around the jutting rock that threatened to send the passersby into the void below. On the way out, Christian and Gaspar talked excitedly about building a mine as soon as a claim was filed.

As I emerged into the sunlight and gazed at the stately mountains with their snowy heads and breathed the invigorating, health-giving air, I watched fondly the two men I had the good fortune to call family. I hugged myself.

Gazing at the vast panorama with its wealth of natural wonders, I knew I was very rich indeed—in much more than gold.